THE BOOKS
OF ANGUISH
(Volume 1)

BY THE SAME AUTHOR

THE BOOKS OF ANGUISH

(Volume 1)

Blood Light
A Shroud of Mist

by
Kurt Steiner

translated by
Sheryl Curtis

A Black Coat Press Book

Acknowledgements: Thanks to Julien Forest, Philippe Curval, Jean-Luc Rivera and Philippe Ward.

Lumière de sang (*Angoisse* No. 44, 1958) Copyright © 2023 by The Estate of André Ruellan; English translation Copyright © 2023 by Sheryl Curtis.
Dans un manteau de brume (*Angoisse* No. 57, 1959) Copyright © 2023 by The Estate of André Ruellan; English translation Copyright © 2023 by Sheryl Curtis.
Introduction, Bibliography & Filmography Copyright © 2023 by Jean-Marc Lofficier.
Foreword Copyright © 2023 by Philippe Curval; English translation Copyright © 2023 by Jean-Marc Lofficier.
Cover illustration Copyright © 2023 by Mariusz Gandzel.

Visit our website at www.blackcoatpress.com

TABLE OF CONTENTS

André RUELLAN

Introduction

André Ruellan, a.k.a. Kurt Steiner, born August 7, 1922, was one of France's most distinguished genre authors, as well as a renowned screenwriter. He passed away on November 10, 2016.

He began his career as a teacher, then decided to become a medical doctor at age 25 and practiced for ten years before embarking on a full-time literary career. In 1948, during his first year as a medical student, he published several articles and poems in a student magazine, *Hebdo Latin*, including a dark and satirical pamphlet in which he suggested that the students were so badly fed by the University restaurant that they would soon be forced to eat the cadavers they were dissecting. This macabre, yet funny, take on ordinary life would become his literary trademark.

In 1950, the newspaper *Le Hérisson* published his first short story, *Méfiez-vous des Veuves* [Beware of Widows], again a dark-humored, twisted tale, whose theme he later expanded in his first horror novel for Fleuve Noir. More crime stories followed, including *La Chaise Infernale* [The Infernal Chair] in *Voir Magazine*.

Ruellan's first published novel was *Alerte aux Monstres* [Alert, Monsters!], published in 1953 under the nom-de-plume of "Kurt Wargar" by the small press Flamme d'Or, as No. 6 in their new science fiction imprint, *Visions Futures* [Future Visions]. That same year, Ruellan also wrote a thriller, *Du Sang jusqu'au Coude* [Blood up to the Elbows], published by Faucon Noir, a publisher specializing in lurid, spicy thrillers. Interestingly, its cover was drawn by Jean-Claude Forest, the creator of *Barbarella*, who was moonlighting as a commercial artist.

In 1954, publisher Fleuve Noir, which had been founded in 1949 by Armand de Caro and Guy Krill, and which published cheap paperbacks devoted to police thrillers, espionage novels, and science fiction, decided to launch a new horror imprint called *Angoisse* [Anguish]. Their first novel in this new imprint was a translation of Donald Wandrei's 1948 dark fantasy, *The Web of Easter Island*.

Fleuve Noir's editorial policy was to rely on a stable of house authors, whose pseudonyms were owned by the publisher. Ruellan, who, at the time, was finishing his fifth year of medical studies, immediately wrote a horror novel which he submitted to the new imprint. It was entitled *Le Bruit du Silence* [The Sound of Silence] and was accepted two weeks later by Fleuve Noir.

A meeting was hurriedly arranged between Ruellan and the imprint's editors, including José-André Lacour who had already penned a few titles under the house pseudonym of "Benoît Becker." [1]

Ruellan was told that not only would *Le Bruit du Silence* soon be released—it was *Angoisse*'s 13th title, published in late 1955—but he was immediately commissioned to write more novels. Since Fleuve Noir demanded ownership of his pseudonym, he decided to adopt that of "Kurt Steiner."

Although Krill soon died following a car accident, Fleuve Noir continued and grew by leaps and bounds, adding new authors to their roster and new imprints to their catalog. Ruellan had been writing six horror novels a year, becoming one of *Angoisse*'s most prized authors. [2] Perhaps because of his

---

[1] That pseudonym was later used by screenwriter Jean-Claude Carrière to write seven novels featuring Mary Shelley's Frankenstein Monster, three sequels of which, by Frank Schildiner, were published by Black Coat Press.

[2] Other writers included André Caroff, the creator of the *Madame Atomos* series, published by Black Coat Press, Maurice Limat, whose *Mephista* was published by Black Coat Press (ISBN 978-1-61227-434-8), and Marc Agapit, whose novel *La*

medical background, the strength of his novels lay in their detailed, almost clinical, atmosphere of heavy, oppressive, bludgeoning horror, which foreshadowed the harder edged, gorier, books of the next decades.

In total, Ruellan penned 22 novels for *Angoisse*, mastering all the classic themes and creating some new ones as well. One of his books, *Le Seuil du Vide* [The Threshold of the Void] (1956) featured modern-day vampires and anticipated many of the themes of *Rosemary's Baby*; it was made into a low-budget horror film in 1971.

The same editor, François Richard,[3] was by then in charge of both the science fiction imprint, *Anticipation*, and *Angoisse*. *Angoisse*, however, was only selling 6000 copies of each title on average, while *Anticipation* was selling nearly 15,000.[4] So, in 1958, having established himself as a valuable author, Ruellan was invited to contribute novels to the science fiction imprint as well.

For *Anticipation*, Ruellan wrote a total of eleven, no less remarkable, novels. *Salamandra* (1959) featured a love story between an Earthman and a Mercurian woman. The ground-breaking *Le 32 Juillet* [The 32nd of July] (1959)[5] described how a man found himself in another dimension and explored the vast insides of a giant, living entity. *Les Improbables* [The Improbables] (1965) told of a time war between two future cities, and the attempts made by their descendants to manipulate events to increase the probability of their existence.[6] *Les*

Bête Immonde was adapted into a screenplay entitled *Despair* published by Black Coat Press (ISBN 978-1-932983-06-7).
[3] Richard was also the partner of science fiction writer Henri Bessière who wrote under the nom-de-plume of Richard Bessière. Four of his novels have been published by Black Coat Press in *The Gardens of the Apocalypse* (ISBN 978-1-935558-68-2) and *The Masters of Silence* (ISBN 978-1-61227-297-9).
[4] *Angoisse* was cancelled in 1974, with its 261st title.
[5] Forthcoming from Black Coat Press.
[6] Ditto.

Océans du Ciel [The Oceans of the Sky] (1967) was a colorful space opera featuring cosmic cross-fertilization between worlds. *Les Enfants de l'Histoire* [The Children of History] (1969) was a thinly disguised allegory of the political events of May 1968 recast in futuristic terms. *Le Disque Rayé* [The Scratched Record] (1970) was the complex tale of a complicated time loop. *Brebis Galeuses* [Black Sheep] (1974) was the story of a medical dystopia.

Ruellan was also the first writer to introduce modern heroic-fantasy into the *Anticipation* imprint with his *Aux Armes d'Ortog* (1960), and its sequel *Ortog et les Ténèbres* (1969), featuring a futuristic Earth where sophisticated science cohabits with a pseudo-medieval society. [7]

In the 1970s, Ruellan's writing skills, vivid imagination, and ability to pen fast-paced thrillers drew the attention of film directors and he found himself increasingly involved in film writing collaborations, including a low-budget adaptation of his *Angoisse* novel *Le Seuil du Vide*. Other genre films included the surreal sci-fi picture *Hu-Man* (1975) and a remarkable modern horror movie, *Les Chiens* [The Dogs] (1979), in which an attack dog trainer, played by Gérard Depardieu, uses people's fears about safety to slowly take over a town. Ruellan also wrote the novelization of his own screenplay.

Other books of note include *Tunnel* (1974), published under his own name, which depicts the hopeless flight of a man through a garbage jungle surrounding a bleak, futuristic Paris. The hero drags his dead lover's body with him, as he searches for a way to resurrect her. In 1984, Ruellan wrote *Mémo*, a novel in which a scientist's experiments with a new drug intended to stimulate memory end in a nightmarish disaster. His final novel, *Big Crunch* (2009), is a Robert Sheckley-like dark and satirical journey through the end of our universe and how it affects a neighboring universe.

Jean-Marc Lofficier

---

[7] Published by Black Coat Press as *Ortog* (ISBN 978-1-935558-28-6).

Bibliography

Alerte aux Monstres [*Alert, Monsters!*] (*as Kurt Wargar*) (Flamme d'Or, *Visions Futures* No. 6, 1953)

Du Sang jusqu'au coude [*Blood up to the Elbows*] (Faucon Noir, 1953)

Le Bruit du silence [*The Sound of Silence*] (*Angoisse* No. 13, 1955)

Pour que vive le Diable [*Long Live the Devil!*] (*Angoisse* No. 17, 1956)

Fenêtres sur l'obscur [*A Window onto the Dark*] (*Angoisse* No. 20, 1956)

De Flamme et d'ombre [*Of Flame and Shadows*] Angoisse (No. 23, 1956)

Le Seuil du vide [*The Threshold of the Void*] (*Angoisse* No. 25, 1956)

Les Rivages de la nuit [*The Shores of Night*] (*Angoisse* No. 27, 1957)

Je suis un autre [*I Am Another*] (*Angoisse* No. 29, 1957)

Les Dents froides [*Cold Teeth*] (*Angoisse* No. 31, 1957)

L'Envers du masque [*Behind the Mask*] (*Angoisse* No. 33, 1957)

Les Pourvoyeurs [*The Purveyors*] (*Angoisse* No. 35, 1957)

Sueurs [*Sweat*] (No. 37, 1957)

L'Herbe aux pendus [*The Herb of the Damned*] (*Angoisse* No. 39, 1958)

La Marque du démon [*The Mark of the Demon*] (*Angoisse* No. 42, 1958)

Menace d'Outre-Terre [*Menace from Beyond Earth*] (*Anticipation* No. 124, 1958)

Lumière de sang [*Blood Light*] (*Angoisse* No. 44, 1958)

Syncope blanche [*White Syncope*] (*Angoisse* No. 45, 1958)

La Village de la foudre [*The Thunderstruck Village*] (*Angoisse* No. 47, 1958)

Le Prix du suicide [*The Price of Suicide*] (*Angoisse* No. 48, 1958)

Salamandra (*Anticipation* No. 131, 1959)

La Chaîne de feu [*The Chain of Fire*] (*Angoisse* No. 52, 1959)

Dans un manteau de brume [*A Shroud of Mist*] (*Angoisse* No. 57, 1959)

Mortefontaine (*Angoisse* No. 59, 1959)

Le 32 juillet [*The 32nd of July*] (*Anticipation* No. 146, 1959)

Glace sanglante [*Bloodied Ice*] (*Angoisse* No. 64, 1960)

Le Masque des regrets [*The Mask of Regrets*] (*Angoisse* No. 68, 1960)

Aux Armes d'Ortog [*Ortog's Arms*] (*Anticipation* No. 155, 1960)

Manuel du Savoir-Mourir [*A Handbook of How To Die*] (*As André Ruellan*) (Horay, 1963)

Les Improbables [*The Improbables*] (*Anticipation* No. 269, 1965)

Les Océans du ciel [*The Oceans of the Sky*] (*Anticipation* No. 315, 1967)

Ortog et les Ténèbres [*Ortog and the Darkness*] (*Anticipation* No. 376, 1969)

Les Enfants de l'Histoire [*The Children of History*] (*Anticipation* No. 388, 1969)

Le Disque rayé [*The Scratched Record*] (*Anticipation* No. 424, 1970)

Tunnel (*as André Ruellan*) (Robert Laffont, *Ailleurs & Demain* No. 25, 1973)

Brebis Galeuses [*Black Sheep*] (*Anticipation* No. 596, 1974)

Les Chiens [*The Dogs*] (*as André Ruellan*) (Titres SF No. 1, 1979)

Un Passe-Temps [*Pastime*] (*Anticipation* No. 944, 1979)

Mémo (*as André Ruellan*) (Denoël, *Présence du Futur* No. 390, 1984)

Grand Guignol 36-88 (Fleuve Noir, *Gore* No. 62, 1988)

On a tiré sur le cercueil [*They Shot at the Coffin*] (*as André Ruellan*) (Denoël, 1997)
Big Crunch (Rivière Blanche No. 2063, 2009)

Filmography

Films:
Le Distrait [*The Daydreamer*] (dir.: Pierre Richard) (1970)
Le Seuil du vide [*Threshold of the Void*] (dir.: Jean-François Davy) (1971)
Les Malheurs d'Alfred [*The Troubles of Alfred*] (dir.: Pierre Richard) (1972)
Les Grands sentiments font les bons gueuletons [*Big Sentiments Make for Good Sports*] (dir.: Michel Berny) (1973)
L'Ombre d'une chance [*The Shadow of a Chance*] (dir.: Jean-Pierre Mocky) (1974)
Hu-Man (dir.: Jérôme Laperrousaz) (1975)
L'Ibis rouge [*The Red Ibis*] (dir.: Jean-Pierre Mocky) (1975)
La Chatte sur un Doight Brûlant [*Village Girls*] (dir.: Cyrille Chardson) (1975) (uncredited)
Infidélités [*Infidelities*] (dir.: Jean-François Davy) (1975)
Le Roi des bricoleurs [*The King of Handymen*] (dir.: Jean-Pierre Mocky) (1977)
Les Chiens [*The Dogs*] (dir.: Alain Jessua) (1979)
Paradis pour tous [*Paradise for All*] (dir.: Alain Jessua) (1982)
Divine enfant [*Divine Child*] (dir.: Jean-Pierre Mocky) (1989)
Il gèle en enfer [*Hell Freezes Over*] (dir.: Jean-Pierre Mocky) (1990)
Ville à vendre [*City for Sale*] (dir.: Jean-Pierre Mocky) (1992)
Bonsoir (dir.: Jean-Pierre Mocky) (1994)
Noir comme le souvenir [*Black as a Remembrance*] (dir.: Jean-Pierre Mocky) (1995)
Vidange [*Tune-Up*] (dir.: Jean-Pierre Mocky) (1998)
La Bête de miséricorde [*The Beast of Mercy*] (dir.: Jean-Pierre Mocky) (2001)
Les Araignées de la nuit [*The Spiders in the Night*] (dir.: Jean-Pierre Mocky) (2002)

Touristes? Oh yes! (dir.: Jean-Pierre Mocky) (2004)
Grabuge! [*Destroy!*] (dir.: Jean-Pierre Mocky) (2005)
Le Deal (dir.: Jean-Pierre Mocky) (2007)
Le Bénévole [*The Benefactor*] (dir.: Jean-Pierre Mocky) (2010)
Le Mentor (dir.: Jean-Pierre Mocky) 2012)
Calomnies [*Slander*] (dir.: Jean-Pierre Mocky) (2014)

Television:
Marie-Mathématique (1965-66)
Dim Dam Dom (1966) (1 episode)
Billet doux [*Love Note*] (1984) (mini-series)
Sa Majesté le flic [*His Majesty the Cop*] (1 episode of the *Série Noire* series) (1984)
Colère [*Anger*] (telefilm) (dir.: Jean-Pierre Mocky)

Foreword

A Conversation Between
Philippe Curval and André Ruellan[8]

"The voice being heavier than air, it necessarily falls into a microphone."

It is thanks to this principle of physics that I am able to tell you about the life of André Ruellan, who told it to me on my tape recorder.

"Can you start before you were still in limbo?"

"I don't remember anything before 1922, which is when I was born. The first image I have of myself is in a bedroom, lying down, the sheets hanging around the bed, swept by the wind blowing in from the window. From what I was able to learn later, this took place in Berck,[9] where I had been sent because I had a broken tibia."

"So you began your life by breaking your bones?"

"Well, I was already two and a half."

"And after that?"

"A big empty hole. I remember the visit of my cousin, born in the United States, who is also called Andrée Ruellan and wore her black hair in buns over the ears. She had hung a

---

[8] Philippe Curval (1929-) is a French journalist and a multiple award-winning science fiction writer, critic and editor. His Apollo Award winner novel *Cette chère humanité* (1977) was translated by Steve Cox as *Brave Old World* and published by Allison & Busby in 1981.

[9] A commune in the northern French department of Pas-de-Calais.

reproduction of Douanier Rousseau's[10] painting of a horse-drawn cart above my little cot. I was six years old.

"Why was she born in the United States?"

"Some of my family had emigrated there around 1910."

"Could you inherit a fortune from a long-lost uncle?"

"No, the last known family member died at age ninety-seven, without leaving any money behind."

"Were does your family come from?"

"Ruellan is a Breton name, from the Côtes-du-Nord. My grandfather, who was a shoemaker, had eight children. That's probably why he moved so often. As a result, my father married my mother in the Auge region: she was from Normandy."

"Then he moved to Paris?"

"Yes. I am a first generation Parisian and the last to bear the name in my family."

"Any other memories of that time?"

"Only fragments; especially, the image of my father returning loaded down with books he had bought on the quays, although he was a welder at Delage.[11] Five of us, including my brother and sister, were crammed into a very small apartment in Bécon-les-Bruyères. The walls were covered by piles of books; a room was full of them; there were even some in the cellar. That was where my brother's collection of Ferenczi and Tallandier novels[12] was, and I devoured them as soon as I learned how to read. There was also a series of magnificent volumes bound in green leather entitled *L'Univers et l'Humanité*, whose illustrations dazzled me."

---

[10] Henri Rousseau (1844-1910), French post-impressionist painter in the Naïve or Primitive manner, also known as *Douanier* (customs officer) for his daytime job.

[11] Delage was a French luxury automobile and racecar company founded in 1905 by Louis Delâge in Levallois-Perret near Paris; it was acquired by Delahaye in 1935 and ceased operation in 1953.

[12] Both publishers of cheap, popular thrillers.

"There were books kept by your father, who must have enjoyed science, esotericism, political works and philosophy."

"Not philosophy as much; above all he was thirsty for knowledge. That is why he also owned a magnificent Nachet microscope, which he had purchased after saving furiously for months. I took full advantage of it. I was a real sponge in this cultural bath, which delighted my father. He was an anarcho-syndicalist; materialistic with respect to God, but on the other hand, rather mystical vis-à-vis the future. Like many socialists towards the end of the last century, he had been influenced by a spiritualist movement from India. Around the age of twelve, for example, he made me read *Les Maisons Hantées* [The Haunted Houses] by Camille Flammarion and I started to strongly believe in ghosts.

"In short, a happy family atmosphere."

"But one with enormous financial difficulties. In 1934, everything went downhill when my father lost his job. The family exploded. I stayed with my mother and my sister."

"Were you the youngest child?"

"Yes—the least of my worries."

"Did you stay in Bécon-les-Bruyères?"

"No, since we never paid the rent, we moved all the time."

"What did you live on?"

"My mother, who had been a cleaning lady, started telling fortunes. It was then that she and some friends of hers tried to build a house with cinder blocks on the slopes of Argenteuil, on a piece of land that didn't belong to them. When the owner drove us away, we took refuge in a hovel in the town's slums. I stayed there until the war."

"What about your schooling during that time?"

"It was normal; first, I attended primary school, then secondary school until age sixteen. Then, I applied simultaneously at the École Normale in Versailles to become a schoolteacher, and at the Lycée Condorcet in Paris to continue with my education. I was accepted by both, and I chose to go to

Versailles to become a teacher, because there, I was housed and fed by the State."

"Did you stay there long?"

"Until the Exodus,[13] when I left for Bordeaux on foot. When I got back from this unintended vacation, I went back to my studies. I was paid; I had signed a contract to be a teacher for ten years."

"What were you thinking?"

"I wanted to write! At fourteen, I had already started a novel about giant insects."

"The result of reading your brother's pulp collection?"

"No doubt, but more ambitious. I had read *The War of the Worlds*, *The Time Machine*, *The Invisible Man*, by Wells and my father's popular science books. All those science fiction ideas were running through my head."

"Did you think you'd become a teacher or a writer?"

"More of a teacher who wrote on the side. In 1942, I embarked on another novel, which I also never finished. But it had a lot of pages, which are all lost today."

"You were about twenty at that time, weren't you? Were you impacted by the S.T.O.?"[14]

"Yes. I did eight days of S.T.O. in Arcachon. I built a tennis court for the crews of the German submarine that lived on a nearby base."

"Was that court at the bottom of the sea?"

"It could have been, if they'd used heavy enough balls. But all joking aside, if I had not benefitted from the protection

---

[13] A massive flight of the French population in May-June 1940 when the German army invaded the majority of French territory. This was one of the largest population movements of the 20th century in Western Europe, involving between 6 and 10 million people.

[14] *Service du travail obligatoire* (Compulsory Work Service), the forced enlistment and deportation of hundreds of thousands of French workers to Nazi Germany to work as forced labor for the German war effort during World War II.

of a lieutenant of the L.V.F.,[15] who had found out that I was a student, I would have been sent, like the others, to build concrete hangars underwater in a diving suit, carrying bags of cement weighing fifty kilos. After a week, we were told to report to a courtyard at six a.m. I understood that we were going to be sent to Germany. Again, thanks to that lieutenant, I was handed an *ausweiss* [16] and instead, I took the train back to Paris."

"What other problems did you encounter during the German occupation?"

"My older brother was a partisan maverick, registered with the Communist Party; my sister was a Trotskyist; my father, an anarchist. The whole spectrum of the Left was represented in my family. Thanks to my brother, I got false papers, which I was supposed to use to go and fight in the maquis of the Vercors.[17] Luckily, my family started crying when I was about to leave, so I stayed; otherwise, I wouldn't be here to tell you my life story today."

"What happened next?"

"I hid, first on a farm in Château-Thierry, then in Mayenne, with my sister, who was married by then."

"In short, a quiet vacation until the end of the war?"

"Not quite, since I almost got shot a fortnight after the Normandy landing."

"By the Americans?"

"No. A German soldier had been shot in the village; all the men under forty were picked up and put against a wall. We

---

[15] Legion of French Volunteers (Against Bolshevism), a unit of the German Army consisting of collaborationist volunteers from France.

[16] German ID card.

[17] The Battle of Vercors in July and August 1944 was a fierce combat between a rural group of the French Forces of the Interior (FFI), or *maquis*, and the armed forces of Nazi Germany. The maquis used the prominent scenic plateau known as the Massif du Vercors as a refuge.

waited there, facing a row of machine guns. We waited three quarters of an hour, which is a long time. Then orders came not to shoot us. We spent the night in a room in the town hall. The next day, we were interrogated. I no longer remembered the birth date on my fake papers. The officer, who saw my doubts, looked at me with his clear eyes surrounded by steel-rimmed glasses, but he let me go."

"The shooting was over."

"He belonged to the Wehrmacht, not the S.S."

"So, after all that, you went back to teaching?"

"No, After the Liberation, I went into business. I traded bottles of Calvados for American products from a nearby G.I.s camp—especially gasoline. My price was a liter of calvados for 5 liters of gasoline; from the farmers, on the other hand, I asked for two liters of calvados for the same quantity of gasoline. The profit provided me with coffee, cigarettes, and K rations."

"Did this traffic last long?"

"About two weeks. After that, I was assigned to be an English teacher in a complementary school, even though I hardly knew the language, but I had registered for an English Certification course at the Sorbonne."

"So you were fulfilling your contractual obligation?"

"I did, for two years."

"What happened after? Did you desert from the National Education Service?"

"No, I repaid my debt. not so long ago, in fact. Ninety-three francs. A ridiculously small amount."

"Is that when you started medical school?"

"Yes, around age 47. I pictured myself as a doctor, writing poems on the side, an activity in which I had been involved for about five years. I was even part of a group organized around Maurice Fombeure."[18]

---

[18] Maurice Fombeure (1906-1981), French writer and poet. Very active in the literary circles of the capital, he was awarded the Grand Prix for poetry by the City of Paris in 1958.

"How did you finance your studies?"

"I got a scholarship. I always had scholarships since the primary school. The financial situation of my parents, being poorer than most immigrants today; explains it."

"In short, you are a Ward of the Republic."

"Totally."

"Did you like your medical studies?"

"Well enough not to start writing any novels until the sixth year of them."

"Was it the emergence of science fiction in France that prompted you to do so?"

"Since my childhood, I had read fantasy and SF, but it is true that it was the publication of one of the first American SF novel, Jack Williamson's *The Humanoids* in 1950 that made me jump out of my seat. At that time, I had written a short story for a magazine called *Le Hérisson*. But what forced a pen into my hand was the start of the *Angoisse* imprint at Fleuve Noir in 1954. I immediately began writing a horror novel, *Le Bruit du silence*, which was accepted at once."

"Not signed Kurt Wargar?"

"No, Kurt Steiner. I had used the pseudonym of Kurt Wargar to publish a short SF novel, *Alerte aux Monstres*, the previous year."

"So why Kurt Steiner?"

"I was tired of seeing French writers use Anglo-Saxon pseudonyms, so instead I chose a German sounding one."

"How did you live at that time?"

"I lived in Enghien with my sister. But I also shared a small flat in Paris with some friends. We sometimes played chess there from noon to midnight. Or we invented funny recipes, like *pain au pain*: 'Fry slices of bread in a pan with any kind of fat, then eat them with croutons.' All of this ended at the same time as my studies, the year I got married."

"Did you ever practice?"

"I had a ready-made practice, but instead, I pocketed my diploma and ran away."

"Why this sudden departure from medicine?"

"As much as I was interested in studying medicine, I found that practicing it did not appeal to me. Through my other brother-in-law, Jean-Claude Forest, the creator of *Barbarella*, I met Georges H. Gallet, who edited a SF book imprint, *Le Rayon fantastique*, and a magazine, *V Magazine*. I had written a few short stories for him, which had whetted my appetite for doing more. Then, I discovered a way to gain more freedom: the editor at Fleuve Noir had told me that my first novel was good, but what they wanted was series by the same author; in other words, he was offering me a kind of open-ended contract. I said yes, but I left the interview terrified because I was convinced that I had used every idea I had in my first book and that I would be incapable of writing another one."

"History has proven you wrong."

"Indeed. During the next five years, I wrote twenty-two horror novels, plus a few science fiction ones."

"It was when you became acquainted with the *milieu* of French SF."

"Yes. One day, Georges Gallet dragged me to a cocktail party at Denoël where I met Alain Dorémieux and Gérard Klein. After an excessive amount of drinking, I took them back to my home where we carried on with the party. The next Monday, they invited me to lunch where I met you, and Valérie Schmidt, Jacques Sternberg, Jacques Bergier, and Michel Pilotin."

"Why did this fabulous collaboration with Fleuve Noir come to an end?"

"Because of a very simple economic principle: the novels of the *Angoisse* imprint barely recouped half of the advance paid by the publisher. Their money allowed me to live a good life. For example, in 1957, as I always loved big cars, I bought a superb used Buick convertible. But, mathematically, every time I delivered a new novel, my debt grew by the same amount."

"Was it a failure of the horror genre since a writer could not live by his pen while producing as much as you did?"

"More like a failure of popular fantasy literature in general. If I had written novels for their *Anticipation* imprint, I would have been fine since their sales were double that of the *Angoisse* books

"Well, you were passionate about writing fantasy and horror."

"The problem is that I only wanted to write the lowest-selling type of books. Nevertheless, there are several novels which use SF elements in my fantasy/horror production."

"So how did it end?"

"Fleuve Noir eventually stopped sending me money because I owed it too much."

"Why didn't you turn to writing police or espionage novels, which sold a lot more?"

"I was not inclined to write police thrillers after a couple of unhappy experiences in the past. As for espionage, I made a half-hearted attempt, and my manuscript was rejected. I must add that the books published in the *Espionage* imprint sold more than a hundred thousand copies, and its editors were not looking favorably upon newcomers."

"You hadn't had a lot of rejections until then."

"No. My novels for *Angoisse* went straight from my typewriter to the printer, bypassing any reviews, probably because they had a low market value."

"Did you ever repay this debt?"

"Oh, yes, like I did with the National Education Service. And as it was not indexed, inflation reduced its value, which allowed me to write only one or two *Anticipation* novels instead of four to repay it."

"During that time, you opened a medical practice in Les Halles."

"Yes, that experience lasted twelve years."

"Did you feel trapped?"

"No, the neighborhood was nice, the people too; few patients, but very loyal."

"Which gave you time to write."

"Yes, I wrote *Les Improbables, Les Océans du Ciel, Ortog, Les Enfants de l'Histoire, Le Disque Rayé*; five books in all."

"They were more elaborate novels than the ones you did when you wrote six books a year."

"Horror is based on the atmosphere, so mainly on the writing; the work in which I was immersed facilitated that. Let's just say that the next period allowed more time for reflection, which is essential for the creation of science fiction books that require very strong structures.

"In 1963, you wrote *Le Manuel du savoir-mourir*. How did the idea come to you?"

"Everything comes at the right time to those who know how to recognize it and, as life is but a preparation for death, it seemed natural to me to talk about it. My contacts with the "Panic" movement, that of Topor, of Arrabal, also helped. This allowed me to meet André Breton. He considered the Manual a reference work."

"So you got along with the medical profession that you had fled."

"Still, I was relieved when I wrote my first film script. It was a form of expression that suited me and turned out to be extremely profitable."

"How did that happen?"

"In 1969, Pierre Richard, who was mostly doing sketches, contacted me. I had written some song lyrics and short stories for *Hara-Kiri*. Sternberg had told him that I was the man for the job. As he was thinking of moving into films, I told him about *Les Caractères* by La Bruyère. He read them that night. The next day, he called me and we got to work. After *Le Distrait*, we collaborated on a second film; he became a star, and I a screenwriter. I haven't stopped since. I have collaborated with Jean-Pierre Mocky, Michel Berny, Jean-François Davy, who adapted my novel *Le Seuil du vide*, Jérôme Laperrousaz, and Alain Jessua."

"Any SF elements in these films?"

"Yes, especially with the last three directors I mentioned. *Hu-man, Les Chiens*, and above all, *Paradis pour Tous*, all have strong SF elements.

"For a while, you were focused on television."

"After fifteen years of screenwriting, I got into it very easily. Michel Berny, with whom I had written three screenplays, without the deals ever coming together, had just directed *Petit-Déjeuner Compris*. The series had been successful. He asked me if I had an idea. So we did *Billet Doux* together; after a string of unlikely acceptances and rejections, it was broadcast in September 1984."

"Do you feel that your work partly reflects your life?"

"For the horror novels, it is indisputable. For the SF novels, there is clearly some connection to my medical background, but in both cases the connection is on the cultural level, not on the affective level."

"Have you ever been tempted by general literature?"

"In 1942, my unfinished manuscript of *Classe 42*, of which I spoke earlier, was vaguely inspired by my life."

"Doesn't it frustrate you to constantly collaborate with directors, without being able to express yourself in your own right?"

"So much so that my last two novels could be read as a kind of compensation."

KURT STEINER

LUMIÈRE DE SANG

M. Gourdon

ANGOISSE

Editions
"FLEUVE NOIR"

BLOOD LIGHT

CHAPTER I

Night was falling. Laurent associated night with rain; both fell. The rest of the scene followed the same slope... branches bending under the weight of the new sap, too early for this poorly fashioned spring, clumsily shaken by the claws of a tenacious winter.

Laurent Prévost was 22 years old. He wondered what combination of reasons had brought him to that particular place, splashing about in a muddy twilight, a few days before a birthday he could have celebrated in joyful company. No. A whim? He had pulled on the straps of his backpack the previous evening and had headed out one of the gates in southern Paris, face towards the road.

Hitchhiking had not been terribly successful; he had barely made it to Fontainebleau... the Mediterranean had seemed, over the past two days, more distant than Australia.

There were two sides to the coin, for a student as for anyone else. In his case, the freedom of "taking to the road" for two weeks during the spring break came with obligation of eating parsimoniously — not to mention using his legs as a means of transportation. How long would it take him to get to Lavandou, if no motorist stopped or if drivers only offered him 10K hops?

A drop fell from the brim of his small Alpine hat and rolled down his nose. He barely felt it, but automatically wiped it away with the back of his hand, as he stepped forward. Over there, at a bend in the tree-lined road, a car was arriving, bright headlights like two eyes staring over the radiator grill drowning in the dark like a gaping mouth.

Laurent had spent nearly an hour leaning against the parapet of a small bridge, using it to support his pack, without removing it. The seven or eight kilometers he'd covered had filled him with disgust for walking and the rain. Cars drove by without stopping, generally filled to overflowing with travelers and luggage... and it was unreasonable to travel no more than 30 km in a day. It was a sporting achievement, of course, but a pointless one. The planned trip was disproportionate to the feat, one that was renewed on a daily basis.

The young man waved his arms. Meanwhile, he had the feeling that the car had slowed even before he'd stepped out of the shadow of the shoulder. The sound of tires on wet asphalt quickly faded, and a long, gray car stopped next to Laurent. An electric car window lowered silently and a voice spoke, a strange voice, a dry crackle.

"Open the back door and put your backpack on the floor. Then climb in the front."

It was clear, precise, methodical. With a glance, Laurent assessed the car, expecting to recognize an American brand. He was surprised; he had no idea what the vehicle was. Yet he was familiar with most cars, from both the New World and the Old... Was the driver Swiss or German? Was the car a rare Mercedes model?

He opened the back door and a dome light turned on, revealing a car seat covered in leather with bloody reflections. It was as if someone had been viciously "bled" in the car, and his blood had been used to dye the leather...

Laurent placed his pack carefully on the black fur covering the floor of the vehicle. He thought of two very dissimilar things at the same time: the unsettling ambience of bloodletting and the damage the fittings of his backpack and the filthy water it was soaked in would cause to the luxurious material. He closed the door.

"I really appreciate you stopping..." he started to say, as he opened the front door.

28

"No problem…" interrupted the driver, as he turned his head away. The window rose as if by magic and the engine purred as gently as a wisp of breath. With the light rocking of a boat, the car started and accelerated without the driver touching anything other than the steering wheel and the gas pedal.

Automatic… thought Laurent.

The vehicle was warm. The windshield wipers operated silently and so quickly that it was almost impossible to track their movement. The man pointed his index in the direction of a row of push bottoms located in the center of the dashboard. Thirty seconds later, a voice spoke.

"…drive very cautiously on the highway we just mentioned; the rain has made certain sections extremely slippery. In particular, we encourage those driving powerful vehicles to…"

The man pushed another button; the speaker's warnings did not seem to please him. Angry rock'n'roll filled the car.

Laurent fell silent, glancing surreptitiously at the silhouette blurred by the thick darkness. The headlights that had just turned on accentuated the fuzziness inside, as they lit up the roadway and the trees.

"I'd still like to thank you," said Laurent in one breath.

When the other man remained silent, he continued, "I was starting to feel like a cube of sugar in a glass of water… By the way, I'm sorry that I've dirtied your cushions with all that mud…"

Silence. Then the man turned off the radio.

"Bad weather…" he observed, in a voice that sounded like a rusty weather vane.

Laurent glanced to the side. The driver was facing forwards and the dashboard light was so weak it did not reveal his features. The passenger did, however, think they matched the sound of the man's voice: a nose that seemed hooked, a pointed chin, bald head. For a second, Laurent thought of a silhouette cut in a piece of aluminum foil… a sort of flat man made of black metal driving this unknown brand of car. He shivered involuntary, and then considered his own appearance, his undisciplined blond locks, the green eyes girls found irresistible. The two men really had nothing in common. He imagined that the man came from nowhere, that he had merely stopped in order to bring an element of life, of youth into this splendid, yet gloomy car. The image of a tarantula slicing the throat of a hummingbird crossed his mind.

"Bad weather for men and animals..." the driver added.

Laurent jumped.

"Animals?" he repeated. "Why animals?"

"Why not?" said the raspy voice.

The young man fell silent. The replies were absurd and inconsistent. It was impossible to determine why the man had mentioned animals. Yet, just before the driver had made his comment, Laurent had been thinking of a tarantula and a hummingbird.

The passenger shifted in his seat, then remained still, eyes fixed on the road at the edge of the range of the headlights.

Night had fallen, thick and almost foreign. The yellow light pierced through it in a fan, bringing millions of sparkling droplets into existence.

...*In particular, we encourage those driving powerful vehicles to...* Laurent recited in his mind. The speaker's mouth had been closed with the tap of a finger. They would never know what piece of advice would have followed. The passenger noted that this "*powerful vehicle*" was driving at a speed outside his comfort zone.

"Bad weather for driving," croaked the man.

Laurent opened his mouth and closed it immediately. He was seriously starting to wonder if the bald man were reading his thoughts. But, upon reflection, the driver's words and his own thoughts could easily be vaguely similar, without there being anything abnormal about that... Laurent was studying for a degree in differential and integral calculus and his training did not give him a propensity for occult meandering.

Why had the color of the cushions made him think of a murder? Many cars had red seats, without necessarily giving travelers bloodthirsty thoughts...

Laurent set those morbid thoughts aside; the rain must have drowned his brains through his small, dented felt hat... Yet he thought about the dagger resting in its sheath hooked to the belt of his blue jeans.

"I suppose you're planning to put a few hundred kilometers behind you?" said the man without turning his head.

Laurent hid a sigh of relief.

Finally, a clear sentence, without any strange undercurrent.

"Yes," he said. "I'm heading south."

He was not unaware that hitchhiking requires cautious diplomacy, and that it was inappropriate to bring up his goal right away. It was better to mention the name of the next village and hope they would drive beyond that... That was how he usually did things, but this man had certainly shaken up those ideas.

"I'm going through Auvergne," said the bald man in his raspy voice. "If that little detour doesn't delay you too much, I see no problem with keeping you on board..."

Laurent agreed, his joy tinged by an undefinable feeling. He had no desire to follow that route, which would increase his travel time and he was not too fond of the driver, although he was courteous. But similar offers did not come up often. He settled back against the car seat.

The car continued to slash through the black rain.

CHAPTER II

A few seconds later, Laurent built up the nerve to ask a question that was burning his lips.

"I thought I knew a lot about the various models of cars..." he said. "But I must admit yours has me confused. It's a beautiful machine... but I have no idea which company made it."

The man sidestepped the question, as if there was some secret about the origin of his vehicle and he considered his passenger's indirect questions indiscreet.

"It's a nice machine, in fact," he said turning his head with a movement that only his nose seemed to take part in. "But you're very young to expect to know everything... There are a great many car manufacturers in the world... They make all kinds, all shapes."

He fell silent and Laurent had the impression that the other man was condensing an idea, placing it under pressure in some way, so as to make it all the more hard-hitting when he got around to expressing it.

"All shapes," he repeated. "Sometimes, in a car, as in any other object, you find lines or mechanical features borrowed from others. At a pinch, you can imagine a sort of combination of everything that provides satisfaction in a field. In the case at hand, you get an ideal vehicle... the flexibility and comfort of American cars, Italian trade-ins, the ability of British vehicles to hold the road, German power... You see what I mean..."

Laurent had no idea what he meant.

"But that's not possible!" he exclaimed.

The driver chuckled dryly, sounding somewhat bird-like.

"Sometimes... sometimes, believe me."

"And which industrial group could achieve such a brilliant combination?" Laurent asked.

"Ah! Ah!" chortled the other. "There you go with your roundabout questions... Unfortunately, I can't enlighten you with respect to that matter. I'd even say..."

He stopped talking and turned the car radio back on. A song by opera singer Élisabeth Duparc was playing. Through the singer's voice, Laurent heard a bizarre comment as an unpleasant counterpoint.

"No industrial group has resolved the problem we're discussing. But it's not impossible to create that impression... yes, that's it... to create the impression."

Laurent wondered what the man meant by that. Was he saying, with a great deal of cold humor, that this conversation was based on a joke, a bluff... or...?

A second interpretation leapt into the passenger's mind, without him being able to prevent it: perhaps the bald man wanted to insinuate that they were both in some sort of imaginary world, *an illusory car, made up of a thousand features borrowed from real ones...?*

Laurent took a damp cigarette out of the pocket of his jacket with shaking fingers.

The soft night preserved its deep cold and the strange vehicle continued its silent race through the pounding rain. For a moment, Laurent believed he was locked up in a submarine; he found that comparison somewhat painful. However, the universe outside was so inhospitable that he could only rejoice in the luck he'd had. As strange as the nameless car and the driver with his beak-like nose seemed, he had to admit that sitting on that upholstered car seat was like relaxing in an easy chair in a comfortably warm lounge.

The song ended. It was *La vie antérieure* — based on a poem by Charles Baudelaire. Laurent had recognized it a while earlier. He'd always managed to mix mathematics and music quite harmoniously. Some of his friends had occasionally observed that the two worlds were connected. In the case of J.S. Bach, it was obvious. Of course, with Duparc, the mathematics was very subtle. Not the math of rational organization, but that of pure intuition, where the framework became invisible.

Duparc had only written seven or eight melodies over the course of her life. No more than that. Laurent was undertaking his eighth long hitchhiking trip. Would it be his last?

"I think you'll flag down another car fairly quickly once I've abandoned you..." said the man.

Once again, Laurent could not help but connect these words with his own thoughts. There was something irritating about so frequently discovering a connection that could be a form of telepathy. Was the driver really reading his thoughts? There were too many of these unsettling observations to consider them repeated coincidences. Laurent thought about that short story by Edgar Allen Poe in which a similar semblance of telepathy was eventually explained by a series of associations of predictable ideas. But in this case, the plot was not as clear and the result was more approximative. It was hard to decide. What did remain was a sort of discomfort created by concern and forced irony which Laurent would have given a lot to get rid of. Of course, there was no way he could coldly ask the driver if he performed in music halls, a blindfold over his eyes... Laurent pulled on his cigarette — the man had refused the one his passenger had offered him.

"I hope you'll enjoy your vacation..." Laurent heard him say.

He cautiously waited for the rest, listening distractedly to a descriptive piece about Honegger.

"I presume you're a student... You're about 22 years old, aren't you? At that age when you take a vacation long enough to travel across France, you're generally a student. What do you think about my little guessing games?"

He was being provoked.

Laurent commented distractedly, "Lots of things. I find your game is bang on and you manage to guess a multitude of details."

The man chuckled dryly and said, "Excuse me for my indiscretion... It's all rather mathematical when you get down to it."

Naturally, mathematics came up like a sequence flowing from a spring. Lips clenched, Laurent waited for the man to turn his head toward him and say, "Come on, admit that you're studying math, your name is Laurent Prévost, your father died six years ago, you live at No. 9 on Rue d'Assas..."

Yet the man said nothing of the kind. Laurent grew even more uncomfortable because he *felt* that he would hardly have been surprised. Only frightened.

With that thought, his concern continued to grow. If the driver had specifically looked him up and acknowledged that fact clearly, perhaps there would be some banal explanation. The man might know him from Paris, in some way or another, without Laurent ever having noticed him... and chance had placed them on the same road.

But the bald man said nothing concrete, settling for ambiguous allusions, leaving the field open for all interpretations... There was something more serious, more irritating, since the shadow was not dissipating, although Laurent was now convinced the bird man knew all about him...

The trip continued, monotonous. Under other circumstances, Laurent would have lost himself in conversation or listening to the radio. He would even have allowed his thoughts to travel to exciting imaginary worlds, simply by allowing himself to be hypnotized by the perpetually distant, yellow horizon, brought by the headlights to an ever-changing life with each spin of the tires.

But his heart was not in it. There was hitchhiking and then there was hitchhiking. You met nice people and you met unpleasant ones. They rarely asked anyone for payment. But, until now, he'd never sat down beside a character so... impenetrable. A character who, with each passing hour, took on a darker significance, a more questionable presence.

South of Nevers, he was starting to wonder if he was dreaming. The purring of the engine could barely be heard by the passengers and the clarity of the radio station relegated the existence of the night and the water to an invented world. Laurent allowed a pleasant drowsiness to wash over him and everything around him melted into enigmatic signs that made up a waking dream.

The man had been silent for a long time. He seemed absorbed with the difficulty of driving in conditions favorable for the slightest accident. But Laurent paid no attention. He was enjoying evoking the image of a blond girl with black eyes, hair tied back, waiting in to be rescued by some modern knight in shining armor... Although half asleep, he still shrugged his shoulders and smiled vaguely. Smiled at what? At this female image forged from the rain or at himself, with that indulgent pity a man always keeps for his dreams?

The car slowed, then stopped on the shoulder. Suddenly brought back to reality, Laurent looked at his watch with surprise. It was almost midnight.

"We've passed Clermont," said the bird. "I'll be heading West. I think that..."

"Of course..." interrupted Laurent. "It's been so kind of you."

He opened the car door, groping his way.

CHAPTER III

The car disappeared into the rain and Laurent found himself alone on a sloped road enveloped in icy darkness. It sloped down along a slight curve and he had to guess at rather than see the fork.

Drawn naturally down the slope, Laurent covered about a hundred meters along between the grass and the asphalt, guiding himself along the edge of the ground under his feet and on the slightly lighter zone between the peaks of the trees: the place for the sky.

The water and the cold suddenly trapped him, like a deer that had found temporary shelter suddenly caught between the paws of the dogs. And the contrast between this world of wet shadows and the cozy comfort to which he had grown accustomed during several hours of relaxation — that contrast made Laurent's abandonment, the immense solitude in which he found himself, even sadder.

He found it impossible to define the surrounding landscape even approximately. The road was the only universe on which he could depend — even though it remained empty and silent as if no vehicle had travelled it in years. For a moment, Laurent thought of a fragile footbridge built over a world of swamps and abysses. He imagined silent reptile people in the depths of an endless forest. Gustave Doré's monstrous landscapes took hold of his mind.

With great effort, he set aside such imaginings. Ahead of him, as if divided into two divergent streams by the tip of an island, the road split with no sign providing the slightest indication to be used to choose an itinerary. Laurent recalled what the man had said: "... I'll be heading West..." since they had travelled South up to that point, he would have to take the road to the left. The young man did just that, continuing to walk along a dark strip, its presence in the seemingly universal darkness announced by the wind.

The road remained empty. In any case, there was no doubt that if a car were to drive by — heading in the right direction — the driver would never stop to pick up a hitchhiker who could potentially be a murderer. After all, it was almost one o'clock in the morning. At that time and given the weather, drivers were right to be suspicious of people they met along a forest road.

Laurent thought all this, putting himself in the shoes of the drivers. After all, he was much more exposed than they were... For the second time that night, he ran his fingers over the handle of his hunting knife, making a little fun of himself nevertheless.

A sudden burst of rain caught him off guard. He felt water run down his face as if he were in a shower. He would have to set up camp here, anywhere.

He removed one strap after the other and the heavy canvas bag fell to the loose ground of the shoulder. Laurent crouched down and patiently searched through the outer pockets. Naturally, the powerful flashlight he had brought with him was hidden under a multitude of objects, boxes, clothing, maps... For that simple reason he had not used it when he climbed out of the car. For that matter, Laurent had never understood why a person like himself, with a methodical and orderly mind suitable for the study of mathematics, could find it so overwhelming to rationally organize a piece of luggage in which everything had a clearly defined purpose...

He sighed and shrugged. The flashlight was sticking out of the upper portion of his pack, stuck between the sleeping bag and the tent. A click. A beam of light.

About ten meters from there, the line of trees stopped, replaced by a rocky expanse; the powerful flashlight only provided a vague image. One thing was certain; he'd have to take shelter where he was. If he continued on his way, Laurent would have to camp out without any natural shelter, on rocky soil which would make it impossible to use tent pegs.

He pulled his pack back on and walked toward the trees, turning his back on the road. The flashlight revealed a shallow ditch ahead of him and he crossed it easily. He made his way through beech and birch trees, recognizing a few pines along his way, and quickly found a spot suitable for camping.

He was starving, but he decided to set up the tent before attacking his provisions. He installed the flashlight in a low fork in a tree and got down to work, as the rain doubled in intensity.

Although old and worn, the canvas tent provided an effective screen. Finally sheltered from the elements, comfortably lit by the flashlight, Laurent lit a small butane gas stove; and an aluminum tray half filled with fragrant was soon steaming on it. The canteen still contained a few large swigs of wine and the solitary traveler took a gulp for his aperitif.

He had taken off his wet clothing; it was hanging from the tent poles, steaming gently in the warmth cast by the stove. He slipped into his sleeping bag and took his meal in this atmosphere of comfort and relaxation.

Tomorrow, he thought, *maybe I'll getting lucky and find just as good a ride...*

The man's profile slipped into his mind. His profile and the composite silhouette of the strange vehicle. But, given the euphoria that washed over him just then, the strange ideas that had sprung into his mind during the trip faded, taking on a more laughable hue. He no longer experienced that discomfort he had found so hard to overcome throughout the trip. And that impression that he was constantly being probed, that his mind was being read, felt like a product of an overactive imagination...

He concluded his meal with an apple and placed the water can, the pouch of sugar and the tin of instant coffee next to the stove for breakfast. That done, he turned off the flashlight and lay down.

The tent was completely dark. Head resting on his inflatable pillow, Laurent listened to the wind whistling through the trees and the music of thousands of raindrops hitting the canvas. He felt peaceful, as if the tent was a cave protected from the elements roaring outside. Better yet: everything was so close, so immediate, making the softness of the shelter all the more priceless.

He laughed quietly, thinking about prowlers. It wasn't the kind of night for people to go about challenging him and his knife in the middle of an uninhabited part of the country... No one would be around to steal the canvas bowl he had set outside to fill...

He turned over in his sleeping bag and soon fell asleep, rocked by the song of the water and the wind.

Chaotic tearing and pounding tore him brutally from his sleep. It was so violent that, for a few seconds, he thought was caught in the grasp of a nightmare.

The next moment he pictured a sudden attack by men or animals Finally, he thought of rocks being rained down by evil peasants.

But it was nothing of the kind. He realized that all too soon. What was happening was much simpler, but more dangerous. Hail was falling outside. Hail such as the kind that is occasionally found in mountainous regions, enormous hailstones capable of destroying everything in their path. The tent had already been damaged beyond repair. Completely shredded, it allowed hailstones as large as nuts to rain down with an infernal clanging on the stove and the aluminum utensils.

Laurent immediately covered his head with his hat, hardened by the water, which kept him from being knocked out. The hailstorm grew even wilder. The beam of the flashlight revealed the scope of the catastrophe: the tent was riddled with holes. It could no longer even be considered a tent, just a pile of rags blowing in the wind. And, to make things even worse, the night had lost none of its impenetrable depth.

During this bombardment, Laurent decided to climb out of his sleeping bag. The damage was beyond repair. He had to find a natural shelter.

After dressing quickly, the young man stuffed everything he had taken out two hours earlier back into his backpack. A glance at his wrist watch revealed that it was barely three o'clock in the morning. Although the tent was beyond repair, he did not have the heart to abandon it and rolled the remnants up hastily.

He recalled that something similar had happened to one of his friends in a campground where everything had been shredded, apart from the American army surplus tents, which had survived intact.

Three times heavier, but three times more solid, he thought, arranging his pack on his back.

The hail storm slowed and turned into a dense, cold rain. Laurent waved the flashlight around, making sure he was not forgetting anything.

That damned hail did its work, he thought, furious... *and now it's gone*.

The water was already drenching his clothes, which had not had time to dry completely. Shivering, he set out in the direction of the road, his head heavy with sleep.

"Let's see," he said to himself. "The trees are too sparse to provide any protection. Over there, beyond the edge, I saw a rocky patch. I may be able to find a large rocky overhang to shelter under. It's not an ideal camp for such a night, but if I use what remains of my poor tent to cover myself..."

He reached the road, followed it, arrived at a moor, and started making its way through it. Ten minutes later, the beam of his long-range flashlight formed a round spot on a strange, massive wall.

CHAPTER IV

Dumbfounded, Laurent stopped dead. A gust of rain whipped his face, blinding him for several seconds. As he directed the beam of light at the obstacle once again, another gust tore off his hat, which vanished into the shadows. Laurent postponed his investigation until later and raced after his hat.

The moor he had just crossed looked as little like the forest where he had camped as a plain looks like a mountain. Not a single bush, not a single weed. Shallow cracks where black water lapped, rocks of various heights, ranging between one and seven meters tall.

When Laurent found his cap, he realized that he had made his way around the short wall which turned out to be as round as the flank of a tower. But the curve was so gentle that the radius must have been very long.

For the first time, he looked at it closely. The wall was apparently very thick, there was no parging and the rough stones were held together at irregular intervals with coarse cement. The light illuminated a strange opening a few meters from the ground; it was almost shapeless and filled with plates of glass of different colors. Laurent saw black joints winding in tortuous directions.

Stained glass: a crooked window, the elements welded together with lead. The rain was rolling down the colored glass, taking on a thousand forgotten hues, as the light created diamonds.

Dumbfounded, Laurent aimed his flashlight higher. The beam did not reveal the roof to him. Did the walls stretch up to a dizzying height or was the rain reducing the range of the light?

He started to walk slowly along the structure. When he had covered a rather large circle, his eyes were drawn to another opening, one that was feebly lit.

It seemed that the light did not come from a room located directly behind the window, but from another one that communicated with it by means of a door. That made the colors of the stained glass look somewhat mysterious and faded. The rain merely accentuated this, giving the window a blurry, shimmering appearance.

There was no outer wall, no garden — what would be the point of a garden in such sterile, tormented terrain? The building stood, formidable, in the middle of a rocky moor.

Automatically, Laurent pulled up the strap of his backpack on his right shoulder. He was cold and his pack was heavy. After all, wasn't it fortunate that this building was located on his way? Wasn't it marvelous that he could see light at such a late hour? All he had to do was go to the door. The people inside would surely not have the heart to leave a homeless, lost wanderer out in the storm... Considering the dark windows, the effort remained problematic. But under these conditions...

Laurent continued walking and finally found a door. A tall, door, with two ornate panels, obviously carved from oak and equipped with ornamental hinges. He stopped, surprised by the distance he'd had to cover to walk around the heavy structure. On the off chance, he tried again to catch a glimpse of the roof and thought he saw, very high up, gutters with irregular overhangs. The presence, in such a place, of such a building, surpassed his understanding. Travel adventures held quite a few surprises...

At least that's what he thought. In actual fact, he felt a certain amount of concern when he considered the dimensions of the building. In the 20th century, people did not build fortified castles with stained glass windows. And real medieval strongholds, or whatever remained of them, did not stand on flat terrain — much less in a valley. Since he had climbed out of the car, he'd been constantly walking downhill.

And that curious car, driven by some sort of soothsayer with a bird's beak? It was the strangest ride he had ever had; the unlikelihoods kept piling up, without ever going totally beyond the possible. What welcome awaited him behind the massive door, behind those black walls and the crooked stained-glass windows?

He hesitated for a moment, pulled his backpack up higher and waded through a few puddles. Reaching a decision, he approached the door and grabbed the heavy iron hammer affixed to the door.

As it struck the wooden panel, the metal hammer woke a deep, lengthy grumble inside, as if the door opened into a cathedral. Laurent took a step back, disconcerted by the racket he had set off. A long moment passed, a moment during which he silenced a furious desire to flee.

No sound inside. Not the slightest sign of life. Laurent did not have the courage to bang the hammer against the door a second time. He allowed himself to be hypnotized by the heavy iron mass, and suddenly realized that it was shaped like the head of a hideous old man, with hollow eyes and a toothless mouth. The rain streamed down over the cheeks half eaten by rust like some sort of red leprosy, covering the face with tears. Laurent started... but at that very instant, the door pivoted on its hinges.

A reddish light cast a blurry beam on the ground, turning the rain in the puddles into fire and blood. The door gaped open on a nebulous hall, yet the light came from farther in, higher up, as if some oven burned in the depths of this rocky citadel, casting flickers of firelight here and there and outside.

Laurent remained motionless on the threshold. He once again saw the seats in the car, seemingly the result of some bloody murder... He felt pursued by that tragic color. But a slight silhouette appeared in the opening as a voice broken by age, called out, tenuous and spindly in the long howl of the wind.

"Step in quickly," Laurent heard. "Don't stay a moment longer in God's wrath!"

Driven solely by reflex, he obeyed and stepped forward, as the shape he took for an old man faded ahead of him. The door closed behind him and he noticed its unusual thickness. The heavy rumble it released in the depths of the rooms filled his mind like a falling gravestone at the entrance to a family vault. But another image replaced that hateful one. The individual who had let him in, the one he had taken for an old man, was actually an old woman. A bald one.

Laurent was unable to find anything positively dangerous, or even threatening, in that anomaly... But the driver of the car had been bald too. The hitchhiker was not being pursued by the color of blood alone; he kept seeing smooth round heads everywhere and, in this case, it was most unusual. Elderly women often cover their heads with hats or scarves... particularly if they are completely bald, something rare in women.

But Laurent's attention was already being turned from that to the décor surrounding him. He'd never seen such a hall before.

Hall... that was not an appropriate term. An enormous room, rather, with an extraordinarily high ceiling lit by a violently red light. The source of the light was located up above, high overhead: a group of three cartwheels, hanging horizontally from chains, candles standing around the circumferences. The material of the candles must have been treated in some strange manner since the flames were red.

Laurent thought about the strontium used in Bengal flames. But his train of thought stopped there. The ambiance in that room was no more like fireworks than a catafalque was like a cradle.

In the back, a gigantic black tapestry with red and gold patterns occupied a large portion of the wall. It was hung directly on the stone, which stood bare, with nothing to smooth the rough edges. It was easy to see the material that made up the wall around the tapestry and that wall, although too close to be part of the enclosure Laurent had walked around outside, was no simple wall.

But the hitchhiker did not have the time to examine the complex patterns of the tapestry before his eyes were drawn to the monumental, copper fireplace that framed a deep hearth carved in the curved wall, to his right. There too, red flames burned with a constant, deep snore.

Laurent's eyes ran over the black flagstones. In the middle of this floor, stood a table that looked more like a druid alter than the piece of furniture commonly known as a table. Two shapeless rocks, the upper portion having been cut with a saw, supported a thick, carefully polished slab of porphyry.

Basically, the chamber was the shape of a semi-circle and the final portion of the wall, which Laurent discovered to his left, contained a slightly convex, pentagon-shaped, black mirror, sealed in the same stone. What was surprising about the mirror was its size; it had to be two and a half meters tall...

Slowly, Laurent returned his gaze to the bald woman.

He was able to see her more clearly. A shapeless black dress covered her, held by a thin rope at her waist. She seemed to be wearing old-fashioned ankle boots.

As he looked at her, she spoke, saying "You are safe here, safe from *His* anger. The master cannot receive you now, but I will take you in."

"Th... thank you," stammered Laurent, his throat tight.

He wanted to apologize for his intrusion at such a late hour, but his tongue had turned to lead and refused to work. The extravagance of the setting, the strange words of the old, bald woman, who spoke of the house like a fortress beyond the reach of God... nothing served to calm a mind exhausted by a lack of sleep in an icy body.

"There will be a fire in your... in your bedroom...," grumbled the old woman. "Here there are fires everywhere, and also light... the same fire... the same light..."

She started to walk through the room. For a second, Laurent felt overwhelmed by a terrible urge to retreat, to open the door with its iron hinges, to go back out into the black rain and spend the night worry-free.

Fatigue won. Although he followed the old woman, a mortal fear constricted his lungs, settling in his heart.

Turning around, he saw a misshapen room in the black mirror. Dark and light played over it, drawing an enormous, grimacing skull.

CHAPTER V

Laurent followed the old woman, a servant no doubt. He suddenly noticed that the enormous fireplace heated the room rather well and the air was warm despite the enormous area of the place. These positive thoughts were out of tune with the sumptuous strangeness of the place and Laurent realized just how at odds they were. From a great distance, he couldn't help but feel a certain sense of irony, given his own actions, skating over his own thoughts which rational training had made to some extent impermeable to the impossible. He did have to admit that everything in the place was not only outside the normal, but also beyond all likelihood.

He recalled a certain enormous room with stone walls that he had walked through during a visit to Mont Saint-Michel. He recalled the gigantic fireplace and the silent comment he had made at that time returned to his mind.

Heating a room such as this would take not one fireplace of this size but at least three...

The fireplace he was walking past at that point was virtually the same size as the one he recalled and the room was about the same size. The proportions seemed to be the same. Yet...

Some great thinker could have built this compromise between Coucy and Argol, that castle from the past seen again in dreams... but he would no longer be simply a great thinker if he defied the laws of physics...

But Laurent would all too soon lose his taste for rational thinking. He felt that with a tinge of confusion and wondered if, instead of being a weapon, a critical mind could instead be a weakness.

There was a low door in the wall the tapestry covered, something Laurent had not noticed before. It stood ajar and the

48

bald woman pushed it completely open, revealing a staircase directly behind it. Laurent noted that the door, like the earlier one, made no sound as it swung on its hinges.

The stairs rose in a spiral, but were wide enough for three people to walk up abreast. As of the first turn, at the edge of visibility, it was possible to see a recess in the wall, which was still rough and uncovered. This recess held three thick candles obviously similar to the first candles he had noticed and their flames cast the same bloody shadows on the steps.

Those steps... Laurent climbed them carefully. They were so worn in the middle that the slightest misstep would have pitched him headlong, and there was no railing to break his fall.

The staircase rose up, the wall punctuated here and there with recesses in which the same candles burned. Hypnotized by the color of their flames, Laurent had not yet clearly noted what they were made of. They were black and grainy, covered with bright dribbles that formed small, solidified lakes at their bases. Howe was someone able to replace them they burned down so they all seemed to be the same height and burned at the same pace?

Was it the old woman? But it seemed as if the dwelling was equipped with the same sort of lighting throughout. The servant hardly seemed up to that...

A crazy idea wormed its way in Laurent's mind. The candles didn't burn down at all. Perhaps their wicks were not really on fire? Perhaps the candles were equipped with tubes containing an inflammable substance? Logical hypotheses seemed somehow even less acceptable in this house in which nothing seemed normal, or even possible.

But the woman stopped on a rounded landing with three doors. She pushed the middle one and stepped back.

"Go in the room and get some sleep,' she said listlessly.

She moved to head back down, turned back, and said, "You'll need it."

49

Laurent thanked the woman., He walked into the room as the servant's footsteps rang out and her rough dress rustled on the stairs.

The room he stepped into looked like the backroom of a museum, one of those warehouses used to store furniture waiting to be restored. Apart from an immense, raised bed covered with black and red fabric, there were few pieces of furniture or useful objects. However, after looking around for a few seconds, Laurent noticed, hidden behind a screen covered with cracked paint, a small table holding a sort of stone trough filled with water, which could possibly be considered a basin. Once again, the light of the six candles standing in a line on a bracket gave the liquid an unpleasant appearance.

This room was warm too. Laurent supposed that the chimney ran through the wall and was enough to heat the room...

The capacities of his mind were so reduced by his fatigue that he was starting to accept the most basic, the least satisfying explications without question.

He threw his backpack down and it landed on the black tile floor. As he sat down on the edge of the bed, he realized there were no windows in the room.

Forcing himself into action yet again, he got up and walked over to close the door. Vaguely concerned, he looked up and down the door frame for some sort of device that would allow him to lock the door until the next morning. He found nothing of the kind.

He glanced quickly at a heavy piece of furniture made of dark wood, a sort of chest, standing along the wall, intending to drag it over to the door. But why did he need a barricade? No one had threatened him...

Yet, the servant had said, "You will need it," when talking about sleep...

"Bah!" said Laurent sighing and yawning. "She saw I was a hitchhiker and she was probably thinking about my next ride."

Fooling himself, he grasped that random interpretation and started to take his clothes off for the second time that night.

"At least now, I won't run the risk of being pummeled by hailstones as large as eggs..."

Barefoot, he walked over to the candles. He blew on them as hard as he could. They continued to burn.

Enraged and dumbfounded, he attempted to squeeze a wick between his fingers. All he succeeded in doing was burning himself slightly. He had to accept the facts; these candles could only be extinguished by...

Half wakened by anger and concern, he walked over to the trough of water, cupped his hands to fill them and threw the liquid at the candles.

A spray of green sparks flew up and the six red flames continued to their imperturbable, seemingly eternal dance.

Fright restricted Laurent's throat. What spell controlled the candles?

Eternal flames! He stopped his train of thought immediately. He was not about to give into unfortunate associations generated by the servant's words about divine anger. There was no way he was about to slip into credulity and from there, imperceptibly, into the worst disorders of the mind. Laurent was not a Christian. As a result, God's wrath and the flames of Hell meant nothing for him. They were nothing more than popular images hiding philosophical symbols... Nothing more.

After all, there was no problem if the candles, obviously made by some obsessed magician, stayed lit all night, although there was no window to bring in fresh air. If the air got too foul, Laurent would notice and he would still have the energy to go back downstairs to the large room where the draw of the fireplace would certainly ensure permanent ventilation.

He discovered the bed, after hanging his clothing on a stack of decorative picture frames. Everything would finally be dry once he got dressed again.

There was nothing particular about the bed, which was covered in dark fabric. A bed like any other, very springy, no doubt covered with white sheets, although the light turned them a violent pink. It was impossible, in the ruby brightness, to see any shades but red and pink and, between those colors and the dark, a multitude of neutral shades that could evoke blue and green, brown and purple... That was the case of the bed spread; its color could have been defined if the light had been white...

But what objects in this sinister house had ever seen white light?

Laurent slipped into the warm sheets and fell asleep as if he'd been on his feet a week.

He sat up suddenly, eyes wide open. Had he slept a minute or an hour? What noise had wakened him? Or what silence?

The candles seemed to be burning less brightly. Eyelids stinging, Laurent looked around. Nothing had changed. He was still alone and the weakness of the light must be nothing more than a product of his imagination. Still the same height, the candles remained in their places, unchanging.

Laurent held his head in his hands and, doing that, noticed that his wristwatch had stopped at 3:05 o'clock.

Was there another reason for him to be awake? He had the impression that, since entering the stone house, he had started to question the nature of time as it flowed there. This bizarre suspicion had not crossed the threshold of his subconscious but had taken root there with such strength that, from that time on, all of his unconscious energy had clung to following the march of the time he carried with him — watching his wristwatch served as some sort of lifebuoy, providing assurance against the evils of other worlds.

He jiggled his wrist, wound the mechanism. Nothing changed. The watch seemed condemned to show the same meaningless time for all eternity. For the first time, Laurent admitted he felt afraid. Not some fear caused by a material danger, but a deep fear caused by brushing up against unspeakable things, things that had no contact with man outside nightmares.

Of the six candles, five suddenly blew out.

CHAPTER VI

In the red half-light, Laurent felt a mortal cold penetrate his body. The sundry objects tangled around him seemed to be moving about in a cunning manner. The sly dance, each item in its own shadow, grew more confused, more threatening.

What harmful influence could have blown out candles Laurent had been unable to extinguish, the flame feeding off water to create sparks? Yet, he was not even certain the liquid had been simple water...

Leaning on an elbow, Laurent glanced about the room. He could no longer see the door and certain objects, certain pieces of furniture seemed to have moved about. As he turned his head, he shifted back violently and held back a cry.

A human shape was stepping away from the wall, slow, blurry, barely visible and yet recognizable. Torn between disbelief, pain and fear, Laurent saw the silhouette of his late father sit down on the foot of the bed.

The shadow had maintained that air of youthfulness with a melancholic, thoughtful face, that Laurent had known. Its posture was somewhat stooped, the head leaning slightly to the left, and it wore the clothing the dead man had worn in the last few months of his life. Everything matched Laurent's affectionate memory of his father. Sorrow overwhelmed fear and affectionate memory and he soon set aside the idea that it might be an hallucination. He considered it a temporary resurrection of a man he had mourned for a long time. Following anguish, the sorrow was in turn replaced by a deep sense of peace and security.

Yet words formed in his mind that did not come from him. Eyes riveted on his father's shadow, Laurent realized the ghost was communicating with him. Initially, he realized that the mystery of the extinguished candles could obviously be explained by some occult action, stronger than that which fed the strange flames.

A combat of inhuman powers had taken place in the red silence and Laurent experienced fear again as he realized the house did actually contain evil enigmas.

Yet the silent dialogue grew more assured, clearer.

"My son," said the shadow. "You are no longer in the world of men here. Forces which I am powerless against threaten you. You have to escape before the spiral swallows you up forever. Leave this house as quickly as you can. Destiny has placed it on your path as a trap. Don't try to understand. Obscure webs are being woven around you and you must break them yourself before it is too late."

Paralyzed, Laurent stared at the shadow, terrified. A few more words formed in his mind then everything grew blurry, indistinct.

"I can't say anything else to you.... Leave, go back to the roads your life must follow. Farewell, my son..."

With those words, the ghost faded into the air like smoke dispersed by a breath. Motionless, Laurent felt a tear bead at the tip of his eyelashes.

After a few moments of dark meditation, Laurent decided the event was the most troubling and the most sinister he had ever experienced. He could have tried to blame the terrifying materialization on the incredible mansion, but the warning was too present in his mind for him to have the strength to doubt it.

Something monstrous was taking shape in the shadows. He realized he had to escape in order to save his life and he should not wait for the danger to be unmasked before fleeing.

He jumped out of bed and dressed quickly. Whatever role the ghost played in aggravating the darkness, the flame of the last candle had not changed. Most of the room remained in shadow and Laurent headed in the direction of the door, feeling his way about like a blind man. The room was much larger than it had first seemed and the light of the single candle was powerless when it came to revealing its full size.

Laurent packed up everything he had taken out of his backpack and bitterly feared that he would have to pack his bags yet again before the night ended...

The door opened without difficulty. The same terrifying light bathed the semi-circular landing, in the same crypt-like silence. Carefully, he walked down the steps he'd climbed behind the servant, fearing he'd rouse the mysterious master who could prevent his departure. At the foot of the spiral stair-case, he recalled his father's words: "You have to escape be-fore the spiral swallows you up forever". He wondered for a moment whether he should view it as simply a metaphor... At the foot of the staircase, he found the same door. He opened it.

It no longer opened into the room through which he had entered.

Laurent saw himself standing at the threshold of a long corridor with several solid doors. The hallway came to a dead end at a wall made of the same rocky material found else-where. The same bloody light and the same silence.

He closed his eyes, ran his hand over his forehead. This had to be delirium, a constant hallucination... How had this staircase, which he'd climbed earlier, suddenly changed place? How could the room with the mirror have disappeared and been replaced by this blind, dungeon-like corridor?

He stepped back. In his disoriented mind, fear was taking possession of everything. He was no longer able to make a healthy examination of the extravagant metamorphoses he'd witnessed. He needed rest, a moment of calm that would ena-ble him to return his thoughts to their normal pace. The last step of the staircase was there behind him. He collapsed onto it.

After a few minutes of confusion, all the while feeling horrifically abandoned, he regained a few vestiges of self-control. The first thing he did was abandon his backpack. It was weighing him down. He stood up, momentarily undecided.

What should he do? Go back up to the bedroom? What if there was no longer a bedroom? Fists against his forehead, he attempted to put the chaos of his mind into some order. No. He had to find out what was going on. Step back as little as possible. If he continued to move ahead, the fantasy he was trapped in might take on an acceptable appearance, a reality sufficiently real to make the exit from this diabolical place accessible to him.

In order to provide concrete support for this burgeoning burst of courage, he drew the long hunting knife from his belt. Its presence had reassured him often. For a moment, he admired the carved handle resting so comfortably in his hand, the slender blade capable of making deep wounds. The hellish light bathing him cast murderous reflections on the blade and he resolved to use it with all his might if enemies appeared. *They* would see their prey was nothing like the inoffensive beasts caught helplessly in traps...

Blade in hand, he walked into the blind corridor.

He reached the end of the corridor and turned around. Nothing had hampered him. If there was an enemy, it was a cowardly and invisible enemy, hunkered down somewhere behind one of the doors, no doubt laughing at his efforts and his anger.

He tried to open the last door. It resisted. He moved onto another one, banging it furiously with his clenched fist.

"Is there anyone there?" he shouted, out of control. "Show yourself! Come out!"

The only response: silence. But the silence suddenly seemed less thick, less heavy. Had he not heard some weak sound coming from behind the walls?

He continued his pounding, moving from one door to the next. There was no mistake about it. Someone, behind the wall, was calling and moaning, in a voice the thick stone rendered weak and distant as if the intruder were worlds away.

Laurent, face red, stopped and stood still, tensing his entire body, waiting for the distant sound, the first he had heard here apart from the old servant's croak. He heard nothing. The silence, as thick as liquid lead, enveloped him. The silence of abandoned vaults.

He allowed his eyes to roam over the corridor. Six black candles in a recess burned with the same flame, making the stone bleed. He felt the wind blowing madness in his ears.

He had to get out of the corridor. There was nothing to be done here. Monstrous secrets might be hidden behind the doors, which seemed to be sealed into the very rock... Those secrets were no concern of his. His thoughts, his efforts should focus on a single goal: escape. Freedom. The dismal message he had received before sliding into sleep clarified his urgency minute by minute...

Minute by minute? The watch remained silent, its hands as motionless as the arms of a cold body. Someone or something had killed the watch, while waiting to attack its owner. Someone whose primary concern was to eliminate anything in this place that could provide a reminder that time was flowing outside, the time of life, the time of night and day, the constantly moving river of human life. There was nothing of the kind here, inside, in a placed petrified in its light of fear, a motionlessness outside the world, locked up in walls, safe from the battering ram, safe from life. Gloomy horror.

Laurent put the ridiculous knife he had brandished against the void back in its sheath. He no longer had the courage to fight, to break the silence with furious cries. He felt as if the red shadow was wrapping closer around him, taking possession of him like a vampire plants its icy teeth in living flesh. Shoulders hunched, he left the corridor.

CHAPTER VII

The spiral staircase opened ahead of him, in its silence and the eternal blood of its tormented stones. Laurent slowly climbed up the steps, paying attention to their unevenness. At the fourth, he turned back.

He had vaguely expected some new metamorphosis and feared, as he turned his head, he would see the door he had first seen when he entered the building. The room, the fireplace, and the mirror. He feared and hoped...

But the door still opened onto the corridor. He abandoned his backpack. He could not carry it everywhere with him throughout this house, with neither beginning nor end, where fever and delirium seemed to reign. As he walked around the first bend, he lost sight of the place he had just left and was tempted for a moment to turn back, feeling that extravagant changes did not take place unless he was watching. But he resisted. Perhaps safety was to be found behind one of the doors on the landing... Perhaps there was another staircase, the right one... the one not intended for naïve people who wanted to get caught in traps...

On the landing, the door to his room was still half open. Ignoring it, he concentrated on the others, but without success. They seemed to be walled up and could have been one with the stone without that changing anything.

Discouraged, he gave up his plans for escape. His eyelids were heavy with sleep and he had no will to focus on a specific goal for long. He was well aware that danger hung over his head. A danger that was all the greater since it was unknown, hidden out of reach of the weakest battle, a danger made all the more present by his memory of the apparition. But sleep, sleep...

When he pushed the door to his room open, he saw another staircase.

Laurent did not have the strength to feel frightened again. The world surrounding him, the world hemming him in with its living stones, was so far beyond him that he could not maintain his desire to fight for long. The incredible is initially frightening, then quickly allows the soul to fall into a deep stupor if there is no rapid return to the tangible.

He did not fight; he did not resume pounding against the blind panels. He had no hope at all he would receive a response. If, by some impossible chance, an exit to the outside were to appear before him now, he would walk through it, abandoning his baggage behind him, delighted beyond belief at finally finding the tenuous link that connected the world of the living with the silent enclosure where he walked about in circles in the deadly light.

This new staircase wound up to an unknown floor. Laurent decided to explore it and walked up it, like a man climbing a scaffold.

This staircase was similar to the first one. The landing Laurent reached was similar enough to the one he had left for the fear of madness to return and swirl around the solitary man, as it had attacked him in the corridor where he had heard the moans.

A single door. Half open. He stopped at the threshold, overwhelmed with fear that he would find the room he had tried to return to. He remained motionless for a long time, frightened of himself. He thought about the mirror in the large room that had vanished, that monumental pentagon of shadows, and realized that if he could have seen his own face he would have run off in horror. His incandescent, dismal image. The expression of a madman, of a miserable wretch torn by obscure worlds from consciousness, wandering in the depths of a geometrical jungle where silence shrieks, where blood serves as light, where his stumbling footsteps constantly carry him back to the mortal point every fiber of his being is trying to forget.

Laurent suddenly realized that his terror was anticipating reality, that he was merely losing his way, without recognizing the keystone of madness. He took a slow, deep breath and opened the door wide.

The room was diamond-shaped. In each corner, three candles stood on a bracket. In the center, there was a lectern on which a book rested, closed.

Laurent stopped short. Above all else, how could all the rooms in this castle be lit up all the time? He imagined a silent person preceding him, everywhere he went, taking a different route, providing light as needed. That could be explained in part by the unusual nature of the eternal candles, as well as the useless light in every nook and cranny of the enormous building. Since, in that case, the house, or the castle rather, remained in darkness and the illusion of constant light was consciously maintained.

Who would that hypothetical person be? The servant? The "master"? The mysterious master the old woman had mentioned?

The old woman? Laurent was beginning to doubt her existence. He wondered if his memory was based on something other than a new illusion. It was quite possible to maintain an incredible architecture of mirages around him without there being anything supernatural in all that. An atmosphere of amazement and fear could easily be created using a few skillfully orchestrated techniques... But why? Simply to reduce the logical thought processes and the calm of the person caught in the trap, so he could be used as a submissive slave... Was someone trying to convince him he'd lost his mind? Would they suddenly present the victim of a recently committed murder to him and take advantage of his disarray to convince him of his guilt? Did they want to make him shoulder responsibility for a crime he had not committed?

Laurent was getting lost in his conjectures. This confusion did nothing to advance his understanding of the facts but, by focusing his thoughts on more material paths, it did serve to distance him from thoughts of annihilation and despair. If there was anything concrete about the danger he faced, there would still be time for rebellion and fighting. In his hypotheses, Laurent found new strength to enter the almost empty room and approach the only object it contained.

The lectern seemed to be made of very old black wood covered with deep carvings. He stepped back upon seeing them. Faces of old men with hateful or terrified expressions decorated the foot of the lectern; two-headed snakes wound around the book in a wreath of worm-eaten wood that had to be several centuries old.

The book itself, bound in very fine, very light leather, was embossed with gold arabesques that converged on the fore edge in a clasp so cleverly worked it brought to mind the work of Cellini. The leather so fine and pale... Laurent shivered as he thought of human skin.

He glanced around, troubled. There was another door in the wall opposite the door he had come in through, giving credence to his suppositions: when he left the corridor, someone could have brought light into this room, left the door half open, and prepared the place for him.

But the silence remained unchanged. Up to that point, it had only been broken by the servant and the anonymous moans. Nothing disturbed it now and, since Laurent was constantly moving about, the person in question had to exercise great caution when moving about... Also, all of Laurent's movements had to be predictable, guided by a system of anonymous open or closed accesses... Laurent suddenly realized how the apparent transformations in the positioning of the rooms and staircases could have been handled. He had not used the same doors each time. That was all.

He felt more clear-headed than he had at the start of this forced stroll. His father' s appearance was the only thing that continued to feel supernatural and unsettling. But if someone could move about around him in the shadow and silence, could that person also have hypnotized him somehow?

He still had to discover the reason for these obscure efforts. Laurent was a total stranger to those who lived in this mad fortress... How could he not go back to the idea of a responsibility to be taken in the place of another?

Laurent reached for the book. Since everything around him seemed to be organized for him alone, this book must have its own place in the strange arrangements and it should be opened.

It was a slim volume of an unusual size. There was no title on the first page, the spine or the cover. As he opened it, Laurent recalled the fear he had felt. Wasn't the book in his hands the keystone to madness which everything could return him to sooner or later? A strange premonition told him that the content of the book should be very important to him.

One strange fact caught his attention initially. The book had not been printed. It was a slim bundle of yellowed sheets of parchment. The tight, loopy writing had obviously been written centuries earlier with a quill and ink that had turned grey over time.

The words were not easy to decipher and Laurent carried the notebook over to the nearest candles.

In the dancing light that gave the parchment a vaguely orange hue, Laurent was able to read a sentence that stopped his heart.

The traveler lost in the blood light did not realize that henceforth only that light would exist for him and the light of the world in which he had been born was to fade from his memory...

CHAPTER VIII

Laurent remained motionless for a long time, book in hand, eyes staring at the wall.

Could this new puzzle also be explained by the secret activity he'd suspected? Had someone written these pages for him? Did their ancient appearance hide yet another trick? He looked back at the text, noting an unpleasant detail. The individual described there in words and expressions dating back to the 18th century was named Lorenzo.

There was no possible error. Lorenzo was the Italian version of Laurent. And the description of the hero was even more disturbing, the same as his own. They were so identical the only details that could have differentiated the two, clothing for example, remained so vague that anything was possible. For example, the text referred to "baggage" which corresponded to the backpack Laurent had abandoned at the foot of the staircase... The same could be said for the rest of the character in the book and his adventure.

Laurent doubted that someone had had the time to write the text since he'd entered the house. Apart from the color of the ink, which could have been created deliberately, and the archaic syntax, which could have been imitated, the volume was still thick enough it would have taken at least a day to write using a quill. Everything led Laurent to believe that the book had been written *before his arrival* — and that was truly frightening. Frightening for two reasons: the prediction, on the one hand, and the content of the book on the other. Laurent read another sentence then suddenly closed the book. He had already fought down his concern, his terror. He'd collected his wavering thoughts and the fear of madness they hid. He would not allow himself to be defeated by this new attempt at intimidation. And the easiest way to get away from it was what he had just done. He'd read too much. Lorenzo's adventures were none of his concern, were of no interest to him. What he, what Laurent wanted was to get away from the people living in this castle.

He put the book back on the lectern and left the room without looking back.

On the stone landing he hesitated as if reconsidering. Not because he regretted closing the book, which seemed to say too much, but because he thought about the second door in the other wall of the room with the lectern.

He retraced his steps, examined the door from a distance. It had obviously been closed with care. They wanted him to take the same route.

On the lower landing the same half open door looked onto the first staircase. He pushed it and continued to walk down, hoping to find a route at the bottom that would finally take him back to the large, ornate room.

That staircase ended with a low door. He opened it easily.

It was one of the doors he'd seen in the underground passage. He found himself back in the corridor where he'd heard the moans. The first staircase started at the other end. At the foot of this staircase, he recognized the dark shape of his backpack. It was still in the same place.

The house had been designed like a labyrinth. An ingenious system of open and closed doors led the victim where someone wanted him to go and Laurent might have got lost if they had given him free access to all the rooms in the building.

He walked down the hallway and automatically checked the contents of his pack. Then he pulled it on, no doubt hoping he'd be better equipped to escape from the place in case he eventually found the large room...

Something had changed in the wall he was walking along. In the middle of the corridor, the wall no longer ended at flagstone floor. At the edge of the flagstone, there was an elongated opening, a window. It was so narrow Laurent could

65

have missed it the first time he walked down the corridor. In any case, it was there this time and the young man stopped when he reached it.

Standing, he was unable to see what purpose it served. There was no way to know if it opened onto a cellar of some kind.

Laurent's curiosity was piqued. He bent down, trying to catch a glimpse of what lay on the other side of what had to be an opening that went straight through the entire thickness of the wall. He finally had to lie down and then he saw.

The narrow window looked into a room below. Only a part of it was visible. It was a room with furniture that seemed much more ordinary than what he had seen in the other rooms. Yet, it was bathed in the same red light.

As he stayed there, spying — pleased to be treating the invisible occupants of the house as they had treated him — a shape moved into his field of vision.

A blonde girl wearing black silk.

Laurent's heart pounded. For the first time during his forced stay, he found himself looking at someone attractive... very attractive.

The girl left his field of vision. He waited impatiently for her to come back, not daring to catch her attention yet. As he was thinking, he suddenly made the connection between her and the moans he had heard.

But no... that was ridiculous. Why had she moaned and sobbed earlier? As far as Laurent could judge from his fleeting glimpse of the girl, the expression on her face was calmly indifferent.

What was important about this "encounter" was the presence of an apparently normal being in a building where everything breathed madness. And although this discovery was the result of indelicate behavior — spying through a basement window was not exactly proper, or so Laurent thought — he had nothing to be sorry for.

All in all, she might turn out to be an ally who would guide him to the room with the mirror, open that hidden door, and finally allow him to return outside, return to the road, find the freedom to continue on his way?

Cheeks burning, Laurent called out in a quiet voice.

The young girl heard him immediately and suddenly appeared in Laurent's field of vision. Laurent though he detected a glimmer of hope in her dumbfounded expression.

"Miss!" Laurent said again. "Excuse my brashness... I believe... I've lost my way in your house..."

Standing in the middle of the room, the girl looked as tense as if she were listening to some celestial voice.

"I have to leave," Laurent continued. "I thought I could accept the hospitality I was offered... but the night must be coming to an end and I have to get on the road first thing..."

He grew bolder. This suddenly direct manner of talking about something he'd considered prohibited made him see the future in a more positive light. Confidence bloomed within him through the magic of unambiguous language and he was starting to believe he would be able to take his leave from his hosts.

After stammering a few incomprehensible words, the young girl uttered a short sentence that froze him to his core.

"So, are you Laurent?" she asked.

Her question destroyed the entire house of cards he'd been so happy to build. It also swept away the reassuring idea he'd conjured up when he supposed someone had written the parchments since his arrival. She knew his name. The master or his henchmen knew it too. That made the invention of that Lorenzo impossible, yet gave much more weight to the idea the book was actually very old. It was so unlikely that someone here would know his name there was no point questioning the authenticity of the parchment. There was no simple series of coincidences and Laurent refused to view the book as a roughly concocted story developed to frighten a possible guest, no matter who it might be...

"How do you know my name?" he asked, short of breath.

Head held high, she stared desperately at what must be for her a simple slot in the ceiling. From where she stood, two meters below Laurent, she would only be able to see a part of Laurent's face while Laurent, his face close to the window, could see half the room.

"But..." she said. "How could you be anyone else?"

A lead blanket fell over Laurent's shoulders. He was taking part, as he should have expected, in a conversation as incoherent, as filled with puzzles, as the house in which it was taking place...

"Let's skip that," he said, reluctantly. "Would you be so kind as to join me in this corridor to help me get out of here?"

The young girl's expression changed from amazement to fear.

"Don't you know that I'm *locked up?*" she asked.

Laurent's disappointment was growing by the minute.

"You're the one I heard crying... a while ago?" he asked with an effort.

Dismay washed over the prisoner's face.

"I... no doubt..." she admitted. "But now... "

Her expression changed. Her face lit up with joy.

"Now you're here," she explained

She said that as if her observation resolved everything, broke down barriers, chased mystery and danger away.

"But I'm locked up too!" shouted Laurent.

"Naturally," she said her voice emotionless. "You didn't read the *book*?"

Laurent felt as if a hand had slapped him on the back of the head. Those hideous parchments again! Just as he finally encountered a living being in that horrible red light, the words uttered by that being plunged him back into the infernal world he was fighting against.

"No..." he grumbled. "One sentence was enough for me."

She looked desperate. Or was it merely the basic, demented light that gave her that appearance?

"You know full well that you'll never get out of here..." she said darkly. "It saddens you to meet me? And I've been waiting for you so long!"

She burst into tears and Laurent, dumbfounded, recognized the sobs he'd heard earlier...

CHAPTER IX

Disoriented, he turned his head away, although she could not see him. Although he realized he had nothing to do with the matter, he felt guilty witnessing the pain of the unknown young girl. More indiscreet than before.

"I can't get out of here, but you can come and get me, if you want," she said through her tears.

He looked at her again.

"But then I'll be a prisoner too," he said in a dull voice.

"Aren't you already a prisoner?"

"Here, I can still explore the house and look for an exit."

She twisted her hands and shouted, "But you won't find anything. Why didn't you read the *book*?"

Laurent felt rage wash over him.

"I don't care about that rag!" he shouted. "I don't want to know what nonsense it contains! If I make the most of my semi-liberty, it won't take long for me to make my way to the exit... All I have to do is break one of those stained-glass windows..."

She looked bewildered.

"What stained-glass windows?" she asked without stressing any of the words, as if the very idea was baroque and of no consequence.

"But..., the stained-glass windows I saw in the walls before I came in..."

She remained silent for a moment before saying, "And once you were inside, did you see them again?"

Laurent bit his lower lip. What had become of those strange windows? He had seen them in the beam of his flashlight as he was walking along the wall... but since then? He'd never found the slightest trace of windows inside the house... Were they fake windows, embedded in the stone like some sort of decoration? Was the air refreshed inside the building by conduits carved in the stone walls equipped with air vents?

No! As he was walking around the building, he'd noticed that one of the stained-glass windows had been lit from *inside*... He explained that vehemently.

"And did you find that room?" she asked in a tone that was now dripping with irony.

He had to admit he had not.

"But it's behind one of these doors!" he added, angrily. "If I have to break it down, I..."

She nodded her head, disappointed.

"You don't want to come and join me..." she concluded.

And that observation seemed to fill her with sadness.

He grew calm. The young girl was a very great beauty and her interest in him touched Laurent more than he wanted to admit. His growing tenderness was mingled with a certain cunning.

"Are you familiar with the house?" he asked.

"Of course, it's mine."

He fell silent. This was no time for lengthy explanations.

"Fine. How can I get to you?"

She clapped her hands as her face lit up. She must either have a very voluble character or be extremely young to demonstrate such a great range of expressions, such unstable behavior. As if to confirm Laurent's thoughts, she suddenly turned serious again.

"Be careful!" she said. "You can't go back."

"We'll see about that..." he said evasively.

There must be a new surprise door somewhere that opened in only one direction. He would simply have to prop it ajar and then they could both escape... He had no idea how naïve his reasoning was.

"Go back to the room with the lectern..." she said in a calm voice. "Then go through the second door. It opens onto a staircase that will bring you to me."

Laurent's head was pounding. Yet another staircase! How was it possible for this house to have so many? It must have been built by a mad man... This was the stuff of dreams.

"Perfect," he said, trying to keep his tone light. "I'm on my way."

He got up and headed for the end of the corridor. But after taking two steps he stopped short.

As they had been talking, his backpack had disappeared. There was nothing at all at the foot of the stairs.

Someone had come, almost under his very nose, and taken away his bag in order to attach him even more firmly to this labyrinth in which the strange young girl seemed to want to trap him as well.

For that matter, had she not played rather odiously on his feelings, exerting pressure on him and adding a trump card to the dark game being played against him? He retraced his footsteps and bent down to the narrow window.

"You're making a mockery of me!" he yelled, furious. "While you kept me here with your lies, someone stole my baggage! Your house is an evil trap. I'll file a complaint as soon as I get out of here."

He thought he heard a quiet chuckle from behind one of the doors.

Those who had stolen his backpack were laughing at his threats. It couldn't be the ancient servant... For the first time he had no doubt heard the master's voice... *the master...*

Teeth clenched, he threw himself against the door behind which he presumed the laugh had come from, then kicked it furiously with his steel-toed boots. He was met by silence, broken by the young girl's sobs rising up once again through the window.

He forced himself to remain still, to stay silent. If he couldn't control himself better, he would slip gently into madness. That was the most likely eventuality...

Soon, he regained enough control to make a decision. It didn't matter whether the young girl was a prisoner or an accomplice of those who were toying with him, he would force her to help him... After all, could he not use her as a hostage?

Boiling with impatience, he returned to the staircase and climbed the steps to the door that stood half open. Relying on his memory, he made sure it was not the one that led to the bedroom, which had closed.

He reached the second staircase and climbed again. *They* were no doubt following his movements with an attentive ear and the sound of his hiking boots on the stone reverberated in his chest.

He reached the room with the lectern, where the light had not changed, and headed for the door on the opposite wall.

It opened easily. He found that detail unsettling; it seemed to prove that *someone* was not making any attempt to obstruct his projects, that *they* were facilitating them even.... And that was just one small step from supposing that he was throwing himself blindly into a new trap.

But what would be the point of locking Laurent up in another cage, located inside an even larger one? He shrugged and walked down the new staircase.

The steps lead to a single door. He hesitated again. Behind the door, if the young girl had not lied to him, he should find the room he had seen through the low window.

That door was the one that should only open in one direction. He pushed it cautiously and glanced inside.

He saw a small, rectangular room furnished with a black couch and a carved, wooden chair. No. It was not the room. There was another door near the couch standing along the wall.

Laurent crossed through the room. The sound of the door closing made him jump. He turned about feverishly and returned to the door. There was no door handle, nothing he could use to pull it.

He finally realized how it was possible to reach the room without being able to leave it. He found himself in a sort of vestibule. If the access to the room had been closed with *a single* rigged door, he could have easily propped it open to let the prisoner out — if she really was a prisoner — without having to enter the room himself. But this two-door system prevented any such undertaking.

He had no choice but to walk ahead. It would no doubt be pointless but at least he would have the satisfaction of asking the young girl what she knew about the sinister house and of finding out how sincere her weeping was.

Above all, he still had his knife. Although the oak doors were thick, with patience he could manage to damage their locking mechanisms...

He pushed the second door.

A voice cried out as he entered the room, the room he had seen through the small, low window. The blond girl stood straight, trembling slightly, in the middle of the room, staring at Laurent.

"It's me," he said affecting a pleasantness he no longer had the heart to feel.

She did not reply, tossing her very long hair over one of her shoulders.

"Give me something to prop this door open with..." he added.

She stared at him with admiring eyes, but did not seem to understand his words.

"A cushion, a chair... anything," he grumbled. "If I let go of this damned door, it will close and we'll have to attack two doors instead of one..."

Moving like a sleepwalker, she finally grabbed a pillow from the bed standing in one corner of the room and handed it to him. As she stood next to him, Laurent had to admit he'd never seen such a beautiful face or such a perfect body before. The dress clung to that body so provocatively the young man looked away. He realized that the greatest danger, possibly the only danger in this house stood before him. She threw the pillow on the floor, preventing the half open door from closing completely.

"What is your name?" Laurent asked, reluctantly.

"Isabelle..." she replied submissively.

Of course, there was a certain Isabella in the parchments. Laurent had read only a few pages, but the name had caught his attention, just like Lorenzo...

"So, tell me everything you know," he murmured.

He stared at her for a moment. He had been about to add, *and don't try to trick me* but the candor in her eyes made that impossible.

"Since you're Laurent..." she said, glancing away.

CHAPTER X

According to Isabelle a two-hundred-year-old text had predicted their births and their meeting in this house.

"If you had read the *book* upstairs, you'd know everything and your attitude would be less cold, less skeptical."

Laurent was surprised by Isabelle's language and some of the deep knowledge her conversation revealed.

"How old are you?" he asked her

"Seventeen. And I know you're 22."

He had to admit she knew an unsettling amount about him... But he didn't forget that, while the manor appeared strange, most of its anomalies could be explained... The same could apply for the incomprehensible amount of information the occupants knew about Laurent. He could not lose sight of the fact that a magic show that seemed to violate the laws of nature was actually based on them. In this manner, a quick glimpse of a rigged universe gives credulous minds an incorrect interpretation of the actual situation.

Isabelle continued, saying, "But don't get the idea I'm going to throw myself at your feet just because I've been waiting for you for years. I was waiting for you, in fact... or rather I was waiting for someone matching your description. But there's something cold and wicked about you that isn't... that I..."

Caught up in a tirade filled with bravery, she got confused and finally turned her face away as tears started to flow. Laurent felt his heart melt and tried to harden himself.

"Stop your play acting," he said, sounding surly.

She went over to sit on the edge of the bed as her tears intensified. Laurent had the strange impression he'd been living with her for a long time and this was a domestic row. He remained standing next to the door, propped open by the pillow, as straight and motionless as a stake, his arms and legs stiff, feeling awkward, incapable of reacting. He realized he felt atrociously embarrassed at seeing Isabelle sitting, face turned to the wall, weeping and sobbing.

"Listen," he said. "We have other things to do than…"

He stopped, walked over to the bed, and sat down next to her.

"You didn't tell me everything," he said in a gentler voice, trying to distract her.

She wept for another moment, patted her eyes and spoke without turning to look at him.

"I can't show you my face," she said quietly. "I've been crying — because of you — and I'm too ugly now."

Laurent smiled. Ugly! How could she say something so stupid?

"You know full well you're very pretty," he replied without thinking. "You're certainly the prettiest girl I've ever seen."

She turned around immediately, smiling hopefully.

"You think…?' she asked.

Laurent didn't have the strength to lie.

"Of course," he replied. "If I had met you in a normal place… I think that…"

"You think that…?" she repeated, in a lively voice.

He hesitated then made a quick decision.

"I would have certainly fallen in love with you…"

To postpone any reaction on her part, he immediately added, "But in this house built by some mad man, I have to be suspicious of you and everything else."

He felt like he was losing ground. Wasn't he *actually* falling in love with Isabelle?

"Oh!" she exclaimed vehemently. "How can you be suspicious of me?"

"You didn't tell me everything. Not by a long shot. Who is that strange-looking bald servant woman?"

"But… that's Maria!" she said, as if that were obvious. "She lost her hair following an illness, years ago."

Obviously, that explanation was quite likely and made the woman seem a little less deathly and repulsive.

"But why doesn't she cover her head or wear a wig?"

Isabelle burst out laughing and the echoes of that laughter under the red light cast by the candles sounded out of place, grating.

"A wig!" repeated Isabelle, laughing. "It's not cold here!"

Apart from the strangeness of that comment — which made it seem that Isabelle considered a wig a piece of winter clothing — Laurent noted that the temperature seemed to be the same in all of the rooms.

"How is this castle heated?" he asked.

"You know the large room?" Isabelle asked. "Well, the heat from the fireplace is carried in pipes through the walls, along with the heat produced by the other three large fireplaces."

Laurent admitted that although it was cold outside that was only normal for the month of March. Nothing like during winter... Isabelle's explanation could possibly be justified.

"This castle is two and a half centuries old, but the man who built it was most ingenious," she added.

Laurent interrupted her, saying "About that, you said little when I asked you about the master of the house and the reasons for your fate."

She remained silent for a moment, then looked at the half-open door and then the small window.

She lowered her voice and said, "Usually, this is not my room and I'm free to go about inside the manor as I please. It hasn't been long since my uncle... locked me up. He's... the master. I call him Uncle Richard. He's a Boisrival."

"Boisrival?"

"That's the name of the paternal side of my family... That's my name. Before the revolution, we had a nobiliary particle and a barony. Four neighborhoods..."

She beamed with pride as she said those words.

"And... what is... your uncle like?"

She fell silent for a moment, searching for her words, then said, "He was very nice to me in the past. He still is, sometimes... But since his illness..."

"What illness?"

"I was at boarding school. He brought me back here... Two years ago. It was the same illness that attacked Maria... a contagious disease... something like typhoid, but not exactly. I don't know which of them caught it first... but Uncle Richard remained... odd. From that time on, he started lighting everything with those candles that cast the red light... and..."

"Those candles..." interrupted Laurent. "It seems to me they don't... burn down?"

"That's almost it. Not quite. They actually last a long time... a very long time. I think it's some sort of ancient formula my uncle found in some old family papers."

Laurent took a deep breath. Things were looking clearer. There was no longer anything mysterious about the house. Just a general strangeness, marked by minds that had grown unhinged over generations...

He thought about his wrist watch, which had stopped working for some mechanical reason, perfectly explicable no doubt. Obviously, time passed here just as it did outside. What made the mind wander was the crazy absence of windows and the eternal red light.

Then Laurent frowned again. There was still his father's appearance. He accepted it awkwardly as an hallucination. He thought for a moment, then postponed that difficult and painful problem for later.

"When did you learn about the... the *book?*"

She stared at the black stone floor.

"Oh..." she said, in a low voice. "They told me about it when I was very young and my parents were still alive..."

She fell silent for a few moments. Childhood memories were no doubt rising up from the depths of mind and she could not ward off a certain emotion.

She continued, "It was a family joke. Everyone knew of the existence of those old things, but no one paid any of it much attention. Yet something happened at the beginning that gave the old jokes a mysterious, questionable aspect. But the family decided it would be good to ignore the strange side of reality."

"What happened?"

"My godfather, a recent yet very close friend of my father, a man who had never heard about the book, was asked to choose my first name…"

"And it was that friend who chose the name Isabelle?' asked Laurent

"Yes. Apparently, when he suggested it, people reacted rather coldly, apart from Uncle Richard who started to laugh. But the decision had been made and that became my name."

Laurent glanced at the door, then at the small window.

"Your uncle… you said he started to laugh?" he asked.

"Yes. His attitude didn't even anger the family. Uncle Richard had a solid reputation within the family for being original… in the sense that people said he was 'one of a kind'."

Laurent ignored that detail, barely noticing it since, as he was listening to Isabelle, his mind was busy thinking about the uncle which some disease had, in all likelihood, caused to fall into some sort of madness... He imagined Richard Boisrival as a man who had once been a colorful and cheery companion, hiding a mystical, nebulous mind. A person who had no doubt turned dry and suspicious following an illness. A man obsessed by the realization of what had once been a state of mind... You had to deal with people like that. Once they got their claws into you it was hard to get away.

"And what does your uncle look like?" he asked Isabelle.

"He was a handsome man, I think. Now he has grown thin and his back is hunched. He has a very long, hooked nose and… just like Maria, he lost all his hair following that terrible illness... His voice changed too. It became grating, unpleasant. He locks me up here, but he's never been mean…. Not as mean as you've been…"

CHAPTER XI

Laurent was no longer listening. He had been brought here by this man. That was no doubt the most difficult fact to accept. But there was no doubt about it. Isabelle had described the bird-like face, the bald head, the grating voice... How had Laurent not thought of that earlier? Maria's appearance had barely suggested a purely fortuitous connection between the two people and yet he should have connected two facts; the strange bald heads and the place where the man had dropped him off. Boisrival had invented his tale of the trip he had to make, intending to drop him off right at the very place he wanted to take him to. No doubt, he hadn't conjured up the hailstorm... but he had to have known that a camper always stops near a source of water and, in that case, he could count on Laurent visiting the manor and trap him. If all his plans went wrong and Laurent camped nearby without noticing anything before leaving the next morning, he most likely had some trick up his sleeve that would produce the desired result...

"I didn't tell you much about myself, "Isabelle said after a lengthy silence.

"You do realize that it was certainly your uncle himself who brought me here."

When he said those words, he ran up against a new mystery. Just as everything seemed to have been cleared up, just as he finally obtained a logical explanation for the supernatural appearance of the manor, he still needed to understand how Boisrival could have been on the road, south of Fontainebleau, at the right time and place to pick him up... him and no one else. A young man named Laurent who was 22 years old... Was it a coincidence? That was hard to believe! He felt, despite everything, that he was the man of destiny for these people just as he felt they were his destiny. In life, there must be neighborhoods you approach with closed eyes, only to find yourself faced with a fait accompli... And for Laurent, destiny wore the face of Isabelle, even more than that of Richard Boisrival.

Of course, he was not admitting it just yet, but he felt it vaguely, like nerves reacting to a change in the electricity of the atmosphere when a storm approaches.

Laurent's last words did not seem to move Isabelle.

"I've wondered about his behavior for a long time,' she said, as if to herself. "I'd never been able to come up with an opinion on that matter — at least during the periods when my condition allowed me enough mental detachment so I could look at it... you've come in time to see the repercussions of one of my depressive crises..."

She had overcome the crisis she was talking about... Laurent noted she now seemed calmly assured and that the newcomer's coldness seemed to move her much less. Her voice and her face clearly indicated she was now taking responsibility for her destiny. The next words she said confirmed the rest of Laurent's impression.

"I should never have hated him as I did so often..." she said. "He took care of me and if he tested me, he did so to keep me for you..."

Laurent frowned. When an attractive young girl makes advances to a young man, he is rarely strong enough or stupid enough to reject them... But when that same girl uses unequivocable language and innocently speaks of the young man as if there were no doubt about their future together... well, then, he steps back. It is more in man's nature to mold the future to his shape than to passively accept a ready-made future even one presented submissively...

As for Boisrival's questionable methods, Laurent wasn't as easily convinced as Isabelle was as to the purity of his intentions. In fact, she would have to be excessively masochistic to be so indulgent in that respect. It was normal for her to rebel against the loss of her freedom — even as passive as some girls may be, they don't generally accept being locked up without feeling some bitterness toward their jailer. Laurent told her as much but either he had taken a prodigious place in Isabelle's heart or she was unconsciously attached to her uncle to an unsettling degree, but he was unable to get anything satisfactory out of her.

He changed the subject, asking "What kind of car does he drive?"

It was a question that had never entered his mind when he was struggling in the labyrinth of staircases... Now, he still had to find reasonable explanations for so few obscure points in order to be able to admit that, during the course of his strange adventure, the existence of such a machine was neither a dream nor an illusion as Laurent had feared.

"A Daimler," said Isabelle, simply.

"But there aren't any modern models," Laurent declared. "They stopped making that car years ago!"

"Uncle Richard explained that to me," she said without blinking. "The firm merged with another and makes nothing under its name. But since my uncle has a very large fortune, he got the managers of the former company and those of the new one to give him a special model that would carry the old name..."

And that was that. Apart from the obscure details Laurent had been thinking about earlier, Boisrival was gradually turning out to be some sort of maniac who wanted to give people a false impression of him by allowing that impression to slip into strangeness, the impossible, and the supernatural.

But could *everything* around *him* be explained?

Impatient anger washed over Laurent.

"Listen," he said to Isabelle, controlling himself. "I'm very flattered that you waited for me so long, like the Messiah or some Prince Charming, but what's important to me is getting out of here. Your uncle may be the greatest man in the world but, in my opinion, his behavior is abnormal and evil — and I'm speaking only about the way he treats you. As for his treatment of me, that's another matter. I'll make a complaint against him as soon as I get away from here. I find enforced hospitality and even more so obligatory engagements horrific. But that doesn't mean I find you loathsome..."

He struggled for a moment to remain silent, but the words came anyway.

"I'd even go so far as to say that, away from this intolerable environment, I wouldn't be opposed to seeing you again..."

Her pout transformed into a smile.

"I think I'd even like that very much," he added in a low voice, looking at her eyes, her hair, her lips.

But how could he appreciate the beauty of a girl in such light? Or more specifically, how could he truly appreciate it without being excessively drawn to the bloody reflections on her skin, by the strangeness of the too tight black silk dress, without allowing himself to be dominated by all sorts of bestial impulses encouraged by the light?

Mathematics and pure esthetics tumbled onto the bed at the same as Isabelle's body as Laurent took her face in his hands to kiss her.

Then Laurent pulled back and stood up as if he had embraced a gorgon. Not that that there was anything repulsive about contact with Isabelle's lips, but he suddenly realized the reality of the danger he'd glimpsed in the young girl's personality. He'd already come to understand that the greatest difficulties would not come from the master of the house, but from his niece. And now everything was confirmed! Now, whether he wanted it to or not, a simple kiss turned the entire situation around. He would start to love his prison as long as Isabelle was there with him... Of course, it was not the kiss that had determined his attitude. That gesture was only the predictable result of everything he had felt about Isabelle since hearing her moans... But it was a sort of abdication at the same time as it revealed the scope of the interest, the liking... perhaps even the love Laurent refused to acknowledge.

He believed he would come back for Isabelle, after he got free from the trap. He did not realize he would never escape unless she accompanied him...

The language of intimacy made rapid progress between them. But their conversation covered a topic Laurent did not feel prepared to abandon...

"You see this knife?" he said. "I'm planning on using it to cut into the second door. Do you understand now why I asked you for a pillow to prop the door open and keep it from closing? This way, I'll only have one to attack. And if we manage to get out of your room, we'll also be able to cut our way through the other doors that lead to the large room with the mirror, since you're familiar with the house..."

She looked frightened and said, "Do you think my uncle will let you do that?"

"So, you no longer believe what you told me earlier, that your uncle was 'keeping' you for me?"

"I... perhaps he'll still refuse to let us leave..."

"I'm certain about that. But if he tries to stop me, I won't spare him. I'm not boasting, but I'm no wimp."

She looked at him with an uncertain, upset expression. Suddenly, she turned around and stared at a point on the wall, near the ceiling.

The place where a narrow window connected the room with the corridor above it...

CHAPTER XII

"He's listening to us…" murmured Isabelle.

Laurent, who felt more concerned than he wanted to show, turned halfway in the direction of the window, hoping to see a moving image through it that would have revealed Boisrival's presence.

"You're sure?" he asked in the same tone. "You heard something?"

"I'm certain although I heard nothing. I *feel* his eyes on us. The ancestor who wrote the *book* had powers like…"

She stopped speaking for a moment, then continued, "He must have gone. Perhaps he didn't hear our conversation…"

"What were you saying about that ancestor?" Laurent reminded her.

"Thomas de Boisrival? Family legend paints him as a man very different from his contemporaries… He is supposed, so people say, to have had a relationship with the Comte de Saint Germain. You may be familiar with his reputation?"

"Yes, that other Cagliostro…"

"Something like that. Thomas had certain skills as a clairvoyant and other aptitudes just as inhuman. Many people of the time claimed he could converse with the dead and act at a distance…

Laurent grinned and attempted to look mocking.

"He didn't prepare some sort of elixir of life?" he asked.

She did not return his smile.

"Some said that if…" she said. "Others that his pacts with ghosts gave him the power to reincarnate from father to son… and so on, if he agreed to die just as his son entered the world."

"And he had no daughter?" said Laurent, chuckling.

"There were daughters, but there were many descendants, and always at least one son."

"So, it always had to be the last one?"

"No. People said that he sometimes rejected his first chance at reincarnation, to wait for a second son — so he could live longer as an adult."

Laurent lost his temper.

"Nonsense!" he shouted. "How can you accept such malicious gossip and believe in it so firmly? Because it's obvious you believe it!"

"No," she said, glancing again in the direction of the small window. I don't believe it as firmly as you say... But I am troubled by all the conversations I've heard when I spent my vacations here... My parents were still alive at the time and Uncle Richard lived somewhere else. He moved into this house that Thomas had built a short while after my parents died in an accident. I was 12 at the time."

Laurent rejected all of this. After his curious adventures in this trap, he was not inclined to give even a little credence to the most unlikely fables. He had to deny everything.

Despite everything, Isabelle's words revealed that Richard Boisrival could seriously *believe* he was the reincarnation of his ancestor, Thomas, which did explain the mythomaniac side of his personality.

And what if he actually was?

If he actually was then, apart from the a few tricks of sleight of hand, there were still certain problems that could not be explained... The appearance of Laurent's father, for example fit in well with the fables concerning the Boisrival family. Richard had retained a certain ability to evoke the shadows, even if those shadows did not take part in his game...

But Laurent preferred to attribute his vision to fatigue, to the fleeting weakness of his mind caused by the strange outcome of such a strange ride. Possibly, if Richard were a skilled illusionist, that appearance could have been suggested from outside. Laurent *had believed* that he'd seen his father and he *had believed* that his father had given him a telepathic message... In this case, it was possible to admit that a telepathic gift also lay behind the divination concerning Laurent's name and age.

But the *book?* Even if Richard had written it himself... No. *The book* existed before Isabelle was born if he believed her, or if he had to believe what she believed...

Laurent decided to sweep all this away and return to a more concrete vision of the situation.

"I want to believe what you're saying," he said to Isabelle. "But only one thing is important to me: getting out of here. Do you have anything in this room that could serve as warm clothing in case we manage to do just that?"

He had not asked Isabelle if she was prepared to flee with him...

She hesitated, then said, "I have... what you asked for... but where are you planning to take me?"

"I will need a witness for the complaint I intend to file. First, we'll have a chat with the police."

She stepped back, saying "I don't want to file a complaint against my uncle!"

Laurent gritted his teeth.

"So, you want to stay here, when I go back to the other side of France? Fine. I see the case that can be made of your declarations."

Although he said those words to exert pressure on Isabelle, he also realized just how intolerable the thought of leaving her felt.

She gave in, quietly saying "As... as you wish."

She added, in an even lower voce, "As long as you don't abandon me..."

Isabelle had put on a large fur-lined cloak fine boots made of tawny leather. The ensemble clashed and Laurent could not help but laugh. That angered him.

But it was time for action. They both walked into the small room Laurent had crossed through to get to her bedroom and it was time to get to work with his knife.

First, Laurent had carefully examined the closing mechanism of the for. door they had propped open, hoping that the mechanism of the other door would be the same. He attacked the polished wood at the same height. The work progressed slowly. They were dealing with an oak panel. A simple knife, no matter how strong the blade had been made, was a weak, insufficient tool. They needed an axe, massive levers...

Time passed as they gnawed away at the door and no one came to interrupt them. It was possible to believe the manor was deserted and they were trying to escape from an abandoned fortress in which they had been left prisoner following a forced retreat. And no one had taken the time to extinguish the red flames providing the light.

Gradually, channels, hollows were carved around the lock. Then came the moment when nothing more than a sliver of wood held it in place, only to be broken when Laurent hammered it with the bone handle of his knife.

The door swung open, revealing the staircase.

"Several times, I feared the blade would break..." panted Laurent.

The noise made by the metal unsettled him. He knew the house was not empty and the silence, the lack of any reaction on the part of the one who was keeping them prisoner did not please him. No doubt he had some emergency system that would stop them with no hope of escaping.

Yet nothing happened. Isabelle turned to Laurent, a concerned expression on her face that the light turned tragic.

"I don't want to go any farther," she said in a low voice. "I know that Uncle Richard doesn't wish me any harm but... I'm afraid."

She was on the verge of tears once again.

Laurent could not control his irritation.

"I want you to come with me, I already told you that..." he finally said, without lowering his voice. "But if you insist on staying here, I'll go alone."

He took a step forward and, with a determined gesture, put the knife back in its sheath.

Isabelle clung to him, murmuring feverishly, "Don't abandon me... And don't shout so loudly... I'm coming with you!"

"Fine. Stop looking so terrified. You'll make me lose my nerve..."

The staircase stood in front of them, empty and red. Was someone waiting for them in silence on the upper landing?

Laurent went first. The joy that had driven him to speak out loud had transformed into unsettled vigilance that compromised his nervous equilibrium. He felt his heart pounding as he placed his feet carefully on one step after the other.

Behind him, Isabelle walked up the stairs, her dress and cloak rustling and her fine leather boots crunching. Laurent could hear her panting and he guessed she was on the lookout, her heart pounding as well.

Before setting foot on the landing, he caressed the handle of the knife he had returned to its sheath. If someone, if Boisrival, the bald man with the beak-like nose, were to appear before him, Laurent knew what he would do. He would leap ahead, planning to use his head, his shoulder to throw him off balance. Even if he were to fall, to be seriously injured, it would be a poor way to thank him for his hospitality... but it would also be the type of adventure he would have sought by making his hospitality look like a trap.

The landing was empty and the door to the room with the lectern was open. Laurent stopped on the threshold. Behind him, Isabelle cried out.

CHAPTER XIII

How could Laurent have thought for a single second that his jailer would appear before him, using both voice and gesture to prohibit an escape he'd certainly followed closely?

No, that was not the way Boisrival, that man who loved secrets, flexibility, affection would act. Disoriented, Laurent had stopped on the threshold of the room when he saw Richard standing still in front of the lectern, hands folded behind his back.

When he saw the man's profile, Laurent immediately recognized, with no possible error, the driver of the hybrid car who had given him a ride. Considering everything, he was a vulgar raptor.

But at that very moment, Boisrival, wearing a dark dressing gown similar to that of the servant, was standing motionless at the lectern, as if lost in meditation. He looked like an unimposing contemplative monk.

Laurent caught himself. The man was faithful to his role. Instead of presenting himself as an enemy, he was trying to strike the minds of his victims through another spectacular trick which he no doubt hoped would have a deeper, more lasting effect. But Laurent was boiling with anger.

He stepped into the room while Isabelle held back, and called out, saying "Sir, you lied to me when you said your trip was not over. You drove me practically all the way to your home where I had no business... and you held me here against my will, using methods of intimidation worthy of the Spanish Inquisition. And to top it all off, you stole my backsack."

Richard did not budge.

"I'm not talking about your treatment of your niece," he continued. "I'm not talking about your odious exploitation of her age and weakness. That's only partially my concern although I do plan to notify the police when I file my complaint against you."

Boisrival turned his head slowly in their direction and Laurent realized he'd made a serious tactical blunder. The man was more locked up than ever in the false character Isabelle had spoken of. He was playing a role and would keep on playing it until the very end. That was not how Laurent should have approached him.

Trampling his own self-esteem, Laurent continued, "You must understand that your hospitality has taken such a strange turn I could almost believe I'm a prisoner."

His mind continued to fill with threats and insults and he had to replace them with politeness and restraint. He was furious.

"Come in, Isabelle," said the grating voice. "Why are you standing there to the side when my guest is defending you?"

That response revealed cleverness. No doubt he was about to tear them apart from one another quite easily. But Laurent did not hear it like that.

"Treat your niece as you see fit," he said dryly. "That's not my business. But return my backsack to me immediately so I can leave this house right away. I've stayed here too long as it is."

"Now, now," said Richard in a tone he intended to be calming. "I suspect you're too interested in Isabelle to abandon her in a situation you consider unfortunate. I prefer to believe that your words surpass your thoughts and I prefer to forget them. Do you think I brought you here for no reason at all?"

"It doesn't matter to me if you had a reason or not," replied Laurent, venting his rage. "My words reflect exactly what I think of you and I order you to return my backpack to me. I warn you that, if you refuse, I will leave here without it. But the authorities will also be informed about that…"

Richard glanced at him sidewise.

"Can I ask you something" he said 'How do you expect to get out of the house?"

Obviously, the situation was growing complicated. Laurent was counting on Isabelle to guide him through the labyrinth... and Richard would oppose that. Left to himself, Laurent would be forced to break through a multitude of locks one by one, which might not result in anything apart from going in circles. He had to work on Isabelle, force her to disobey, to be stronger.

He turned to her and took a step back. Leaning against the wall, Isabelle was staring at her uncle with dilated eyes, distraught.

"Isabelle!" shouted Laurent.

She didn't blink an eye. Laurent turned back to Boisrival, furious. The man was looking at his niece from beneath hooded eyes, without talking. Laurent realized that it was hypnosis. The man might have exaggerated his abilities.... But given a suggestible subject like Isabelle, he was at least capable of that.

If Boisrival was also capable of telepathy and suggestion, Laurent did not have to look any further for the explanation of everything that remained incomprehensible in the house. What was left was nothing but architectural tricks.

"Isabelle!" Laurent repeated, taking her by the arm. "Listen to me! Don't look at him! Do you want to leave with me or not? You have to guide me!"

She remained unresponsive, as if deaf. Laurent placed his hands in front of her eyes, trying to cut off the invisible flow that deprived her of will. But the damage had been done.

Richard turned away from her and addressed Laurent, "There's no point," he said with a thin smile. "She'll remain like that until I permit her to move and she'll have no memory of my control over her mind. She didn't tell you anything about this, did she? Well, it's not the first time I've conducted this interesting little experiment..."

To jump at the man. Strangle him, pound his head against the floor, throw his body down the stone staircase... Laurent lost all control.

He took a step forward.

The room vanished. He stopped, bewildered, frightened.

He suddenly found himself standing in a place of gigantic dimensions. The sky was red and his feet stood on a black, uneven surface. About a kilometer from where he stood, he saw an immensely tall tower, topped with an enormous black block to which red lights clung. He thought he must have been transported, by means of some sort of spell, to a vast plain where the sun was setting, on a lava foundation cracked by bad weather.

In the distance, to his left, something titanic and indistinct was moving like the tall column of a waterspout over the sea. Beyond the tower, another mass lost itself in the horizon. A thick wind blew over the plain. Laurent tripped, rolled into a crevasse that was deeper than his height.

He stood up, uninjured. He had fallen almost slowly, like in a dream. But this was no dream. He had felt his fingers touch the stone and using his arms and legs, he returned to the wrinkled surface that reminded him of basalt... Yes, basalt rather than lava.

He suddenly realized that the horizon, far behind the tower, was closed by a cliff, its peak invisible.

The same questions ran in circles in his scattered mind: Isabelle... What had happened to her? Where am I? And that man... how had he done this What had he done?

A vague explanation surfaced.

"He's not a magician. Magicians only exist in fairy tales. He hypnotized me too and made my mind wander... He's making me see what he wants me to see. It's an hallucination he provoked. Meanwhile, he's running away with Isabelle, locking her up again in some inaccessible cellar!"

He had to escape from *this* as quickly as possible. He closed his eyes, focused his thoughts on the room where he had been a few moments earlier, trying to exercise his own will to regain control over his senses.

When he looked around once again, nothing had changed. He saw the same furrowed soil, the immense tower, the cliff on the horizon, as tall as the sky, and the same setting sun.

That sun... He had to turn his back on it, based on how nightmares were constructed. He turned around.

A second cliff, closer, blocked the horizon behind him. In a cavern as large as a city, carved in the flank of the cliff, a monstrous fire burned. The light was coming from there, from the fire, not the sun. To the right, to the left, distant cliffs. No sun anywhere. He spun about. Several kilometers from the cavern, the cliff came to an abrupt end. A gap with infinitely tall walls cut through it seemed to connect the plain with another one. "Plain" was not the right word... Laurent compared this landscape to a sort of geometrical basin over which mountains unlike anything that existed on Earth looked down.

He would never get out of this impossible landscape. He could walk as much as he liked... After days of efforts in the basalt ruts, he would reach the foot of the cliff, no matter which direction he took. It didn't matter. He had to walk towards the breach. Perhaps it would lead him to the moor where the manor stood...

"No," thought Laurent, filled with fear. "Nothing like that exists... I'm dreaming while awake. I'm under the influence of that…"

He interrupted those thoughts. A sudden discovery made the truth explode in his mind. He held his head in his hands and looked up at the red sky with a feeling of horror.

CHAPTER XIV

He did not know if he was caught up some simple illusion or some monstrous metamorphosis. He had been made into something other than a man, but he was still in the same place, in the room in the manor, in the room with the lectern.

It was just that he was smaller. Two thousand times smaller.

The wrinkled soil? The black tiles. The monstrous tower? The lectern. The cliffs? The walls... It was the same for the cavern in the flank of the mountain, which was actually the nook in which the red candles burned. As for the breach in the cliff, it was the door through which Laurent and Isabelle had entered the room.

He recalled the gigantic, indistinct shapes. Isabelle and her uncle leaving the room through the other door. The crazy dimensions had masked the nature of all these things to Laurent's microscopic eyes...

This chain of dumbfounding observations was aggravated by his ignorance of the causes behind the phenomenon. What if Isabelle had told the truth? What if Boisrival did actually have the supernatural powers she had mentioned? Was... Was Laurent *really* now one millimeter tall?

He shook his head furiously and shrugged. No. That was ridiculous. Yet... that strange fall into the crevasse — a crevasse that was one millimeter deep as well — that fall had been as slow, or almost as slow, as the fall of a tiny grain of dust.

"Of course," Laurent said to himself. "I weigh so little that the resistance of the air — always the same — was enough to slow my fall. Had that terrible transformation really taken place? Once again, madness beat against his burning forehead, like the current of air that Isabelle, the giant Isabelle, had created just a bit earlier, as she moved away from the wall to obey Richard's orders.

Plunged into a gloomy stupor, Laurent fell to the monstrous ground. He closed his eyes.

He did not feel his position change. Yet, when he opened his eyes, everything around him had transformed.

"Rest assured," said an unpleasant voice close at hand. "You're the same as you were."

He glanced around, frightened. He was sitting upright in a gothic chair to which his arms and legs were tied. In front of him, on the other side of a large stone table, Isabelle was also sitting on a chair. But she was not bound.

"Isabelle!" he shouted, trying in vain to get free.

"There's no point..." said Boisrival, standing at the end of the porphyry table, both hands placed on top of it.

He observed them attentively.

"She can't hear you," he added.

Laurent fell silent. He was out of breath. A violent anger was replacing his fear.

"She can't hear you, since she's still in a trance. As for you, well I had to use the same method to bring you to your senses, the same method, and adding a few hallucinations in order to help you..."

"Help me?" grumbled Laurent.

"Yes... to help you see a healthier vision of things. You tend to overestimate yourself. You were able to see how weak and unarmed you would be if the size of your body were reduced..."

He smiled.

"And yet, I did not show you the dangers that such a situation included. A mouse, for example... Can you imagine what a mouse could do in such a situation?"

Laurent shivered.

"That's crazy," he said with an effort. "Since it was an hallucination, I was in no danger..."

"Of course... But *you did not know that...* I would be very comfortable using that to teach you a lesson. I have many other methods for convincing you."

Laurent twisted furiously on his chair.

"To convince me of what?" he said. "What is the purpose of this trap? What do you want from me?"

"I'm getting to that," Boisrival said calmly. "But let me just say that if I've tied you up that was only because you were behaving like a maniac. I don't get the same results with you as with Isabelle... Just a small suggestion lasting a few minutes, just the time to bring you here without creating an unpleasant scene... I must say that you came here with no problem. While you were walking ahead of me, your mind thought it was in a much smaller body, in the place you had just left... But that's enough of that. You want to know why I need you?"

Laurent remained silent. He had just recognized the room he had been brought to. It was the large room with the mirror, with the same tapestry, the fireplace where the same fire still snored. He had seen all that since he opened his eyes — or thought he opened them — but his mind was only restoring the memory now.

"I need you for a spiritual seance I've been waiting for some years now," concluded Boisrival.

"Please explain," said Laurent coldly, as he ended his struggles. "Why didn't you say anything to me about this when I was with you in the car?"

"Because you would have refused. You would have refused for a very simple reason. You would have asked 'Why me?'"

Laurent had to admit that was true.

"You would have also refused for two or three other reasons," Boisrival added calmly. "First, because you're skeptical about anything that concerns spiritualism or the supernatural... Then because the light of favorable doubt you conserve would have made you fear the harmful consequences for yourself... And for other reasons that it would be tedious to mention."

"Unfortunately, here I am, forced to ask the same question you said I would earlier," replied Laurent with a hint of irony.

"And yet it was in order to answer you that I had Maria welcome you. Yes, I know that Isabelle gave you her name. And also that's why I guided you to the *book*."

"Ah yes," chuckled Laurent. "The *book*..."

"It doesn't matter whether you believe me or not, but those pages were actually written two centuries ago. It was as I told you, to allow the facts to speak for themselves, that I guided you to the pages. I also wanted you to meet my niece before the experiment took place, to give myself every chance of success."

Laurent wanted nothing more than to keep the conversation going, in the hope of being able to use his knife, which Boisrival had carelessly neglected, to cut through his bonds...

"And what do you hope to get out of this 'spiritual séance'?" he asked, emphasizing the last two words insolently.

Boisrival smiled as he watched the young man's clumsy efforts to grasp the handle of his knife.

"You can see that you won't succeed," he said shaking his head. "But I will answer your question. Both of you, Isabelle and you, were mentioned in the parchments. That's obvious. But Maria and I are not. That's strange and I merely want to verify the thoughts of the author, Thomas de Boisrival."

Laurent gave up his project. He started looking for another means of salvation in Isabelle's eyes. But she was staring straight ahead without seeming to see anyone.

"You are planning to contact the... the ghost of that man?" Laurent asked in a toneless voice.

He was not interested in the conversation. The man Isabelle had described to him as a maniac obsessed with the beyond and reincarnation only captured half of his mind. Someone else was standing in the shadow, at the corner of the fireplace, someone silent, someone Laurent could only see if he turned his head... Maria, the bald servant. Could he get help from her?

"I plan to try. I make no claim that I will succeed, but the presence of the two of you will make things much easier for me. Although I'm telling you all this, don't see it as proof of any sense of guilt... I don't feel anything of the kind since my intentions are pure. But the more you know, the more likely it is that the experiment will succeed.... That's all that counts."

"Yeah?" Laurent said negligently.

The he turned his head toward the servant and shouted, "Maria! You know that you are your master's accomplice and that when the police are informed about all this you will go to prison with him!"

Boisrival fell silent.

Laurent stretched his neck to the side trying to see her face, which was hidden in the shadow and continued, "If you help me in any manner whatsoever to get out of here, I will help you with the judges and you won't have any problems."

He could have been talking to a wall.

Why, he thought, *didn't I accept the maniac's proposal? I could have used the opportunity to escape with Isabelle...* In fact, he knew full well why he'd refused. He didn't know the full scope of the abilities of this man who had just demonstrated an astonishing and terrible power of suggestion. He didn't know his true motives.

Stretching his head back, he saw Maria clearly and cried out in horror. The servant was not standing. She was hanging on the wall in an iron necklace, her swollen tongue sticking out of her mouth.

CHAPTER XV

Boisrival had followed Laurent's gaze. He showed no signs of emotion.

"Yes," he said in a paternalistic tone. "The poor woman killed herself barely an hour ago... I've had so much to do that I haven't yet found the time to piously take care of her mortal remains..."

Frightened, Laurent turned accusatory eyes on him.

"You claim she killed herself!" he said in a deep voice. "And you dare talk about cynicism..."

He stopped in mid-sentence. Everything seemed to indicate that Richard had murdered the servant. But what motive could he have had? It was an incomprehensible crime, a mad crime.

"I must admit that this desperate action in the result of solitude that no doubt disturbed her mind," Boisrival explained in the same hypocritical tone. Perhaps I should have sent her back to her village at the first signs of trouble... She had grown very quiet, closed in, yes, truly... About a year ago, at least. Two perhaps...

Laurent recalled Isabelle's revelations. If there were someone in this castle with a disturbed mind, it was certainly the master. The dates coincided. Two years...

The bald man continued, "I should say that this unfortunate death does not fit in the framework provided by my ancestor Thomas since there is no mention of Maria in his writings."

That was it! Even madness has its motives: to force far-flung, vague predictions to mesh with reality. At the price of a human life, if need be.

At the price of how many human lives? Laurent realized that his refusal to bend to his host's preposterous claims was dictated by a certain intuition. When someone took part in this maniac's game, they had no idea where they were headed. Any bizarre reason that appeared in his tortured mind could make the situation take a turn for the worse and transform a benign, vain spiritualist séance into carnage.

There was no longer any question of taking the high road, of talking about judges and punishment. He had to dodge and weave, deceive, enter the game partway in order to keep his hands free. Laurent had never been so close to danger and the fear that preceded that danger doubled in the presence of Isabelle.

The man, of course, was not following the normal paths. But the peril did not lie solely with his relative obsession with the parchments. Whether Laurent wanted to or not, he had to admit that Boisrival was behaving in a coherent manner, in keeping with his obsession. It was not a matter of a solely aggressive activity made inefficient by a demented inconsistency. Not at all. Richard remained faithful to a well-defined line of conduct, one on which he based all of his actions, to the extreme.

And then there was the in disputable gift of suggestion that made the man infinitely more dangerous. There was no way to parry the weapon he could use at any moment.

Laurent cleared his throat then said, "I recall I found that women unsettling when she opened the door..."

"Unsettling to say the least," chortled Richard without changing his position. "Bald, elderly women don't usually exhibit their skulls as trophies."

Laurent was starting to see that the man saw straight through him. And there was that diabolical telepathy... Just how successful could he be at hiding his thoughts?

He looked at Isabelle, still motionless, on the other side of the table. Her eyes remained empty. She still wore the cloak Laurent had urged her to put on in the event of a problematic escape...

Everything is ready for casting off, thought Laurent. *All I have to do is get free. Then I'll take care of that villain...*

"You have a mental barrier that makes your thoughts rather blurry," Boisrival said coldly. "But I can still make out their color, their direction... And I can see that you retain an unpleasant aggressivity. Your words are forced. You make a great effort to appear in my sight while reserving some stupid plan for rebellion."

Laurent looked at him with an innocent air.

"You don't understand," added the other man. "Whether you submit to me or not, the lines have all been drawn and you have no power to change them since they are the expression of an infallible vision..."

"Listen, don't take into account the thoughts you may see in me," Laurent said, in a conciliatory tone. "I may have thoughts of rebelling, but I am fighting against them through reason, since an attitude of opposition will not get me out of this situation. I know that."

Boisrival looked at him sharply.

"Let's suppose... Let's suppose that you're telling the truth," he admitted with a smile. "In any case, you can't do anything against me and we're going to proceed, starting now, with the experiment I told you about."

He looked in the direction of the fireplace.

"The presence of this cadaver will help things..." he added in a light tone.

All the candles standing on the cartwheels hanging from the ceiling had burned out. Using a sort of pothook Boisrival had lowered an iron plate in front of the fire roaring behind Laurent's back. He had left a small opening, about ten centimeters high, between the plate and the tiles. It allowed no more than a weak, orange light through.

He returned to where he had been standing earlier, pulled a chair from under the table and sat down.

In the shadow, Laurent was still able to see Isabelle, petrified in front of him, sitting on a third chair. The lighting from the distant fire at ground level highlighted her chin, her cheeks, leaving her eyes and her lips in a strange darkness.

Nearby, Boisrival was highlighted sidewise, his head reduced to a half face, like a mask sliced in two from the forehead to the neck. The silence was heavy.

"You have nothing to do but stay still and keep your thoughts to a minimum..." murmured the half face, barely moving its lips. "Isabelle is fine as she is and I can keep her in this state with no effort. I would have willingly done the same for you, but you're different. It would have taken too much effort for me."

Laurent did not say a word. He was convinced that nothing would come from this absurd effort and did not plan to make an effort to sabotage it in advance by refusing to respect the instructions he had been given.

Silence and motionlessness. Only, from time to time, a sudden variation in the light cast by the fire or the roaring of the flames. Laurent made no effort to agitate his thoughts but he could no prevent them from flowing freely. So, he asked himself questions about details. What fuel was used in the fireplace where enormous flames roared constantly? He thought he'd seen half burned logs, but was there some hidden installation? Oil burners hidden under fake logs?

The room seemed to start spinning slowly.

Through some curious doubling effect, Laurent gradually felt himself to be in two places at the same time. He saw himself from the front, as if in a mirror — or as Isabelle was seeing him, as she did the same as him. He was no longer able to turn his head, but all of the items in the room appeared clearly in an omnivision unimpeded by the shadow.

That sensation... being in Isabelle's mind as she was in his!

He thought quickly. Despite his apparent desire to join them, Richard was pursuing another goal, an acknowledged goal, but one that had nothing to do with them. Was there also another one, unacknowledged, one that could be deadly for them?

Laurent realized that he was communicating telepathically not with Richard, but with Isabelle. It was she who had suggested that question to him. He suddenly saw himself standing in front of the large, pentagon-shaped, black mirror. Isabelle was standing close to him. Yet, neither of them had actually changed place. He continued to see his body, seated, bound, and Isabelle's body motionless opposite him.

There had been a splitting — two splittings — more hallucinations, no doubt. Perhaps the apparent intervention of spirits had been a necessary means to achieve that result?

But Laurent could also see that the hallucinations caused by Isabelle's uncle did not put him in any danger. There was no reason for the young girl to be in any peril...

As he was thinking that thought, with a strange sense of detachment, he received a clear mental message from Isabelle.

"Yes," she thought. "He is pursuing another goal and I know what it is."

Laurent remained attentive.

"He has designed some sort of way to verify the theories I told you about in my room. I can say this and I don't think he will know about it. His mind is too busy directing us and imposing his visions on us for him to be able to catch the thoughts we exchange..."

There was a void — like a silence.

"He believes he is the reincarnation of Thomas de Boisrival..." continued Isabelle. "He undertook this séance in the hope of verifying that. He has tried to obtain results several times by hypnotizing me. When I'm awake, I don't remember any of that."

"But what sort of verification can he make?" asked Laurent.

"It's simple. If he can use us to make contact with Thomas, that means he is *not* that reincarnation. He's counting on the experiment to fail *definitively*."

CHAPTER XVI

An invisible force was pushing them toward the mirror.

Laurent still had time to reply, "But that's terrible! The experiment will fail without a doubt... and he will use that failure to consider himself an incarnation of Thomas! God knows what will come of that..."

"That's where the danger lies. There will no longer be anything to slow his wandering... He will no longer play *a role;* he *will be* the person — even if that is fake and meaningless."

Laurent and Isabelle, or what they recognized as their split bodies, were now standing against the mirror.

Without making an effort to turn around, Laurent could still see his other body, bound to the chair, along with Isabelle's other body as she continued to sit across from him, petrified.

"I wonder..." he thought vaguely, without going further.

"You wonder what?" Isabelle replied, echoing his thought. Now none of his thoughts escaped her.

"I wonder if this entire story of reincarnation is not actually some kind of fantasy," he said. "What's happening to us now is not terribly frightening, rather interesting and strange, but it does go against all of the notions that have shaped me. So... Why wouldn't other phenomena, rather close to this one in fact, be proof of their existence?"

Isabelle was unable to answer. A sort of energy whirlpool had caught them both up and was carrying them, like a violent current in a mountain torrent. They saw themselves projected into an empty, black space. Behind them, a pentagon-shaped opening, weakly tinted red was growing smaller and smaller. Through it, as if through a window, they could see three people sitting motionless around a table.

Isabelle's silent cry crossed through Laurent's mind like a red-hot steel arrow.

She had disappeared. Laurent found himself alone in a dark space and unable to re-establish mental communication with her. The mirror-window had vanished. Shadows reigned everywhere. And solitude.

Whatever likelihood there was that Boisrival's attempt would succeed, Laurent could not question this result. No doubt, it did not correspond to Richard's effort, but represented, despite everything, an incursion into the unknown, at least for those serving as pawns on the chess board. Under other circumstances and, above all, if Isabelle's existence had not profoundly changed the situation, Laurent would have been most interested in this adventure; his interest would have been so great that he would have been able to overcome the fear caused by his depersonalization and his plunge through the looking glass...

But Isabelle was there. Or rather her form, which had been present a moment earlier, had drowned in the ocean of shadow that reigned here. This disappearance, the countless dangers that must be surrounding her, weighed more heavily on Laurent's heart than the fear of the perils to which he felt exposed.

What perils? Although he no longer had a physical body, Laurent had retained a form of knowledge of the new world, which corresponded rather closely to vision. But the mysterious void provided nothing this inner eye could rest on. Dangers were hidden there, like carnivorous creatures hiding in the depths... Laurent felt like a deep-sea diver, the cable connecting him to his ship cut off...

No... Boisrival was capable of submerging them in these depths, but nothing indicated that the strings connecting the man to his marionettes in this drama had been cut... Laurent found the strength to reject such fears and focused all his energy on Isabelle, attempting to form a new mental link with her. As the young girl's silent cry had crossed through the shadow, Laurent cried out in response. Perhaps he would have had to use all of his strength from the very start to ensure the best chance of succeeding... but the following moment would reveal the ruin and sterility of future efforts... Too bad. Caution was useless.

"Isabelle!"

After shouting, Laurent realized that he had bet on the wrong color. His cry had not reached Isabelle. Instead, it had provoked certain confused movements in the shadows, denouncing the presence of... a certain form of life Laurent just knew was evil and dangerous.

But that was how it was around him... What had happened around Isabelle when she had first cried out?

Suddenly, Laurent forgot Isabelle. What he felt vaguely was so very frightful that everything that did not concern him personally seemed to be swept away by panic.

During his early childhood, Laurent had for a long time felt a deep terror with respect to a man living in his parents' house. A man wearing a very loose-fitting, black overcoat and a round felt hat — Laurent had never seen him in anything else. He had a mastiff on a leash. The dog never barked.

Laurent had constructed a strange tale about this character in which the man and his dog melted into a single inhuman being, similar to those mystical creatures people threaten children with. The bogeyman.

By a disturbing coincidence, the man and his dog died at the same time, asphyxiated in the sordid apartment where they lived, the year Laurent turned ten.

The fable constructed by the child around these two beings immediately took on a formidable value. In his eyes they became an irrefutable demonstration through the fusion, in death, of two elements that had been separated, in life, in different bodies.

Until he turned fifteen, Laurent had experienced that retrospective terror on several occasions, a terror of having rubbed shoulders with something unlike anything that is human for such a long time. It was only when he started to take part in truly absorbing studies, studies requiring a stable, rational mind, that Laurent had abandoned this mystical side of his character, along with the inexpressible emotions bound to it.

Just then two shapes stepped out of the shadow and approached him: an old man wearing a loose-fitting, black overcoat and a round, felt hat leading a mastiff with crooked legs on a leash...

Laurent's shriek had to have been heard in the real world. But the man had already reached him. Blurry and dull like those nightmare characters that pursue you slowly along endless factory walls, he stood a few steps away, his waxy face emerging from the shadows. Laurent felt — as if he were in his flesh and bone body — the dog's deep bite in his leg.

He shrieked a second time, in this silent, endless nightmare. At that moment he discovered escape was possible. A certain strength of will was enough to tear him from the horror and he saw still fuzzy images form around him at a dizzying speed. They slowed, then stopped. Laurent was floating, motionless, in a place lit by red light. He thought he'd been finally released from the nebulous world into which he'd been tossed and had returned to the room in the castle, on the other side of the looking glass.

But that was just an illusion. He was not standing on his feet, feeling his weight, his material body. He was floating in space and the frame surrounding him was nothing like those in the rooms in the manor. He found himself in a sort of rather wide corridor. The end, in the distance, seemed to open a new void. The light was coming from there. Laurent wanted to go there hoping to finally escape from the man and the dog and find Isabelle.

He felt a double presence behind him, rather distant. And his efforts to race to the end of the corridor were frightfully slow. The exit shone in the distance, but the double presence was closer. Laurent started a viscous advance down the corridor, the black man and his silent dog progressing silently behind him.

After struggling for a few moments, he stopped. For two reasons. First, he'd passed several side hallways and he hoped to be able to lose his follower there. Second, he no longer felt the terrifying presence behind him.

Turning back was no longer a problem. Laurent found walking back much easier than advancing toward the light.

He walked past two hallways, staying alert. His concern multiplied as he felt, for the first time, an *abstract* fear, a mental fear that his body was not involved with. For good cause. He imagined he would have been partly relieved of his fear if he had limbs that could shiver, a heart that could pound. He had nothing of the kind. He was condemned to feel at fear that had no support, no reactions similar to those of a terrestrial body. Apart from escape.

As he walked past the third hallway, Isabelle's cry rang out in him. She was shouting his name, somewhere on the side where the man and the dog were.

CHAPTER XVII

What served as air gradually grew thicker. Laurent moved about awkwardly, painfully. The space itself exerted a resistance that was not inert, but active. Laurent was moving about *in fear...*

That was it. His terror was not inside him but around him. He was fighting against the glacial river to advance despite the currents, despite the invisible eyes he could just make out on the shores, despite the motionless walls that made the corridor walls tremble, walls he soon realized were built from thousands of clasped hands.

Yet Isabelle's dull cry continued beyond the hallways and their frozen whirlpools, as if cast out behind a world. Around the cry, around Laurent, fear, curled in a double figure, half chalky, like a skull, half tawny, like the bestial muzzle and the teeth Laurent had run from.

In the eyes of another, the danger Isabelle faced would have been meaningless, incomprehensible — even doubtful. In Laurent's eyes, there could be no greater danger, revealing greater horror. The double personality of the dog and the man provided a rich symbol of all childhood fears, fears that are intense and profound. It was this crystal of fear which, slow and mineral like, had changed direction to attack the young girl.

While continuing to struggle, Laurent responded to Isabelle's cry.

"I'm here! Isabelle! Be brave..."

The word, the concept of *brave* crossed through the trembling waves like blasphemy... Everything here was threat, fear. Bravery was the worst enemy — in the walls, the Trojan horse.

The sticky fibers that limited Laurent's progress seemed to give way, to break. He found the strength to move faster in the direction of the uninterrupted cry. But he felt despair well up deep inside.

Then he saw a shape moving toward him. A shape with a stooped back, head slightly bent, thoughtful eyes.

"Father!" shouted Laurent. "Can you..."

"I'm here for that... My actions have more force in this world. I'll you."

He was already fading through the walls... Isabelle's cry stopped. Just then Laurent realized that, alone, he was not capable of saving her. Perhaps he had reached her, but had he pushed the man in black aside? And what sort of injuries had Isabelle sustained?

With that thought, fear returned. What had happened to Isabelle? In what situation had Laurent's father found her? Had her cry stopped because she had been saved or because she had been lost?

The shadow reappeared, nebulous.

"My intervention has shortened your stay here for both of you" he said. "That's fortunate because your childhood fears were founded and I had to work hard to make the double being depart. But this is not all over for you. All I can do is repeat what I said to you earlier. You must leave this house in which you will now regain consciousness. The slightest delay will mean that you'll stay here for eternity."

Laurent had only enough time to think of the link between his father's words and those of the parchment. Everything was fleeing around him. The corridor, the hallways were fading and Laurent felt himself plunged back into the dark space he had first crossed through.

An opening was growing in the distance. The red dot expanded into a pentagon-shaped window. Laurent crossed through the mirror like a ball and...

He looked around. In the red-tinted half-darkness, Boisrival was standing. On the other side of the heavy table,

Isabelle turned her head, moaning weakly. Laurent felt himself bound to the chair as pain moved up his leg.

"Perfect," Richard said in a deep voice as he walked over to Isabelle.

He bent over her, surprised.

"What is this injury?" he asked. "What happened?"

Throat tight, Laurent realized that his former enemies had spared no one. What horrors had been perpetrated behind the black eye opened in the wall?

Richard walked over to Laurent then rushed over to the fireplace. Scarlet light swept over the red shadows.

"You too!" he said, examining Laurent's leg.

The injuries inflicted on the astral body appeared deep on the material body. Everything that had occurred behind the mirror left a trace in reality.

"This is the result of your 'experiment'," Laurent said weakly, holding back a moan.

The injury in his calf, was throbbing terribly.

"Start by taking care of Isabelle!" he added. "Can't you see she's about to faint?"

Richard was moving about, visibly concerned about something else.

"Yes, yes," he said, voice filled with regret. "I'll get what's needed."

"You can free me now…" said Laurent.

"So you can wait for me, knife in hand? You must be joking."

Richard raced off. His long, black dressing gown flapped against the tapestry as he walked through the door.

"Isabelle!" Laurent called out. "Hold on… We'll take care of you. You were bitten too!"

She did not reply. Her head lay, inert, against the back of the chair.

"First, I'll get rid of an object that is weighing you down," said Boisrival as he placed bandages on the table.

He walked over to Laurent, quickly grabbed his hunting knife and threw it into the fireplace.

"You damaged one of my doors with that knife," he said. "That's enough."

Without another word, he started bandaging Isabelle's leg.

"I'd be surprised if the wound got infected..." he said, tone ironic. "Moreover, if it did grow infected, I don't know which antiseptic would work... But tell me what happened to you..."

He slapped the palms of Isabelle's hands, wiped her forehead with a damp cloth. The wound had been covered with a bandage.

"If you don't know what happened, then you are conducting your experiment blindly," said Laurent. "And I'm not the one to guide you."

"I won't use your insolence as a pretext to refuse to treat you," said Boisrival cunningly.

As the man was rolling up the fabric Laurent's blue jeans in order to wind a second strip of gauze around his leg, he glanced at the bite. It was deep, but barely bleeding.

"Ah!" exclaimed Richard. "My niece is coming to... Soon I'll be able to tell you about the results of my attempt."

Isabelle had in fact raised her head and moaned weakly.

"Laurent!" she said in a low voice... "What a nightmare!"

The young man did not disabuse her. She had told him, behind the mirror, that she regularly lost her memory of the hypnosis sessions to which her uncle subjected her...

The same could not be said for Laurent.

"You recall your nightmare clearly?" he asked, ignoring Boisrival.

She made an effort to flex her leg and moaned quietly.

"No..." she admitted. "But what happened?"

"Oh... one of the consequences of your uncle's pastimes..."

Boisrival stood up. He had finished bandaging Laurent.

"Shut up both of you," he said dryly. "I have to speak with you seriously."

"That so?" asked Laurent in a tone he intended to sound scornful, but the pain of his wound made it dull and contracted.

Boisrival ignored the interruption.

He continued, saying, "Do you know that one of my ancestors, a man named Thomas de Boisrival, was assigned to the Court of Louis XV as a soothsayer. I'll skip the details. Isabelle already knows them and has shared them with my respected guest."

He fell silent for a moment and Laurent used that time to attack.

"There's no point dreaming up new lies!" he shouted. "I know the purpose of your experiment was not to learn your ancestor's thoughts but to determine, as you claimed, why your name is not in the parchments. I know your goal was precisely *not to* contact Thomas de Boisrival... to convince yourself in all possible manners that the project would fail... and all to convince yourself that, if contact were impossible, there was only one reason for that, that *you were* Thomas yourself. That would resolve the problem of your name not being in the documents since mentioning it would have caused Boisrival to betray himself, at least in his mind... And since he also had to be filled with the legend that dictates your actions, he would have simply failed to name himself, namely to name *you*."

Laurent took a deep breath and continued, "All as a natural part of the fake position you have placed yourself in. Reason takes hold when we accept the sophisms that provide the foundation. Since you're blinded by a preconceived idea, you're prepared to interpret an *absence* of the phenomenon in the most extravagant sense possible. That's just madness."

Laurent had gone too far.

"Fine," interrupted Richard, his face icy. "I'll behave better."

He walked slowly toward Laurent.

115

CHAPTER XVIII

Appalled, Isabelle, had followed Laurent's ardent discourse with consternation, without recognizing her own words, since she had no recollection of the forced excursions behind the black mirror.

All she recalled was the information she had given Laurent when in her normal state... information about the old soothsayer's obsession, transmitted down through the family by word of mouth. But the experiment was a new matter for her. She had believed her uncle when he had explained his attempt in his own manner. Laurent had revealed a new face of Richard's behavior. Fortunately for her, she had no idea what it entailed.

"My young friend..." said Richard in a tone both intentionally protective and hurtful. "My young friend, I am not keeping you here because destiny has decided otherwise. And I do not go against the decisions made by destiny."

He fell silent, smiling smugly, then continued, "Particularly since I'm the one who represents destiny. Yes, you're right when you say that I expected our séance to confirm my *immortality.*"

He had uttered that word with a certain emphasis. Laurent shivered. There was no more to be done to keep the man on the fatal slope which his feverish mind was racing down.

"If that is so, as everything seems to prove, then I was the one who wrote, two centuries ago, the parchments informing everyone about our future. I suppose that if you took your reasoning to the logical conclusion, you have realized that if my name is not found in the *book* then Thomas... then Thomas-Richard wanted to avoid betraying himself in advance."

Laurent shrugged and said, "Your story about parchments doesn't hold water. Two centuries ago, people wrote on paper..."

Richard nodded and said, "For great ideas, when building the future, it is important to select a noble material."

Laurent fell silent. No one could make Richard hear reason. Perhaps the man was not truly mad... just stubborn. Many people have an indestructible faith that can go as far as making them commit unreasonable acts... That was not the problem. Whether Richard Boisrival was of healthy mind or not, the result remained the same.

"I was saying earlier that I should keep you here," the man continued. "Isabelle too. That does not mean that I'll be so stupid as to give you free rein."

He stared Laurent straight in the eyes. The young man saw the double reflection of the fire roaring behind his back dancing in Richard's pupils.

Boisrival proposed to hypnotize him a second time. Laurent initially resisted and thought he saw a glimmer of concern in the man's eyes.

But his resistance was futile. Laurent, his head heavy, first felt immensely tired. He fought furiously for seconds that seemed like hours to him. In the background, he vaguely saw the blurry shape of Isabelle's face and tried in vain to recover the mental contact he'd shared with her behind the mirror, hoping to beseech her to do something, to come to his rescue.

Impossible. Consciousness flowed away like the blood of an injured man. He felt as if he were falling into a pit. The servant's body seemed to be waiting for him at the bottom.

When he woke from that unfortunate sleep, he recognized Isabelle's room around him. He took him a moment to adapt since his brain was still filled with the fog of the artificial sleep he had been plunged into. But gradually, everything grew organized around him and the framework of their first encounter seemed familiar to him.

He shifted his position.

"Laurent!" called a trembling voice.

He smiled vaguely. Isabelle was there. He could not see her yet, but he recognized the voice that was now his only connection to hope.

He turned his head with difficulty, lifted it up off the pillow on which been lying, and saw that he was stretched out on Isabelle's bed. Motionless, face turned toward him, the young girl sitting at the foot of the bed was staring at him intensely. For the first time since entering the house, Laurent recalled a brief vision he had had while travelling in Boisrival's car: that of a young blond girl.

The memory was strange not only because it had taken so long to resurface in his conscious mind but above all because of the obvious similarity between the image he had seen and the one now before him. Had he projected his vision in the future to such an extent that he knew what Isabelle's face would look like in advance? Was that one of Boisrival's first occult influences?

The man's power of suggestion and telepathy were undeniable. So undeniable that Laurent wondered if the man's claims about reincarnation and immortality were not based on something real. Gradually, the master of the manor upset standards and, using certain spectacular gifts that could nevertheless be explained, he managed to make people doubt reality and credit him with essentially unlimited powers.

He had to be one of those charlatans use a curious trait specific to their nature and make the most of it to exploit the credulity of those around them.

All of these thoughts passed through Laurent's mind in the brief moment he had looked at Isabelle's face, a face that had suggested them... A thought travels fast when it is clear and conscious, but it is sometimes even faster at the poorly defined borders that separate hypnotic sleep from refound lucidity. Then it transforms easily into a series of images and symbols in which silent words are only barely formulated...

That's when Laurent noticed the tears beading on the tips of Isabelle's eyelashes. In the scarlet light, each tear looked like a tiny ruby.

He sat up.

"What happened?" he asked.

She shook her head without replying. Laurent got up and went over to sit by her. His movements revived the pain of the inexplicable injury to his leg. He automatically looked at Isabelle's legs. The left one was bandaged and he recalled everything.

"Did he hypnotize you as well to bring you back to your room?" he asked.

She swallowed, then said, "I... don't know. But..."

"But what?"

"Everything... everything you said to him. I'm afraid..."

He placed his arm around her shoulders and said, "Don't be afraid. I'm with you."

She looked at him. Looking at her eyes so close, Laurent felt tenderness wash over him. He would have liked to protect her from the gravest perils. A bit of that warmth must have flowed into Isabelle's heart since Laurent felt his arm around the young girl's shoulders rise a little as she murmured, "It's all so terrible. We'll never get out of here."

Laurent noted that her words constituted an acknowledgement. Isabelle had never once spoken about escape. She had docilely gone along with the abortive attempt undertaken by her companion, but without taking the slightest initiative. She'd even been very reticent about acting as a witness in the event that Laurent decided to file a complaint with the police about his kidnapping. Something seemed to have guided her in another direction...

"Of course, we will," he said. "The next time I face him, I'll take my precautions."

"What precautions do you plan to take?" she asked, turning away, discouraged.

"I have only a vague idea. I'll have to consider this seriously. But you said you were afraid. Are you afraid of being locked up in here?"

She did not reply immediately.

"I don't know," she finally said. "I have a feeling the future holds something terrible in store for me."

Laurent tried to distract her, saying "So stop thinking about the future. Your uncle has already been predicting the future for two hundred years..."

She gave him a look in which he read lack of understanding and a sort of distrust. No sign of a smile. No doubt she didn't appreciate his sense of humor, particularly considering the conditions they found themselves in.

"I meant to say that your sense of foreboding is no doubt misleading you," he explained. "Now that I'm familiar with the weapon being used against us, I won't be caught off guard. I'll take care not to injure your uncle, but I will render him incapable of causing harm."

She thought for a moment then said, "Did you know that we came back to my room a long time ago?"

Laurent leapt up and ran over to the door. It was closed and, unfortunately, he no longer had his knife.

"A long time ago, you said?"

"Hours and hours ago... I don't have a watch and I don't know if it's day or night outside... but over the past two years I've developed a rather accurate sense of time."

So, the absurdities Laurent had considered for a moment did not exist. Time, or rather duration, flowed here as it did everywhere else. The young man looked at Isabelle seated in front of him, her face raised, her throat taut.

I have in fact wasted too much time! He thought as he embraced her.

CHAPTER XIX

"Gently, my lambs..." said Richard's voice through the small window. "I have urgent business to attend to and I see that you are making the most of your solitude."

Laurent abruptly moved away from Isabelle, as the young girl hastily fastened her robe.

"You scoundrel!" shouted Laurent. "Come and speak with me down here instead of hiding like a rat in a hole!"

"I'm coming... I'm coming... don't be so impatient."

A slight scarping sound came through the small window, followed by Boisrival's voice.

"However, before I join you, I have to warn you that Laurent will leave this room since it is unacceptable for a stranger to have access to my niece's apartments..."

What did this change of heart mean? Richard was the one who had encouraged Laurent and Isabelle to get together... Perhaps it meant Laurent was no longer of any use to Boisrival?

The voice continued, "He will be free to go about the house as he sees fit since the *book* has decided he is to remain here. But Isabelle's bedroom will be off limits to him for a very good reason."

Silence.

"It will be mine."

What did he mean by that? A furious sense of disgust washed over Laurent, making him tremble. No... it could not be what he imagined...

"Mine and hers at the same time," added Richard as if taunting them.

Another silence. He was spying on them.

"You should understand why," he continued. "Yet you both know that I can only ensure my immortality by way of reincarnation through my son..."

121

A chuckle.

"And for that I have to have a son... And who here could be the mother of my son, apart from Isabelle?"

Laurent cried out in rage and disgust.

"Shut up, fool!" shouted Boisrival through the small window. "I'll teach you for trying to rape my niece!"

He fell silent, laughed dryly, then added, "That's it... I'll teach you. You'll be free to stand where I'm standing right now."

The laugh faded in the distance.

Laurent, eyes wide, face twisted in fear and hatred, had taken Isabelle back into his arms. She was shivering. After his initial indignation, he started to think furiously.

The man had invented all of these tales solely to justify the erotic lunacy he could not satisfy with his niece. Now, there was nothing holding him back. No moral barrier to stop him from acting on his impulses. Given the mental chaos of his mind, there was a chance he no longer mastered his exceptional abilities. Laurent acted accordingly.

He propped Isabelle against the wall, near the closed door and took a stance in front of it, prepared to strike.

The door opened violently.

The man had rushed in without taking the lightest precaution, just as Laurent had hoped. Boisrival was met by a right hook to his belly. He doubled over. In a fraction of a second, Laurent pummeled him on the nape of his neck, completing his welcome.

Boisrival fell to the floor as Isabelle screamed. But Laurent was already on him crushing his throat with fingers strengthened by blind rage. Isabelle threw herself at Laurent in an attempt to make him release his grip. She continued to scream, punching and kicking, as the fingers around Richard's throat tightened. It was as if they had a will of their own and nothing in the world could loosen their grasp.

When Laurent got up, Isabelle was lying unconscious on the tiles. Boisrival was dead.

Terrified by what he'd done, concerned about Isabelle's state, Laurent stood there stupidly. Then he carried the young girl to the bed, then slapped her to bring her out of her faint.

She regained consciousness, sat up with difficulty and glanced, distraught, at Boisrival's body.

"Murderer!" she shouted. "You're a murderer. You killed my uncle!"

He looked at her, frightened.

"But he would have raped you!" he said in a toneless voice.

She turned away, stared at the basement window and said, "Murderer! You talked about judges in courts! You're the guilty one…"

Laurent stepped back, dumbfounded. Isabelle's words filled him with horror, decreasing his awareness of his deed.

Shameful bonds had been woven between these two beings, cloistered in the extravagant building…

He had come as an intruder. While Maria's murder had eliminated the only witness to this hermetic existence, it had also destroyed everything.

Isabelle did not love him. She too was abnormal, unbalanced… What 17-year-old girl would have hesitated to choose between a well-built 22-year-old youth and a half-mad old man?

Now that the man was dead, she barely hid the secret bonds that had connected them. With perverse naivety, she revealed that she had only pretended to fear the rape…

The very next moment, Laurent swept away the whirlpool of ideas that had obliterated his judgement. After all, it was natural for this girl to react as she did to the violent death of a member of her family, the last member, one who represented her entire horizon!

He walked over to her, trying to find a way to justify himself in less direct terms. But she was looking at him in horror and moving away from him. Perhaps she did not have all her wits?

Or the shock she had suffered...

Inspiration suddenly swept over him.

"I'm just the instrument of destiny!" he said vehemently. "Remember what concerned your uncle. He didn't understand why his name was not mentioned in the parchments... It was because he had to disappear after I arrived... I'm just a pair of arms. Perhaps your ancestor was the brain two centuries ago."

She shrugged, furious.

"Murderer! Don't come near me!" she said again. The body on the floor placed an impassable wall between them. Laurent silenced the burgeoning love he felt for Isabelle and bent over Boisrival. Digging through the pockets of the man's dressing gown, he found what he was looking for: a sort of handle with a square metal stem. It had to be a key. This was what he was going to use to get out of the manor... with Isabelle if possible.

"Let's go," he said, approaching the closed door. "Come with me."

She glanced at him, her expression filled with disgust.

"No," she replied. "You're a murderer and a body robber."

Laurent had grown attached to the young girl, even more so since she had given herself to him... But her gift... it was becoming obvious that it had nothing to do with love. She would have given herself to Boisrival with the same ease and long ago if the man had not maintained such self-control... Laurent even wondered if she had not been aware of Richard's presence behind the small window well before hearing his voice...

There was no need now to invoke such complex troubles to justify his actions. She was naturally deceitful and perverted. That was enough to explain her attitude.

Laurent felt his heart ache. The ache of love that you tear from yourself, leaving on its way a few deeply embedded, poisoned thorns.

"As you wish..." he said, feigning indifference. "But I can't leave this in your room.'

He bent down, pulled Boisrival's body onto his shoulder, then headed heavily in the direction of the door.

Isabelle threw herself onto the bed, screaming.

Out of breath, he said, "Hysterics are of no use. You'll find the murderer in the large room, next to his victim."

The curious key he had found made his search much easier. He did however, have to abandon the cadaver on a landing to make his way through the maze of staircases.

The key opened all the doors. The locks were all the same. But he still had to find the right way after countless errors. By chance, he entered the only room that had a window and stopped to admire the incredible wealth of the space.

It was most certainly Boisrival's office. A large Louis XV desk stood below the stained-glass window and Laurent noted in passing that not a single ray of light crossed through the colored glass. Outside, it was night. He had already spent 24 hours in this trap since arriving late one night... Unless he'd stayed there longer? It was unlikely.

He looked back at the desk, covered with papers, books, and an indescribable jumble. Elsewhere in the room he saw chairs in the same style, in perfect condition, and more tapestries and black mirrors. A thick carpet covered the floor, damping his footsteps into a gentle rustle.

As he stood there, surprised and admiring, he realized that the strange light cast by the eternal black candles was progressively dimming.

He must not allow himself to be caught in total darkness. He turned about abruptly and bumped into an object. His bag.

He was happy to see his backpack! He quickly pulled out the flashlight that was still in his pack and left the room, preceded by a white beam the ambient red light turned pink.

Hands free, he finally reached the room with the large mirror.

The fire had gone out in the fireplace and at the front door a series of carefully cemented rocky plates blocked the exit.

CHAPTER XX

Through the small window, Boisrival had said, "I have important business to attend to..." Well, he had said that or something like it.

What had he done? He'd walled up the exit. Overcome by a brutal feeling of claustrophobia, Laurent rushed over to the staircase he'd just descended, as the flames of all the candles continued to dim and the beam from his flashlight turned whiter.

He found the office with difficulty and headed for the desk. Using a bronze statue he found standing on a stack of papers, he struck the stained-glass windows violently.

A few small fragments of glass rained down, injuring his face. He picked up one of the fragments. The windows were made of quartz plates of various colors... plates of an unknown thickness.

He attacked the extraordinary windows again, without success. Of course, there was no mechanism to open the window... if it really was a window. The embedded quartz made that unlikely.

He ran over to his backpack and dragged it into the large room after losing his way a dozen times. Through the thick walls, Isabelle's cries came to him like the tiny chirping of mice in the depths of a cupboard. He blocked his ears, pacing around the table like a wild animal.

It was starting to grow cold and the dark was thickening. Should he abandon Isabelle in the depths of this labyrinth where darkness lurked? No. He would go to her and bring her back by force if necessary. At least in this room they would be close to freedom even if a wall still blocked their way. Yet Boisrival must have had a few tools to build this wall. If such tools existed, Laurent would find them and use them to demolish what they had helped build...

He set out to look for Isabelle. First, he found Boisrival's body, which he dragged into the large room. Why did he do that? A remnant of guilt perhaps? Or the intention to reunite the torturer with his victim?

Then he attacked the iron necklace that held the servant's body up. It was easy to undo; the body fell next to Boisrival's.

Laurent went back to looking. He finally found the door he'd broken. He crossed the room with three steps and pushed the door to Isabelle's room, which was now cloaked in thick silence.

Darkness was invading everything, like black water infiltrates a submarine. And the fire in the fireplace had gone out — Laurent had never found another one despite Isabelle's claims — the cold had intensified and bit at his skin. An unusual cold for the season... but what connection was there between the house and outside?

Shivering, Laurent waved the beam of his flashlight around the room. He discovered Isabelle curled up in a ball on the bed, her hair tousled, covering her face. She bit her wrist convulsively as she watched the slice of light, blinking.

"Get up," said Laurent forcibly. "Don't waste time. We have to find a way out of here immediately or we will be frozen alive. This house turned into a refrigerator in a matter of minutes."

She did not move. Laurent heard her murmuring in a strange voice, "It's... the cold of death. There were four of us here. Two are dead. Death... death."

Laurent walked over to the bed.

"I don't want to know if you've lost your mind, you too," he said. "You'll follow me willingly or by force and I will get you out of here."

She stammered, "That's impossible... The *book* predicted everything... Dead or alive, we'll never get out. And that's just..."

He grabbed her by the waist, pulling her up. She fought, scratching him. The flashlight fell on the bed and turned off. Frightened by the thought of staying in the labyrinth without light, Laurent released Isabelle and groped around for his flashlight. When he found it, he sighed with relief. A white beam surged under his finger. The light was not dead.

Isabelle had obviously decided to remain in the same position no matter what happened. He would have to carry her off by force.

Laurent struck her on the back of her neck unexpectedly, with his fist. It was not a violent blow. He had been afraid of hurting her. She screamed again. He hit her again.

The staircase yawned before him. But the shadow filled was casting a dark curtain over it and he was carrying an inanimate body over his shoulders. For a moment, he imagined a swimmer carrying the body of person he'd forced to knock out to keep him from drowning and pulling the two of them down.

He held the flashlight and the key in his left hand and supported Isabelle's body with his right, concentrating on keeping her head from banging against the stone walls.

When he finally reached the large room, he gently placed his burden on the porphyry table and checked to make sure her heart was still beating. He felt nauseous as he thought about hitting her and, oddly enough, that nausea made him then feel atrociously hungry.

That posed the problem: darkness, cold... hunger. Did these people eat? He'd never heard any mention of it... Laurent had not been concerned about that since he had spent no more than one night in the place... one night or 24 hours... no more than that. And he had unconsciously accepted the fact that his hosts had eaten one or two meals on their own... without inviting him.

The more he thought about it, the more this banal side of his adventure seemed to retreat from strangeness. Making an effort to concentrate on more immediate problems, he abandoned Isabelle in the midst of the cadavers and set out to look for hypothetical tools Boisrival could have used to wall up the door.

He had no idea how long he had spent searching. But he came back, teeth chattering, empty-handed and discouraged. There did not appear to be anything of the kind in the manor.

Of course, the shadows did nothing to help him... But his blind searching through the labyrinth convinced Laurent that Boisrival had hidden everything he'd used. It should not be very difficult... The house no doubt contained nooks and crannies Laurent had not explored — and perhaps would never discover...

When he got back, he found Isabelle shivering, kneeling on the tiles near her uncle's body. She blinked in the glow of the flashlight, like a night bird. Since then, she'd remained silent and motionless in the dark.

Laurent went over to examine the cemented tiles. Close up, they looked nothing at all like a man-made structure, but a wall made of volcanic rocks welded together naturally.

Fear flowed into him, deeper and deeper, along with the cold. He felt as if he were to be walled up forever, condemned to die like a rat in a hole, with Isabelle, on the road to madness. He could not bear that silent presence in the dark — he had turned off the flashlight so it would last longer — and he left the room to escape it rather than pursue problematic searches.

He was walking into the room with the lectern when a thought caused a shiver of hope to run over his skin... *The book!* If there were any truth in the words written about him... and in the parchments themselves, was the condemnation they implied unforgiveable? Was it destiny or bewitchment?

Laurent thought the frightening phenomena he'd witnessed — imaginary or real — had weakened his mind. Too bad. He had to try.

When he left the room with the mirror, he took a box of matches he'd taken out of his backpack. He had taken the matches because the battery in his flashlight was starting to die and he feared he would find himself in the dark in the depths of the mansion.

He did not touch the parchments placed on the lectern. He lit a match and walked towards the sheets.

With a deep groan, an enormous, bloody flame burned up the book and was immediately extinguished. Terrified, Laurent leapt back. As he aimed his flashlight at the lectern, he noticed that it was empty and that *the book* had left no ashes as it burned.

At that instant, a deep vibration rumbled under his feet and the building seemed to shake on its foundations. He staggered out of the room.

In the large room where he had abandoned Isabelle, the rock plates that had walled up the door had collapsed and broken into pieces. The beam of the flashlight revealed the polished wood of the door, which was finally accessible.

Laurent rushed toward it and placed the key in the lock. He immediately felt more anguished than he ever had before since arriving.

Soundlessly, the heavy door opened. The heavy scent of leaves and damp soil caught Laurent by the throat.

Outside, it was night. Driven by a desire that seemed to come from outside him, Laurent pulled his backpack and the two cadavers over the rocks, and returned a final time to look for Isabelle who allowed herself to be carried along without saying a word. Once that was done, he was overcome with a sudden drowsiness and fell to the ground, unable to resist.

Laurent regained consciousness under the caress of a warm sun that blinded him when he opened his eyes. He stood up painfully and what he saw immediately awoke no feeling in him. One leg of his jeans was torn at his calf and through the tear he saw his skin, a strange scar covering it.

He slept near a very tall rock, a rock shaped like a tower, where odd agglomerations of quartz reminded him of stained-glass windows.

Memories rushed in. He got up, heart aching, and walked around the erratic shaped block, limping. Naturally, there was no hole, no door, at the base of this rock...

But on the other side, he saw two large, dead bats lying on the ground, their black, downy wings spread. A third pulled itself up clumsily. It flew off with a sharp cry.

Torn to the very depths of his fiber, Laurent painfully pulled his backpack on and set out for the road without turning back. Tears blurred his vision.

KURT STEINER

DANS un MANTEAU DE BRUME

M. Gourdon

ANGOISSE

Éditions
"FLEUVE NOIR"

A SHROUD OF MIST

"And I saw an angel standing in the sun,
who cried in a loud voice to all the birds
flying in midair,
"Come, gather together for the great supper of God,
so that you may eat the flesh of kings, generals,
and the mighty, of horses and their riders,
and the flesh of all people, free and slave,
great and small."
Revelation 19: 17-18

CHAPTER I

It was October. The small village of Langrune-sur-Mer, huddled around its church, shivering in the damp cold. The stones of the old, low houses and the roofs of abandoned villas dripped with a fine rain that had been falling for weeks with no sign of stopping. The storm, always prompt to unfurl over the coast, battered the two-story granite dike and large, gray waves crashed against the closest houses.

The wind spat waves of rain mingled with sea spray against the blind windows, their shutters banging on rusty, creaking hinges.

Grazing the rooftops, thick leaden clouds broke over the stone church spire, a wound that constantly opened and closed, accompanied by the sharp cries of distressed sea gulls.

Large strips of kelp, carried by the wind, leapt about in the deserted streets like shiny, black serpents that had escaped from the depths of the sea.

Old women, sitting next to fireplaces, poked at the coals, worn wool shawls wrapped around rounded shoulders and curved spines. Their husbands, fishermen or farmers, huddled in low tavern rooms, sou'westers drying near roaring, red fireplaces. Thick steam, weighed down by smoke, drowned the yellowish light cast by gas lamps. The strong-smelling smoke from pipes stuffed with rough-cut tobacco mingled with the odor of rum and the stench of fish. The herring season was in full swing and there was no time to go home for pampering... if the storm calmed even slightly, they could all hope to go back out. Even in the dark of night, the banks of phosphorescent herring provide more light than the moon... And the landlubbers would return to their housewives at dinner time.

At home, the women darned as they watched their pots. From time to time, they would glance furtively at the large, stolid clock that had not as yet decided to sound four o'clock, an hour that released the children from school. Soon they would be heard running, bawling and bringing life to the streets for a few moments, shouting in their high, determined voices, stronger than the wind, stronger than the birds.

Four o'clock and night was already falling. Had day ever actually risen? At noon, people had had to turn the oil lamps on to "see into their plate and avoid swallowing fish bones".

The church clock had no doubt struck four o'clock but quite indistinctly. The wind carried sounds, noises away with the clouds and even the cavalcade of the children arrived only in waves. They had to return home, hoods pulled low, books sheltered under raincoats, and run in their clogs to get there as quickly and as dryly as possible. The filthiest were entitled to a good clout. And there was no question about letting such expensive books get damp. In passageways protected from the wind, this was possible, but in the alleys where the wind rushed, the children had to turn their backs to the enemy and walk backwards.

Once a child reached home, the greatest difficulty was standing on tiptoe to reach the latch, panting, arms laden with books, notebooks or a school bag, to finally open the door and furtively sneak in, accompanied by a squall of wind and a burst of rain, then vigorously close the door with a kick of his heel...

The operation did not always go smoothly. The school boy still had to wipe his feet on the doormat or the mop. Eyes reddened, tearing, whipped by rain and salt, cheeks frozen, suddenly turned beet red by the heat of the fireplace, the homecoming child merely had to blow his nose and say good day.

Ah! A truly good day!

Fortunately, the teacher, known by all as Schoolmaster Bourru, had had the good idea to prolong the lesson on the colonies and, in the damp warmth of the classroom, he had transported all of his children, from the youngest to the oldest, on the most wonderful school outing possible, a trip to Timbuctoo, Dakar, Abidjan, Bamako, across the Sahara, a blinding sun, camels, lions, gazelles, giraffes, over the savannah, and through virgin forest, then more sun, and a blue sky, as blue as the sea, butterflies as large as dinner plates, as well as panthers, both the ordinary ones and the black ones, bananas, peanuts, pineapples, cacao, oranges and naked children without clogs, sweaters or face coverings, then still more sun! What a wonderful country, what a marvelous trip! Something to make the students dream of new vocations... sign up, sign up again for the Colonial Infantry! What a temptation!

But the sad reality was that when they left school, it was raining over Langrune, it was cold and almost dark, and winter was only starting. Christmas was still far off!

They had to head courageously home, eat their snacks quickly, a crust of bread and a piece of chocolate, drink a glass of cider or milk and plunge into their homework for the evening, plunge into the shadowy problems of a tank that needed filling, while some simpleton had left the tap open...

The oldest students, the fortunate ones, stayed behind for a study group, making the most of the teacher's efficient assistance, and the possibility of copying from their neighbors.

Unfortunately, they had to head home in the dark of night, walking through a village that was already sleeping and occasionally toward an isolated house near the constantly roaring ocean, spitting threats, or in the direction of the plots that lay along an immense, dreary, mysterious plain.

A few boys, notably the two Jagu brothers, came from a neighboring village. There had been some mysterious disagreement between their father and the local teacher. So, a decision had been made to send them to the Langrune school. This meant they had to travel a few kilometers over sodden roads, along a line of elm trees twisted by the wind and menacing bushes, filled with indistinct sounds and the cries of beasts roaming the night.

The Jagu brothers' father, a non-commissioned officer in the colonial forces, had returned from campaigns in sun-drenched lands ill, bilious, and a Bonapartist. He did not appreciate the resolutely republican history lessons of the local school teacher. He made his sons travel a league and a half every day to take part in the lessons provided by a schoolmaster who was just as resolutely republican.

The two Jagu brothers were strong headed. Accustomed to dealing with their military father, they constantly displayed an air of bravado. Conjugating verbs and writing lines did not intimidate them. It was possible to believe that nothing moved them. After all, every evening, after nightfall, they crossed through the field at Manvieu, a small sinister wood where, in a not-so-distant past, the body of the butcher's wife had been found, chopped into pieces, in a basket.

Their courage, their heroism, renewed each day, earned them boundless admiration from all the boys at the school. They willingly related horror stories about owls, wild cats, foxes and even wolves. If you believed the brothers, these evil beasts waited for them on their way, playing mean tricks on them. They invariably managed to extricate themselves from such delicate situations and owed their salvation to a weapon that never left the pocket of their velvet pants: a sling, made by their own hands, from a hazel tree branch and a solid piece of inner tube. They displayed it with pride and spoke of it lovingly as Roland would have spoken about Durandal. The Jagu brothers were skilled at using their sling. With a single rock, they killed a bird no larger than a titmouse or a wagtail perched high on top a wall...

The next morning when he got up, Schoolmaster Bourru realized that the day would be as desperately rainy as the previous one, that the light would remain on in the classroom throughout the entire day and that he would have to make a real effort to vanquish the children's boredom through some subterfuge. What would he do? Talking about Christmas, that oasis of light in the gray immensity of winter, would be a little premature. They only started learning Christmas songs in November, after reviewing the *Marseillaise* for the celebration of the Armistice and the ceremony at the monument of those who had given their lives in two wars. He, who had fought in the first war, had always been angered by the idea that those who had fought in the second, were honored at the same time, placed in the same basket so to speak.

While shaving, his cheeks covered with soap, Schoolmaster Bourru pushed the curtains covering his window aside with his elbow, and glanced at the street.

Under the gas lamp, hidden by a veil of rain, near the school crossing sign, the Jagu brothers were holding forth to a gaggle of schoolmates whose eyes were still heavy with sleep.

He witnessed the same scene every morning. The concerned teacher walked from his bathroom to his bedroom, to consult his empire clock, a distant gift once given to graduates. 7:10 a.m.! No. They were not late. The little rascals were always ahead of time. Couldn't they sleep an extra thirty minutes at their age?

He shouted down to the maid who was busy at the stove in the kitchen downstairs:

"Janette! Let the children in and tell them to take shelter under the canopy in the schoolyard! Is the coffee hot?"

Without waiting for an answer, he returned to his morning ablutions.

CHAPTER II

Under the canopy, where it was darker than in an oven, the Jagu brothers were recounting a new chapter of their novel. But this time, their listeners, arriving one by one or in small groups, suddenly fell silent, listening to the whispering of the two adventurers. They did not dare interrupt them that morning. Their story was so unusual.

The Jagu brothers had relegated owls, foxes and even wolves to the prop storeroom. For once, they admitted that their sling had not "come to their rescue" and with supreme and stupefying honesty they acknowledged they had scampered off like rabbits, tripping in puddles of water, tearing the skin off their hands on brambles and almost putting their eyes out on the low branches of thickets.

What had they seen?

First, a greenish light, off in the distance, behind the mesh of tree trunks. A greenish light, flickering in the gusts of rain, appeared then faded, only to come back more intensely as they advanced toward it.

"Maybe it was a will-'o'-the'-wisp?" said one boy.

"No," said the boy next to him who lived next to the cemetery. "It's not possible in this weather. I've seen them. They appear when it's warm at night and things are working in the coffins. Plus, they're no larger than a pumpkin."

"Exactly," said one Jagu boy. "Ours was larger than a Bengal light on July 14. And we didn't even see it up close... It was green... grayish green!"

"And that's not all!" said the other Jagu boy, repeating himself for the 100th time. "We also saw a completely white ghost, an immense man, surely more than two meters tall. On his shoulder, he carried a white ball that shone in the rain, like a large, moldy, skull."

"Did he have a sheet?" asked one of the younger children, panting.

"No, no sheet."

"So, it wasn't a ghost…"

"We didn't have time to see everything. We were afraid and we ran off."

"I fell to my hands and knees and I glanced back quickly to see if he was following us. I saw him disappear into the trees… He might have been afraid too!"

The details of this tale were reviewed several times, examined by everyone and commented on passionately by all. It was all quite out of the ordinary, a complete change from the usual Jagu bestiary. A completely white giant, with an enormous skull. It was impossible to make something like that up!

No, it was impossible.

Yet, some of the students, a few nasty types, said that this time, they were being fed nonsense, that the story of the Bengal light was too much. First of all, a Bengal light cannot be lit under pounding rain.

Two camps formed immediately; those who believed and those who did not. And they were about to come to blows when the school bell rang, ordering them to form rows at the classroom door.

Each student took his place, frowning, preoccupied with this mystery.

The teacher started the day, as he always did, with a moral lesson. To a completely silent room, he related the edifying story of an accident that took place on the scaffolding of a house under construction. Two bricklayers were left hanging in the void from a plank so weak it could not support the weight of two men until people could come to rescue them…

"You're married and have four children," the younger man said to his colleague. "I should sacrifice myself."

As he uttered those words, he let go and crashed to the ground, killing himself. The other man was saved.

"Rigaud!" said the teacher. "What do you think about this sacrifice, this selflessness?"

140

Rigaud, torn from a dream, was in no condition to say what he thought. He had no idea what they were talking about. He was coming straight from the Manvieu wood, along with all his little classmates, who were thinking only about the Jagu boys' story.

A providential arm was raised two rows ahead, that of Gaston Leprêtre, an attentive, conscientious student.

"Well, Gaston," said the conciliatory teacher. "What's your opinion?"

"The moral of the story is that you should anchor your scaffolding carefully," said Gaston.

"Of course, of course, my young friend. But that is not what I was trying to suggest. What you should conclude from my example is that the younger man immediately realized he had to sacrifice himself for a father who was of more use to his children and society. That's what you should have retained. Understood?"

A few voices, scattered here and there, called out "yes, but Schoolmaster Bourru was satisfied and continued with a lesson on matters that would be suitable, or so he thought, for drawing his kids away from their day dreams: the examination of the herbarium, fragrant evocation of flower-covered prairies and scented glades.

"This periwinkle was picked in the Manvieu wood," he said.

After uttering the magic word, although quite involuntarily, the brave man was pleased to see that he had caught his students' attention and they were quite passionate.

He invited his boys to look closely at the plants and they all rushed to the front of the classroom, racing to look at the periwinkle, a plant torn from the cursed wood that possibly knew more than the Jagu brothers about the mysterious being and the lights.

But the flower said nothing. A fresh, young, scented, pretty flower could possibly say a few words. But this one was wilted, dried up, mummified, dead a hundred times over, and smelled of hay and dust like all the other plants in the herbarium. It had been dead a very long time and no longer remembered anything.

The boys returned to their places, dragging their feet, pouting.

The disappointed teacher carefully put his herbarium away and desperately looked for some idea that could revive all those little brains befuddled by rain, cold and shadow.

The water flowed endlessly down from the sky over the classroom windows. The white-hot stove transformed the dampness of the clothing into vapor. The smocks of those closest were visibly steaming.

"Take out your notebooks," said the teacher. "We're going to have a dictation."

The children busily set about looking for their notebooks in their desks, taking out their pens, and writing the date...

Schoolmaster Bourru paced up and down the rows, saying, "Come on now. Are we ready?"

After five long minutes, silence fell over the room and the teacher returned to his own desk. He opened a thick, worn notebook in which he made it a habit to copy, in a very fine hand, passages from his personal readings that he deemed suitable for a dictation, not too difficult, not too easy and, above all, interesting.

Having returned to the Manvieu wood, the students were perfectly silent, which certainly intrigued him.

"Boys," he said. "I have a surprise for you. I'm going to dictate a passage from *The Brave Little Goat of Monsieur Seguin.*"

The children fidgeted. Monsieur Séguin's little goat was a real treat. They never tired hearing the story, even if it was reduced to an extract. It had drama, blood, tenderness and they willingly forgot there was a moral to the story. They had read the book over and over the previous year and, with a bit of luck, they might just remember how the words were spelled. Well, at least the important ones!

Their reaction was favorable, particularly since this story about a wolf fit in well with the Jagu brothers' adventures and it was a good thing to make that sort of connection in one way or another.

But when the teacher had finished reading the text, they all had to admit that the author, one Daudet Alphonse, was nowhere near as talented as the Jagu boys. Once the dictation was over, little Bernard, tore a page from his notebook, wrote a single sentence on it, folded it carefully in four, got up discreetly and slipped it into the slot of a piggybank made from a cardboard box. The teacher had made an opening in the top of the box and glued a label under it bearing these presumptuous words: Who, why, how?

Little Bernard's maneuver had not gone unnoticed by Schoolmaster Bourru who instructed his students to close their notebooks.

"We'll continue this dictation next week," he said. "I'll take your questions now."

And he headed over to the window ledge where the "Who, why, how" box stood, next to a jar containing frogs, a jam jar containing cotton and chrysalids, a camembert cheese box filled with foam on which large beans, Soissons beans, were germinating.

He grabbed the question box and opened it as he returned to his lectern and pulled two small notes from it, waving his hands like a magician.

He unfolded them, then said, "First question."

The students were amazed. Their teacher usually answered questions on Saturday afternoon when the program for the week was drawing to an end. This time was allocated for a few dreams, manual work, singing and recitations.

It was only Saturday morning. This was a serious violation of the program, traditions and established customs.

Something really strange was going on.

The first question was extremely complex in its simplicity. The anonymous author asked, "Why is the sum of the squares of two sides of the right angle equal to the square of the hypotenuse?"

That was enough to embarrass Pythagoras himself.

Schoolmaster Bourru was used to that type of trap. He knew his students and was familiar with their trick questions. He did not beat around the bush.

"I don't know," he replied. "But I can assure you that no one knows the answer to that question. The priest will tell you it's a mystery. I can tell you it's a basic truth. In fact, it's like asking why fire is hot and why the rain falling just now is cold and damp. But I can tell you one thing, the theorem is perfectly true. I noted that on my own while conducting the land survey."

The teacher, who also served as the secretary at the town hall, enhanced his meager budget by working as a surveyor.

He continued, "In the 'Top Part' (a term used to designate the portion of the plain located above the church and the ancient Roman road), there are three fields that belong to the farmers of our village. These three fields are square and lie along the three sides of a fourth field which is a right triangle. I measured these plots of land myself. The area of the square lying next to the hypotenuse of the triangular field is equal to the area of the two other fields lying along the two sides of the right angle."

The teacher paused, then continued, "I verified the truth of this theorem myself and I encourage you to do so on your own."

They took him at his word. A sense of satisfaction washed over the students as they noted that Langrune took pride in providing a concrete geographic demonstration of such profound theories. In a way, it was as important as if the municipal council had decided to erect a statue honoring Pythagoras in front of the town hall.

"Second question," said the teacher, trying not to reveal his satisfaction at seeing all the students' ears perk up in interest.

"Second and final question: Do ghosts exist?"

That was little Bernard's question.

It was really was turning into a bad week! Nothing but traps! No comfortable questions like: What is the exact height of the tallest mountain in the world? or What is the deepest ocean?

No, the question was "Do ghosts exist?"

He read the question out loud then reflected on it in dead silence for a long moment. Of course, it was little Bernard's handwriting. Where could he have got that idea from? His parents were very religious, reasonable people... The note was not signed but he recognized the handwriting and the way in which little Bernard forgot the "s" and then added it later, separated, a good distance from the word.

"Do ghosts exist?" Now that was a serious question, one he had asked himself a thousand times honestly and he had to respond honestly. What was going on in that little brain? Where did the idea come from? A story told by his grandmother? Something he read?

He glanced around at his students. The intensity of their attention gripped him immediately. He realized it was not the question of a single child, but the concern of an entire class. Accustomed to feeling for his boys, loving them, understanding them, he immediately knew he had to respond, not to one of them, but to the problem that concerned them all, because they did look unsettled, distressed even. The depth of their trust in him surprised him, as it always had throughout his career.

He could not pussyfoot around this. He could not pass it off with the hurtful chuckle of a self-centered adult.

He had never been a truly great person; he could not disappoint this immense, profound trust.

He stepped away from his lectern, walked over to a table to sit down, filled his pipe, something he never did in class but only during recess, and started to speak, or rather to think out loud.

"Logic dictates that there are no ghosts, that they are nothing more than superstitious beliefs on the part of the most backward of people... A French mind, a Cartesian mind moreover, is not entitled to debase itself by giving any credit to ghost stories. Yet, such stories have been circulating for thou-

145

sands of years, dating back to the most distant past, while remaining vivid in our century, braving the most astonishing scientific discoveries."

The teacher thought a few seconds, then continued, "We cannot deny the fact that in our cities, in our rural areas, many people believe in fantastic appearances, claiming to have witnessed..."

The children were fidgeting about, not because they were distracted, but out of nervousness. They were passionate about the topic and the teacher was not responding clearly enough. They needed a clear, decisive answer... and they weren't getting one.

The teacher paused for a moment that seemed eternal to them, then continued, "There is something unsettling about the persistence of this belief in the supernatural. That is true. It could be tempting to say that there is no smoke without fire. There are too many similar reports, coming from people who are considered sensible, for us to be able to reject, beyond question, the existence of such apparitions... Unfortunately, no scholar has studied such phenomena with the rigorous methods of science. And while a few rare researchers may have undertaken such an effort, they have rarely presented impartial conclusions to their fellow citizens..."

The citizens wearing short pants bitterly regretted that shortcoming. The Jagu mystery remained cloaked in shadow and both those for and against held on to their positions. While it did raise the tone of the debate, the teacher's response provided arguments for both sides.

The students whispered. The whispers grew louder. The time came for recess, giving them an opportunity to continue their discussions freely.

The teacher pulled his gold watch from his pocket and wound it calmly. He glanced at the low cloud, then lit his pipe, which he had allowed to go out.

He picked up his beret, white with chalk dust, pulled on an old, threadbare, black overcoat, wrapped a scarf hastily knitted with loose stiches by his wife around his neck and started to pace around the schoolyard in his clogs, making sure no one injured themselves and hoping to catch a few snatches of conversation that could explain his students' strange behavior.

But the students were particularly distrustful and, considering the importance of the events, they remained so cautious the teacher learned nothing about what was upsetting them.

The maid called him to offer him mulled wine to ward off any potential cold, the cruel enemy of orators.

CHAPTER III

A car stopped at the fence surrounding the schoolyard: an old Citroën covered with a thick shell of mud. Its owner, Mr. Bellière, had long since given up on taking care of the vehicle. He was a veterinarian, accustomed to driving night and day on rutted roads filled with potholes. In his mud-covered rubber boots, his faded corduroy pants and his dusty jacket, he seemed even more earthy than usual. Spending his life in fields and stables, he would no doubt find it difficult to dress up in fancy clothes.

He entered the schoolyard, a place most familiar to him, knowing full well his friend the schoolmaster would willingly chat with him for five minutes and would unfailingly offer him a coffee or a mulled wine.

"Guess what just happened to me out of the blue! Well, I've just come back from the Dumont farm. Someone injured one of their most beautiful cows and it bled to death. I arrived just in time to see it take its last breath!"

"An act of vengeance, jealousy?" asked the schoolmaster, dubiously.

He could never understand how such feelings could be expressed so basely.

"Only a transfusion could have saved it," continued the vet, putting the animal first. "But it would have taken a barrel of blood! Can you imagine this happening here? What's abnormal is that the injury looked nothing like anything I've ever seen. Generally, people just cut the animal's hamstrings. That's how they cripple horses. But in this case, someone cut, perhaps tore, an enormous slice of flesh from the animal's thigh, about 50 cm long…"

Thoughtfully, the teacher replied, "We need some animal rights' legislation."

"Of course, I keep going over and over what could have caused the wound. It was so jagged it couldn't have been done with a sharp object. A bite would be more plausible, but it seems like the flesh was removed in a single piece and no carnivore in our region is capable of such a feat."

"A lion that escaped from a circus?" asked the teacher, thinking about his African tales.

"If a lion had escaped, people would know about it. I'd have been among the first to be told. Moreover, there were no claw marks and I doubt a tiger or a lion could have torn off such a large mouthful. It's all highly unlikely!"

"Could the animal have injured itself?"

"On what? The bark of an apple tree, barbed wire? It isn't all that easy to carve a wound right down to the bone! We're not in the Middle Ages here and we can't attribute this inexplicable phenomenon to some demon!"

The teacher jumped, turned about suddenly and grabbed little Bernard by the ear, saying "Instead of listening behind my back, you'd be better off playing with your little friends!"

The child took off in a flash.

"Let's go have a coffee Mr. Bellière. It's not good for the children to hear such things. Their imaginations will run wild. Their minds are filled with ghost stories right now and I have no idea where that's coming from. When they learn what's happened at the Dumont farm…"

They already knew. Little Bernard had heard everything the vet had said and told his friends.

As the two men walked off, the teacher said, "I'd like it better if they were passionately debating the municipal elections. That would be healthier."

In the study group that evening, the Jagu brothers were the first to complete their assignments. That prodigious activity contrasted starkly with the dejection they had felt since the morning recess. Little Bernard's revelations did not concern them excessively, but they did make a vague connection between their ghost and the drama that had taken place at the

Dumont farm. They knew the pastures there lay along the Manvieu wood. They were willing to bet the cow had been attacked...

After completing their assignments and reciting their lessons, they asked, with affected and unusual politeness, for permission to go home.

The teacher agreed and just to be sure asked, "Marignan?"

"1515," the Jagu brothers answered together, satisfied with their maneuver and pleased to get off so easily.

They rushed into the black night. It was raining. Their classmates heard their galoshes rapidly run across the schoolyard and fade in the distance.

Concerned, the boys in the study group kept their noses up, their ears perked, but all they heard was the pouring rain, the shrieking wind and the crackling stove.

"Let's get to work," said Schoolmaster Bourru, with a severity that hid his own concern.

In fact, the Jagu brothers had decided to take a route that would allow them to avoid the fateful wood. They took a long hook along the edge of the sea to Saint-Aubin and from there took a small provincial road that wound through fields to Douvres la Délivrande.

Even walking quickly and running half the way, they knew they would arrive late and would get a good slap for that. They debated that possibility at length but, after weighing everything, they decided it was better than another encounter in the wood.

When they got home, they received the expected discipline and went to bed without supper.

The next day, two police officers arrived at the school during the afternoon recess. They leaned their bikes against the wire mesh fence surrounding the schoolyard. Alerted by Dumont who had made a complaint against X, they were starting their investigation with a visit to the school teacher.

Schoolmaster Bourru would not refuse them the traditional cup of coffee with calvados or the information only he knew about the region as a result of his eminent situation. After all, he was the secretary at the town hall.

"Don't count on me to point out the guilty party," he said. "I'm not Sherlock Holmes, much less a police informer..."

The two cops protested, saying that was not the situation, but they did need to guide the investigation in one direction or another and they had to start at one end. Vengeance perhaps? Had Dumont leased a pasture a neighbor wanted? Situations like that could generate a lot of anger. Unless it involved the sale of livestock? A butcher who might had been conned by the clever Dumont?

"And a butcher has instruments capable of causing such a large injury," added one police officer with a sly smile.

"You're forgetting, chief, that the meat was torn, not cut with a sharp blade," said the other.

"That's true, that's true," the first man replied, grudgingly. "We need to think about this." It was obvious that he found thinking quite painful.

"Just between us, what do you think, sir?" he asked the school teacher.

"Nothing. I don't think anything at all. It's beyond comprehension. I didn't see the wound, but the veterinarian told me about it and I'd willingly believe that it was caused by the bite of a wild animal, a lion..."

The two police officers looked at one another, perplexed, dumbfounded.

"In that case," said the older one. "We have to ring the bell, gather the firemen and the able-bodied men in the region and organize a hunt. The two of us won't be able to trap a lion, if there is such a wild beast in the area, on our own."

"Well, here's what we are going to do, Teacher," said the police officer. "We'll go take a look at the cow's body right now. It the injury seems suspicious to me, my captain will

151

warn the mayors of the neighboring municipalities and you can rest assured we'll get your lion!"

The teacher protested, "Don't put words in my mouth! I only gave you my impressions based on the testimony of the vet, Mr. Bellière. I don't want you to use that as a pretext to organize an entire region to capture a... a..."

He stopped suddenly. He had been about to say "to capture a ghost" The children had definitely upset him with their ridiculous questions!

"Of a what?" the police officer asked firmly.

"I don't know anything," said Schoolmaster Bourru dryly. "And it's none of my business. Have another drop of calvados and don't waste your time here. I have nothing else to tell you and the recess has gone on too long. I have to get my students back inside."

He said that much like the farmers would say, "It's time to get the calves back in the barn."

The recess had lasted too long for the police officers as well. They got up sadly, thanking the teacher with forced politeness. They climbed on their bikes and headed for the Dumont farm.

The schoolmaster's wife, who was also a teacher and taught the younger children to read, was watching the schoolyard and the inner courtyard during her husband's absence. She was finding it difficult to stem the flow of questions asked by all the children who wanted to know why the police had come to Langrune.

The woman knew barely any more than the children and she was the first to rush toward her husband to ask about the reasons for the unexpected visit.

"Something strange is going on here," said Schoolmaster Bourru.

Then, turning to the children, he raised his voice and declared, "The police recommend that the children go home before nightfall and say they should not linger in the streets. Things could be dangerous now for some unfortunately unknown reason."

Everyone fell silent. All eyes turned in the direction of the Jagu brothers who, visibly upset, were wondering how they could avoid going out at night when the days were so short and their studies ended so late. Those police officers sure came up with some good recommendations...

When the day came to an end, the Jagu brothers rushed through their assignments in the study group with the same haste as the previous day. The teacher, surprised, attributed it to their understandable nervousness and let them leave before the others.

CHAPTER IV

As they left the school, the two brothers looked at one another. Night had not quite fallen and the rain had stopped an hour earlier. The clouds, which were not as low, provided glimpses of the twilight sky.

They were tormented by the desire to take the longer, and most certainly safer, way home. However, the discipline they had endured the previous evening incited them to get home as quickly as possible!

"Bah!" said the older brother. "If we hurry, we might get lucky enough to cross through the Manvieu wood before it gets completely dark."

The younger brother was not convinced. He felt they would not even reach the cross at the new cemetery before night fell completely.

"Plus, the tide is rising" he said "It's the new moon and that will bring back the rain as sure as sure can be."

"Too bad," decided the older boy. "We're not sissies. We just have to plunge on!"

And they raced off.

When they reached the cross protecting the new cemetery, they had to stop running to catch their breath. A large gust of wind accompanied by a gloomy moan announced the arrival of the first drops of rain.

"I told you so," said the younger boy, resigned.

Panting, they looked at the walls of this sinister enclosure, all the more alarming since it was empty, containing no tombs. What could be deader than a cemetery without tombs?

Noticing that the small ancestral cemetery, huddled around the church in the heart of the small village, was filled to bursting with dead people, the municipality had decided to build a more comfortable cemetery in the middle of a field.

154

Unfortunately, in the past five years since the cemetery had been created, no one had wanted to place their dead there and people continued to bury them in the shadow of the bell tower, digging up cadavers that had barely been forgotten, had barely decomposed, to make room for the new occupants.

The new cemetery remained empty, battered by the winds. Grass gradually grew over the field and the fence was starting to rust.

The Jagu brothers looked at this desert made even more desolate looking by the stubble and furrows stretching to infinity. The last light of day faded at the horizon just above the cursed wood.

They felt like turning back, making their way along the large loop through Saint-Aubin and braving their father's punishment... But, no, that was too much! The consequences of arriving late two days in a row would be too serious. They might even be sent to a new school yet again... Their punishment would be exemplary. No, they had to keep going!

And they set off at a good pace, firm, determined, whistling to give themselves courage and trying to think of anything, like the words of the national anthem, for example, thinking it might be a good opportunity to review their knowledge of the song...

The road was muddy and chaotic, bordered by deep ruts. They had to walk in the middle of it, the younger boy stumbling at the heels of his older brother.

"We can't be far now," he said.

The younger boy knew what he was talking about. The way ahead of them seemed interminable.

The wind had risen sweeping bursts of rain that rippled down their faces and necks. They picked up their pace.

The road, like all roads in the region, was almost straight, rigorously stretching from one bell tower to another. Yet, they were aware of a slight curve, a few hundred meters before the wood. Had they already passed it without realizing it? Each boy silently asked himself the same question, not daring to utter it out loud.

They continued to walk. The older boy thought he heard the younger one sniffling, or perhaps whimpering, behind him. He felt like crying too, he was shivering with fear...

Soon, the darkness surrounding them seemed to grow thicker. The gusts grew less brutal. They heard branches cracking and the wind whistling in the twigs.

They entered the wood.

"We're there," whispered the older boy.

But the younger one did not reply. Had he heard? Or did he think a response was superfluous... He merely sniffled a little louder...

"There's no point crying," said his brother, taking care not to raise his voice. "There's no point..."

He walked faster. He was almost running, trotting, stumbling, staggering as he slid in the viscous mud.

A vague burning scent wafted over them, arriving through the dampness... the scent of burning horns... then it disappeared and came back, carried by the wind.

Where could it be coming from?

This was no time to be burning pig bristles and no one in the area could handle that kind of work.

The smell did not upset them particularly. Just the contrary. It evoked the exciting activities involved in killing a pig, cutting its throat, blood flowing so abundantly it was hard to catch it all in a basin, the beasts' sharp cries and jerking, its surprising vitality and then the straw fire for burning the bristles, a joyous fire announcing amazing feasts... In fact, the burning odor was not alarming, just a little surprising at such an hour. It must be coming from a distant farm, carried by the wind.

They walked on bravely. They would soon leave the wood and arrive at home, well ahead of time. Although they would never be congratulated, at least they would not be beaten and the evening would pass without drama. Suddenly a branch cracked very near them and fell to the damp ground with a dull thump.

Was it the wind? A dead branch? Panic washed over them. They ran as fast as they could, running like madmen, each for himself...

The older Jagu boy reached the edge of the wood. A light appeared, the light of the first house in the village, a few hundred meters away. He was safe!

He slowed, then stopped.

He chanced a glance back. He could barely make out the dark mass of the trees drowned in a compact shadow. And then he started to shout! His brother was not there! Nothing! A void! A frightening silence!

Ears pricked, he heard no voice crying out. Only the lament of the wind...

Silently, he started to cry and slowly, step by step, headed back toward the wood. Then he stopped, paralyzed with fear, heart pounding, unable to breathe. He took another step, then listened for a long moment.

Nothing. Eternal silence.

He suddenly understood. He knew he would never see his younger brother again. He had disappeared forever, swallowed up by the shadows.

Blindly, he pictured the cursed wood as a plant monster, stretching thousands of fingers to trap its prey, then swallowing them and digesting them, like exotic flowers close their mouths around butterflies and eat them.

He backed away and suddenly ran off screaming.

CHAPTER V

The next day, the news swept over all the villages in the region and even as far as the most distant farms. Although the older Jagu boy had not returned to school, all the students knew that morning that his little brother had disappeared.

The children looked tense, their eyes were round with anxiety and their frail faces suddenly seemed older. They had turned into a gathering of adults in bodies that were too small.

Starting at eleven o'clock, mothers of families started arriving, busy and cackling, at the schoolyard fence to take their children home. Everyone knew the police had searched the Manvieu wood during a large part of the night, assisted by farmers, carrying torches and lanterns, as well as pitchforks and guns.

In the morning, at dawn, the searchers returned to their task but at noon they had still found nothing. No binder, no scarf, no beret. Not the slightest trace, not the smallest clue.

Throughout the day, men and women, left their homes, following the route taken by the two children, searching the surrounding fields meter by meter, exploring the wood, bush by bush, using pitchforks to turn over piles of leaves and dead branches.

Mr. Jagu swore, cursed and wept by turn. The mother, small and unassuming, paced back and forth, wringing her hands, wrapping her shawl tightly around her thin shoulders and quickly pulling back a lock of gray hair that kept escaping from her loose bun. From time to time, she crossed herself, begging the gods to return her little one to her.

The older brother, who had remained in bed, watched over by a relative, had developed a high fever. In his delirium, he spoke about an "apparition" and the priests immediately decided to pray for him.

No one made a logical connection with the mysterious accident involving the Dumont cow, but unquiet minds could not help but think there was some strange sort of coincidence.

The two events had occurred at basically the same location.

During the course of the afternoon, Schoolmaster Bourru arrived, guiding a gaggle of boys selected from among the older students. In any case, it was impossible to set them to work on their studies and it was appropriate for them to take part in the search.

He released them like a pack of hunting dogs and they dispersed, running off, aware of the importance of their mission and convinced they were better informed about the situation than all the stupid, harassed big people.

They had been made to promise they would stay in view of the adults and return well before night started to fall. That was quite superfluous...

They headed off in small groups in clearly defined directions. They were familiar with all the little hiding places, clumps of shrubs, rabbit holes, partridge nests where they used to hide during their free, wild play times on Thursdays or during the freedom of the summer holidays.

The schoolmaster and the police captain, who had insisted on directing the search in person, met for a break, sitting on a stone bench next to the new cemetery.

"I read my sergeant's report," said the officer. "It mentions your suggestions. I can accept that there is some ferocious beast... if the matter of the Dumont farm and the disappearance of the child do have a point in comment. But, of course, I don't believe in the story of the apparition..."

Schoolmaster Bourru nodded. He had nothing to say. He did not know what to think.

"The child suffered a shock. He's delirious and the slap his father gave him when he got home did nothing to improve matters. When the fever falls, I'll go and question him. The doctor is against that for the time being. However, I don't expect any great revelations. According to Mr. Jagu, the older boy was running in front of the younger one. He didn't see or hear anything. In any case, the body is not in this area."

"If it was a ferocious beast, it could have carried the child quite a distance from here," said the schoolmaster.

"No circus has travelled through our area this season and no one has reported the disappearance of a lion in several years. I consulted my bulletins. Five years ago, an old lion got out of its cage during the Caen fair. His trainer found it the same day on the racecourse. He placed a rope around its neck and brought it back to the circus, pulling it behind him, like a farmer taking his calf to market!"

"A wolf perhaps," continued Schoolmaster Bourru. "Wolves used to carry off sheep as heavy as children. But there haven't been any wolves in our region since the Middle Ages."

"Why not a werewolf?" asked the officer sarcastically. "I suggest you drop that hypothesis. The people in our part of the country are superstitious and backward enough to believe in such things and I don't want to have to fight with them on that. People already tend to drag the police into such ridiculous matters!"

"Don't be cross," said the teacher in a conciliatory tone. "You do have to admit that this disappearance is mysterious!"

"Any disappearance is mysterious until you find the body. I called to have a police dog sent to me. It may sniff out a trail. We'll get on to that tomorrow at dawn, although this rainy weather doesn't make searching any easier!"

"If the child is only injured..." Schoolmaster Bourru said, thinking out loud. "We've wasted so much time. Will he survive two nights in the cold and the rain?"

"Night is falling," said the police officer, getting up. "We've systematically swept the entire sector over an area of several kilometers. I'm convinced that if the child were here, we would have found him. I'm going to order people to stop searching for the day."

The teacher remained sitting for a few more minutes. He thought of the little Jagu boy's dirty face and tears swelled in his eyes... He would have to take the children back to school. They were already returning from the four corners of the darkening horizon, dragging their feet, their boots covered with heavy mud. Heads down, eyes fixed on the ground... they were discouraged that none of them had found a single clue.

Their mothers arrived from the village, coming to pick them up and escort them home and the teacher informed them he had cancelled the study group temporarily.

The police gathered in a field, formed ranks and marched off.

The farmers watched them leave, looking vaguely suspicious. They criticized them for their inefficiency... "Just good for handing out tickets for not having lights or a hunting permit!"

Then the villagers left as well, in small groups, each heading for its own hamlet, silent and weary.

The Jagu parents remained there alone, clinging to one another, abandoned, not knowing what to do.

Schoolmaster Bourru noticed them.

He turned back to them and said firmly, "You have to go home. There's no point standing there. Tomorrow, we'll find him and I forbid you to discipline him!"

The way he spoke of the child, as if he had been involved in nothing more than a hugely stupid prank, gave them back their courage and they headed home in the fine, icy rain.

At the school, the schoolmaster's wife had prepared a large bowl of mulled wine for her husband. He drank it in a single gulp, took off his shoes and asked the maid to bring him his slippers. Then, seated at the kitchen table, near the purring stove, he started to correct the assignments.

But his calm air was just a pretense and the work did not progress. All those errors he corrected in red ink seemed so unimportant to him. This was no time to be severe with respect to such thoughtless blunders, which had grown more numerous in recent days. He understood his students' concerns. Their thoughts were elsewhere. They scented danger like the little animals they were.

And they believed in ghosts...

When dinner time arrived, he had only corrected a half dozen assignments.

He swallowed his boiling soup. The meal was eaten in silence.

His wife hazarded a few questions but it was obvious he had nothing to say. They could well place some hope on the police dog... and yet... in this weather...

The same oppressive silence enveloped dinner tables in all the houses in the village. And the wind shrieked at the doors and windows. Torrential rain struck the windows.

"And if he's only injured, he'll die of fear..." thought the schoolmaster.

After dinner, the maid washed the dishes. The schoolmaster went back to correcting his students' assignments.

His wife, who taught the youngest ones, did not have that kind of chore. She picked up her knitting, spent 15 minutes on her work, then feeling stress wash over her she decided to prepare some herbal tea.

"We won't be able to close our eyes tonight," she said. "A little verbena tea will do some good."

Finally, she went up to bed.

"Don't stay up too late, the fire will go out and you'll catch cold."

He grumbled a vague response and pretended to be engrossed in his corrections.

Alone, he listened to the groans of the storm. Although old and solid, the house was vibrating like a ship under the pounding of the waves. He heard the floor creak overhead, his wife's footsteps as she prepared for bed, then nothing living, nothing familiar. She would be lying in bed, the light out, trying to sleep.

He felt like joining her but, convinced he would not fall asleep easily, he poured himself another cup of tea, which was almost cold by that point, and filled his pipe.

His thoughts were so tense they were almost painful. He felt furious with himself for his powerlessness to discover the slightest explanation for this disappearance, apart from absurd and childish hypotheses about lions, tigers and werewolves, and they were the ones that kept running around in his head, over and over. He imagined that madmen kept turning the same nonsense over in their poor, cracked minds...

A dog started howling at the moon, a long, gloomy, guttural lament that never ended. But was it really a dog? It was possible to doubt that... The wind occasionally creates similar moans while blowing through the trees over through telegraph wires...

Schoolmaster Bourru shivered. The fire weas dead and his pipe had gone out. He shook out the ashes and relit it.

He felt as if he had been dreaming there for a long time, a match in his hand. While puffing his pipe, he glanced at the clock. It was almost midnight. Unbelievable. And yet the teapot was empty. He must have poured several cups of tea automatically, without thinking...

Suddenly, the light went out and he remained there, in the shadows, a small flame flickering at the ends of his fingertips. Vaguely concerned. He was thinking about the child.

Burning pulled him from his torpor. He threw the match in the direction of the stove then remained seated for a long time.

The power failure was no doubt a result of the storm. There was no need to worry; he could just wait quietly for the light to return.

Yet he felt anguish fill him. He was surprised to find himself puffing nervously at his pipe, as if the reddish light he revived was going to reassure him.

"My wife must be asleep," he thought. "Otherwise, she would have grown concerned about my absence a long time ago."

The dog howled again.

In total darkness, sounds grow terrifying. It was possible to believe that the entire house was being swallowed up into a waterspout. The staggering roar of a waterfall unfurled around him. The sea, in an immense tide, was sweeping over the village, leaping over houses, cutting down the clock tower and below it, the granite wayside cross, submerging the new cemetery, invading the plain, drowning the wood...

The teacher leapt to his feet, turning the chair over. He kept from crying out and desperately tried to control himself, to calm his racing imagination. He thought: *It was a nightmare, I must have fallen asleep. I'm trembling and that damned light has not come back...*

He struck a match, groping about. Then, trying to make no sound, he looked for a candle on the fireplace mantle. After he finally lit it, he placed it in the middle of the table. The room seemed to be transfigured to him, unreal, vacillating, with supple, undulating shadows.

The house started to pitch and toss again. He righted his chair and sat down on it, thinking it might be better to go to bed. The candle was looking more and more like one used at a wake. He imagined the cemetery and suddenly an idea burst into his mind! The cemetery! How could it be! It was crazy! No one had thought to go into it!

He had chatted outside its walls for ten minutes without... But he had no doubt whatsoever! There wasn't a moment to be lost!

Grabbing the candlestick, he silently made his way down into the basement, pulled on his fishing boots and an old raincoat he used when going out on the sea. He picked up the rifle he used for duck hunting, hesitated for a long moment before shouldering it, then lit an old storm lantern that seemed to contain a bit of oil. He would have liked to fill it but, in his haste, he was unable to find the bottle he was looking for.

He returned to the ground floor, picked up the key to the town hall, which was next to the school and still dimly lit. Taking care not to make a sound, he entered his secretary's office. There, in a cupboard, he picked up the large key that would unlock the new cemetery.

He went out, closing the double door behind himself.

CHAPTER VI

The squall slapped him furiously. He felt frozen to the bone, but was determined. He crossed the schoolyard with a firm step, gave his bedroom window one final glance and headed, his weapon strapped across his back, onto the road leading to the plain.

Rushed by the cold and perhaps by a deep sense of anguish he did not want to acknowledge, he walked as quickly as he could.

His rubber boots slipped on the damp soil.

The furious wind blowing in from the sea pushed him violently from behind, as if wanting to drive him into an infernal, shadowy abyss as quickly as possible. But the poor man thought only of the child... He was certain he would find him. Dead or alive. He did not want to think of the possibility of a dangerous encounter and yet the veterinarian's words played over and over in his mind.

...A piece of flesh torn... enormous... extraordinary strength...

No! No! He could not think of that. If there was the slightest chance of saving the child, nothing else mattered. Going for help, waking a few neighbors, would have wasted precious time. Did the heroes he described to his students every morning put their own safety first? And did all those sailors who, each year, tore shipwreck victims from the jaws of death, hesitate to launch their boats into raging seas?

The teacher was now walking along a dirt road so drowned in mud that he had to hold his lantern level with the ground to make sure he didn't sink into some tilled field.

And the damned lantern kept threatening to die. He had to shake it constantly to use up the small amount of oil in the font and he had to raise the wick from time to time since it constantly burned out for lack of fuel.

He feared losing the light, even as feeble as it was. If the lantern died, he would lose his way and wander through the plain the entire night, like a blind man.

He almost ran into the wall of the cemetery. Raising his lantern, he reached out his arm to measure the height, which he estimated at three meters. The dead seemed well protected; no one would be able to climb it without a ladder. Then he suddenly thought that a child could no doubt climb the fence and, for some reason or other, remain trapped inside.

As he headed for the fence, Schoolmaster Bourru was once again surprised no one had thought to explore this enclosure. The kingdom of the dead must have a deeply sacred character so that, unconsciously, each individual had shoved back the thought of searching there. It was also true the child had disappeared in the wood more than a kilometer away and, and in everyone's minds, the search had concerned the area around the wood.

The angry wind intensified, roaring against the stones of the wall that dripped with rain and shone palely in the light of the lantern. And the wall was interminably long. The teacher slipped in a puddle, almost fell, stopped for a moment, then continued on his way.

The wall stretched slowly, infinitely, like in a nightmare.

Suddenly a metallic vibration warned the teacher that he must have reached the cemetery gate. At the same time, the lantern flame decreased suddenly to the point he thought it would go out.

In the total darkness, the iron gate started to vibrate brutally, as if shaken by some herculean force.

And it was not the wind...

It was not the wind since he heard the violent vibration precisely between two squalls, in a brief moment of calm.

Frightened, the teacher leapt back and flattened himself against the wall. He waited for a new respite, holding his breath, heart pounding. Once again, the wind dropped for a few seconds and the fence, the immense wrought iron fence,

167

was shaken with such force it seemed as if it would be torn from its hinges.

Schoolmaster Bourru jumped, chilled to the bone in horror. A living being was shaking the metal fence nearby. And it was not a child.

He placed his rifle on his hip and slipped a numb, wet finger over the trigger.

The lantern, tossed about by the teacher's swift movements, came back to life, as if by some miracle and, in the weak glow, he saw two enormous, white hands gripping the iron bars.

The light dimmed, but he thought he caught a glimpse of the fingers releasing their grip and disappearing into the night, beyond the fence...

As if driven by a will of its own, the teacher's index finger tensed on the trigger, although the man was caught up in an inner duel, as he tried to force himself to control his feelings and avoid any action that could compromise the search for the child.

However, everything happened very quickly as the finger, continuing to obey an appeal to defense launched by the body on its own, despite what the mind might think, pulled on the trigger.

There was a metallic click, nothing else, no explosion. The bullet remained lodged in the barrel.

Schoolmaster Bourru was both relieved and distressed. He did not feel like a murderer and the sensation of shooting at a living being filled him with horror while the impression that a defective weapon had failed to defend him merely increased his nervousness.

He shook the lantern hoping to light up the cemetery gate once again. He could not believe what he had seen and questioned the reality of those enormous, pale hands. Yet, he vaguely felt a terrifying presence. He peered through the shadow beyond the moving curtain of rain eyes burned by the cold and wind.

He waited like that, for what seemed like an eternity, jumping at the slightest sound, but all the sounds seemed strange to him.

Yet, the fence had stopped vibrating. The wind alone filled it with indistinct murmurs, transforming it into a Dantean harp.

Schoolmaster Bourru felt his breathing grow calm. His confidence returned.

After placing his dead lantern on the ground, he ejected the defective bullet and, digging through the pockets of his old raincoat, found another one. Presuming that it had been well preserved, he loaded his rifle.

While doing so, he repeated over and over, as if reciting a lesson, that no matter what happened he would not shoot at anything.

The diabolical lantern came back to life, comforting the teacher.

He decided to open the cemetery gate.

He thought that might be a little difficult. The lock was new, but completely rusted. It must not have been opened in five years...

Things did not go as he had feared. The key slipped smoothly into the lock. It had not actually been locked.

He withdrew the key and noted that it showed signs of recent use. Finally, he shifted the latch and the immense wrought iron, double gate opened on its own, a slow movement accompanied by sinister creaking.

He was dumbfounded by the black hole of shadows as the gates opened wide, inviting him to enter this kingdom of darkness and solitude...

The wind at his back was pushing him, thumping him jerkily. Almost despite himself, Schoolmaster Bourru entered the cemetery.

He advanced cautiously, with measured steps, among the tall weeds, the wild grasses, dead since the fall, woody stems still standing despite the wind.

There were also treacherous crawling brambles, stunted shrubs ready to grab his clothing and throw him to the ground.

Schoolmaster Bourru advanced painfully, stumbling here and there. He was convinced the giant with the white hands was wandering about in the shadows surrounding him. He could hear him walking with long strides, then stopping, whenever the schoolmaster stopped walking.

Suddenly, an irresistible squall threw the elderly school teacher to the ground, feet tangled. It had been impossible for him to keep his balance.

Had the squall been unpredictable? He doubted that.

Ears pricked, he made no effort to move, to get up. He didn't dare. He felt as if he were about to be killed here, to be devoured like some poor animal, to disappear like the little Jagu boy.

He stayed there, like a soldier, stretched out in the tall weeds, his cheek leaning against a heap of rotten, spongy plants, hand tense on his rifle, a ridiculous weapon, useless, not at all reassuring.

He shivered... Weariness swept over him. He thought he would never find the strength to get up.

Water slipped into his clothing, freezing his innards, numbing him. He felt he was on the verge of fainting, perhaps even at the doors of death...

He closed his eyes, then opened them a moment later. A reddish light was dancing on the ground, a few meters in front of him. A blurry shape appeared, fleeting, beyond the light, a vaguely human silhouette that seemed immense and high above, very high above it, two pale eyes, with irises as luminous as a cat's... Then nothing, nothing other than the red light...

He lifted his head and immediately realized the light was coming from his lantern, which he had dropped during his fall. It had tipped over and was rapidly finishing up the last few drops of precious fuel.

The fear of being permanently deprived of the support of that feeble light drove all other thoughts from his mind. Forgetting any concern for safety, Schoolmaster Bourru got to his knees, then rushed over to grab the lantern.

He knew that if it went out, he would die too...

He grabbed the lantern, raised it and looked around.

A new discovery awaited him.

CHAPTER VII

Three steps ahead of him, he discovered a cement slab the size of a tombstone, placed in the middle of a square of soil that had been turned recently.

There was no doubt about it. A grave had been dug there. The little Jagu boy was the first dead person to be buried in the new cemetery...

There was nothing to be done for him and there was no point in spending time facing the danger lurking in the night...

The rain pounded twice as hard. The teacher turned about partway, in the approximative direction of the gate and, when he found it, after a few seconds, he headed for the road.

A familiar creaking forced him to turn back.

He heard the gates close, banging brutally.

He could not see a thing but, through the rain, he detected the movement of the wrought iron gates.

The image of the vast, white hands, gripping the bars, burst into his mind. He raced off, convinced something was pursuing him, and resolved to find any clue he could about the demonic presence. He knew now that it could only be the little Jagu boy's murderer.

As he approached the village the wind carried the sound of the church bell ringing two o'clock.

The rain continued to pound.

The lantern died just as he reached the paved road. He was walking into the wind which pitched fistfuls of muddy water against his rain-sodden clothing. But Schoolmaster Bourru no longer felt the cold. He was walking like a robot, his mind burning with chaotic, frightful images.

The next morning, he would notify the mayor, the police and, accompanied by the gravedigger, they would raise the cement slab, open the tomb, and discover the murderer...

He had to be an extremely strong madman. Where had he found the heavy cement slab? How had he transported it? No doubt, he fed off raw or partially cooked flesh, in the depths of the wood... His satanic strength could also account for the death of the Dumont cow, the enormous piece of flesh torn from the living animal.

The little Jagu boy's final moments must have been dreadfully frightful, defying imagination. What could remain of the small body?

When the teacher reached the school buildings, he saw that the windows of his bedroom and the ground floor were lit. Power had returned and no doubt his wife had noticed his absence.

She was waiting for him, in fact, shivering, in her nightgown, close to the stove where the fire had gone out.

On the verge of tears, she had been about to wake the neighbors.

Her fear grew when she saw her husband walk in, pale, eyes wide, incapable of saying a distinct, understandable sentence, one hand clutching his rifle, the other grasping a dead lantern.

His clothing was so wet she was convinced that he had gone onto the dikes, slipped into the water and was returning half drowned. She could get nothing out of him to either confirm or disprove this explanation.

After lighting the fire, she prepared some grog and hot water bottles. She helped him into bed and he immediately collapsed into a deep sleep.

The schoolmaster's wife did not shut her eyes the rest of the night, turning thousands of hypotheses over and over in her mind, each more implausible than the last. The storm had not calmed. It roared, swirling around the house, water streaming down everywhere.

The endless hours were chimed by the nearby church bell. Then it was time for the angelus. It was time to get up, wake her husband and, perhaps, learn what he had gone out to do during that horrible night.

She lit the light.

The schoolmaster woke immediately. He blinked, then stared fixedly at the curtains covering his bedroom window.

His memories were quickly organized in his mind. First, he thought he had dreamed. Unbelievable images swirled about in his head, a nightmarish fresco: the cemetery gate, the gigantic hands, the freshly dug grave...

Suddenly, he sat up in bed.

He stared so fixedly and so intensely that his wife believed, for a moment, he had lost his mind.

He jumped out of bed and, recalling his professional obligations, he said, "You'll take care of both classes today. I have to see the mayor right away. I went to the new cemetery last night and discovered where the boy's body has been buried..."

He said no more, dressed quickly, pulled on his rain coat and, without drinking the cup of coffee hastily prepared by his wife, went out into the night. The rain had not stopped falling.

The mayor lived at the other end of the hamlet, close to the cliffs.

When he arrived, the schoolmaster saw a light in one of the windows and was pleased he would not have to wake the region's senior magistrate. The tale he was planning to tell was not one of the most likely and he was fully aware of the difficulty inherent in pulling a man from his sleep to give him such news.

The more he thought about it, the more impossible it seemed that he could even relate his adventure. People would think he was crazy... He was already considered unusual, rather eccentric, in the region...

He opened a wooden door, walked through a small garden, and rang the doorbell of the house.

Inside, a dog immediately started barking. It must be a German shepherd, a formidable beast. The mayor was well protected.

He heard a voice curse the "filthy beast" and imperatively order it to lie down.

The door opened.

The mayor was partially dressed, having obviously pulled pants on over his pajamas.

Surprised by this early morning intrusion, he guided the teacher into a poorly heated room apparently reserved for visitors.

Boiling coffee was brought.

"What brings you here, sir, at such an hour?" asked the mayor. "You don't look well... I imagine it's that deplorable disappearance. I wonder why Mr. Jagu didn't send his children to the local school... If he did like everyone else does, we wouldn't have all these problems. We wouldn't be in this situation!"

Feeling that his words might contain some sort of indirect criticism of the schoolmaster, he added, "Of course, I'm not criticizing you for accepting children from the neighboring areas. My administrators are proud to have such an excellent teacher... and people elsewhere are aware of this! No one could have predicted such a situation!"

Schoolmaster Bourru said, "I understand that, two months away from the municipal elections, this could create complications for you, but you do know that your re-election is assured... You can't be held responsible for how the search is conducted. That's police business. Moreover, I've come to tell you that there is no longer any need for searching."

Startled, the mayor asked, "You found him?"

"Almost! I found the place where he must be buried."

"So, he's dead?"

"I think so. I've come to ask you to do what's needed to exhume him. The gravedigger has to be notified. There's not a minute to waste... I believe the police should also be notified. You have a telephone..."

"Fine, I'll call them immediately and I'll also notify the sub-prefect. He sent me a letter yesterday, instructing me to be diligent. That's a good one... But tell me, sir, you're certain you've found a tomb? I don't want to put everything in motion for an error."

"I can assure you, Mayor, that I found a freshly dug grave. I'd swear on it. Why would anyone have dug up soil in a cemetery if not to bury a body there?"

"In the cemetery, you say? The murderer had the audacity to bury his victim in the cemetery? But that's crazy!"

"It's the work of a crazy person. There's no doubt about that! And he must have the strength of ten mental patients to have placed a cement slab the size of the one I saw on the tomb..."

Schoolmaster Bourru did not dare say he had glimpsed the murderer or at least his impressive hands... It would be too difficult to talk about that without looking crazy...

"But that complicates everything!" said the mayor, suddenly considering the administrative side of things... "If the body is in the cemetery, that will cause of heap of problems for exhuming it! And then there's moving the other tombs!... The cemetery is filled to brimming! And dragging a slab and doing all that under the windows of everyone... That's unlikely!"

"Excuse me," said the schoolmaster. "You misunderstand me... It's not a matter of the old cemetery, but the new one, the one no one wants to..."

The expression on the mayor's face suddenly changed. He leaned closer to the school teacher and asked in a concerned voice, "Did you speak of this to any one before coming to see me?"

The teacher was surprised. Were they going to ask him what he knew? What shadowy maneuver was hidden behind that question? No... he hadn't mentioned it to anyone, not even his wife. Thinking about it, he hadn't had the time...

"Perfect!" said the mayor, sounding more and more enigmatic. "Just by chance, while looking for one cadaver, you
found another..."

Dumbfounded, Schoolmaster Bourru was trying desperately to understand the words he had just heard. Was the mystery going to grow even deeper? What was this new drama?
Was it possible for such a series of horrors to strike at village
as peaceful as Langrune?

The mayor continued, "I would have liked to keep the
existence of a dead body in the new cemetery secret for a
while. That's why I'm going to ask you a very huge personal
service. I'm asking you not to say a word about what I'm going to tell you... Moreover, you will have consulted the civil
register and you will have noticed the fraud... But I understand
you have not done your daily reading. Here are the facts. Very
early Monday morning, at about four o'clock, the sea spat out
the body of a drowned man. It was Rigot, the gravedigger as
you know (and you will see that this is important to the case at
hand), who discovered it on the shore, opposite my place. He
was going out fishing on the rocks. He came to me immediately and said, 'Look what I fished out!' It was a body, in a rather
advanced state of decomposition, as we see all too frequently
around here... He was wearing a sailor's peacoat and he must
no doubt have been a captain of a cargo ship or a coastal ship,
based on certain clues... But he had no papers. Based on his
size, he was much taller than average, I figured he was of
Norman stock, or perhaps a Scandinavian sailor...

"And that's when, God forbid me, I got an idea, which I
regretted the next day (and I regret even more now). I came up
with the idea of using the cadaver to inaugurate, in a certain
manner of speaking, the new cemetery...

"The man was not from around here and I thought people
would accept things more easily in the future if one burial
would create a precedent and thereby provide company for
others to be buried there in the future...

"I needed a first dead body and I had it, sent by God as it were! Just then I said to myself: Governing means anticipating!

"Initially, I only saw that aspect of the problem. When I told Rigot about it, he opposed it immediately (as I expect all our fellow citizens will also object in the future). He said it would be dishonest to bury the poor devil in the plain, all alone, in a place where no one from around here had yet agreed to bury one of their dead, that it went against Christian charity and we shouldn't do to someone else what we wouldn't want someone to do to us..."

The schoolmaster was smiling. He knew Rigot. He frequently hired him to dig beds in the school's vegetable garden and his gravedigger's spade made short work of it. He turned the soil over deeply...

Rigot was a good man, filled with good intentions, reading his bible every night, and the schoolmaster had heard the man, in his garden, wiping his sweat-covered forehead with the back of his hand, staring at the ground, frequently say "We come from this earth and we will return to this earth..."

Obviously, the gravedigger had strong feelings...

"I was wrong to insist," continued the mayor. "Using my authority, I convinced Rigot to bury the drowned man immediately in the new cemetery... Rigot said 'Like a dog, without even a tombstone. I offered him a concrete slab that was lying about in my garage and, using my van, I transported the slab and the corpse to the plain.

"In any case, I assured the man that the burial was only temporary, that certain formalities would be required, that I would handle everything, and that, in the meantime, I required absolute silence on his part... Apparently, he kept his word!"

"Do you realize that this is all completely illegal?" asked the schoolmaster. "Apart from the autopsy that should have been performed immediately, did you even think about the poor man's family. They may be looking for him as we speak..."

"I do admit I ignored the autopsy. There's no doubt he died of drowning. He must have been shipwrecked in the North Sea or off the coast of England..."

"And what if it was a crime? You know nothing! Only a doctor could make such a declaration and only after carefully examining the body..."

"I admit that I didn't think of that," said the mayor, visibly upset. "I only thought about my new cemetery. As for any possible family, I did what was necessary. Without your knowledge (and I apologize for this), I informed the authorities and the navy. As for the navy, I did what they said needed to be done but, as for the authorities, they wanted to know who had jurisdiction in the matter..."

The schoolmaster could well imagine the sort of deliberately vague letter, that had been received by some administrative bureau more interested in 'filing' it as quickly as possible than in looking into the problematic situation...

"We'll get this all sorted out later,' he said. "You can count on my discretion. Let's hope no one claims the body before the elections. In a certain sense, what you've told me is comforting. It gives me hope that all is not lost and we'll find the Jagu boy alive. That's what counts. I'll be on my way. The children will grow impatient if they don't see me and they're already too tense right now!"

Schoolmaster Bourru headed back to the school, panting like a student who was late. He ran down streets where he thought no one would see him and arrived out of breath.

When he reached the schoolyard, he was surprised by the silence there. He thought it was deserted, given the total absence of the feverish clamor and the unbridled yelling that usually reigned there. Yet all the students were there.

All of them without exception. *Even the two Jagu boys...*

CHAPTER VIII

They were there, hugging each other, in the middle of the schoolyard, surrounded by the students from both classes who watched them silently, like idle onlookers observing a two-headed calf in a fairground shed.

Schoolmaster Bourru almost fainted.

He saw his wife, apart from the group, leaning against the school wall.

He headed in her direction initially, but at first glance realized he had little chance of obtaining any clarifications from her. Her face was a portrait of confusion.

"He came running," she said. "He said he was afraid of being late. He apologized for being absent. He said he got lost in the wood and only managed to find his way this morning."

"That's unlikely," objected the schoolmaster. "He knows that wood better than anyone. He's played there many times and he had an entire day to find his way out. Plus, hundreds of people looked for him in the thickets, in the plain, everywhere. And the Manvieu wood is not that large. It's nothing like a forest in which someone could get lost forever!"

Schoolmaster Bourru was overcome by a fit of coughing. He had caught cold during his nighttime outing. But that was not what concerned him most. He felt vaguely ridiculous. What was the mayor going to think when he learned of the little Jagu boy's resurrection? Why did he have to discover that secret tomb? Fever had overtaken his mind... and he had not realized the soil had not been turned as recently as he had wanted to imagine... As for the ghostly hands shaking the fence, he had to admit that could not be anything but a hallucination...

He headed toward the little Jagu boy, painfully making his way through the tight ranks of children.

He took the child by the arm and pulled him away from the group.

Schoolmaster Bourru was trying very hard not to reveal his emotions at finding his student fresh and smiling as if nothing had happened.

He clasped the child's face in his hands and turned it toward the yellowish light shining out of the tall classroom windows.

The child looked a little tired but did not seem to have suffered otherwise...

"What happened to you?" the schoolmaster asked for the tenth time.

"Nothing sir. I got lost in the Manvieu wood. I only managed to find my way this morning. I was afraid of getting to school late. I already missed yesterday and that was enough."

And, after thinking for a moment, he added, "What is my father going to do to me?"

"No one will scold you," stated the schoolmaster, paternally. "Everyone is too happy to have found you! But tell me what you did during two nights and one day. You don't look like you've gone without food or sleep!"

But the child did not answer. He stubbornly refused eye contact and laconically replied that he "had got lost". He intended to keep his secret. It was exasperating and Schoolmaster Bourru had enough experience with children to know it would take a lot of time and patience to clarify such a jealously guarded mystery. He postponed his interrogation for later and had his students enter the school.

The morning was most dismal. Apparently, the children knew no more than the schoolmaster about the events that had filled the life of the little Jagu boy during his disappearance and each boy allowed his imagination to run wild, paying little attention to the day's program, their schoolwork and their lessons.

181

The ten o'clock recess was every bit as dismal and, when noon came, the group of mothers who came to pick up their offspring were surprised to learn about the reappearance of a child they had imagined dead, eaten or buried. They were devoured by curiosity and hounded the hero, each interrogating him in keeping with her own temperament: tender, brutal, concerned or cunning.

But the answer was always the same: "I got lost!"

"He already told you he got lost," added the older Jagu boy, always at his brother's side and determined to defend him.

Wearied by all this, the housewives returned home, dragging their offspring and their shopping bags along with them.

Considering the distance they had to travel to come to school, the Jagu brothers never went home to eat with their family. They would bring their lunch boxes with them and the schoolmaster's wife would heat their food on a corner of her stove. They would then devour the unrecognizable contents in the classroom, during the winter, or under the canopy, in the summer.

Although each child usually had his own lunch box, the schoolmaster noted he had only been given one to heat. That seemed to prove the boy had not gone home and had headed straight for the school... The older boy had made the trip on his own. Since he had apparently recovered from his shock and his fever had faded, his father, a man not known for his tenderness, had probably decided one day of rest was enough and his son should not laze about. Moreover, since the after-school studies had been temporarily cancelled, the boy would be able to get home before nightfall.

The two brothers headed off to devour their meal. However, the schoolmaster's wife had decided the portion was too meager and had supplemented it with items from her own meal: two slices of cold roast pork, some bread, and two magnificent pears from her own garden.

After eating, the schoolmaster, pipe in mouth, looking paternal, walked through the classroom and pretended to look for something on his desk. The brothers' conversation stopped immediately and Schoolmaster Bourru was saddened to see how little they trusted him. He went back home for his coffee, leaving the Jagu boys to their chatter.

Suddenly he had an idea. If they had not heard the rumors, the parents had most likely not been notified about their son's return.

He asked the children.

The youngest replied, "There's time enough to let them know. I'm not in any hurry to be disciplined..."

There was something surprising about the child's calmness. The more their schoolmaster thought about it, the more abnormal it seemed. Where and with whom had he spent the two stormy nights and the agonizing day during which the entire population and the police department had been mobilized to look for him?

Of course, the schoolmaster made an effort to reject the memory of that enigmatic presence in the rain-drenched cemetery. But, all in all, if that being did truly exist, it was possible to imagine he had confined the little Jagu boy for thirty-six hours... For what reason? It was a ridiculous hypothesis! And why was the child not afraid? Because it was obvious that the child had returned from his adventure perfectly calm. He did not look like a child who had been terrorized, who had lived through a nightmare... Quite the contrary! He did not even seem to understand the significance of his absence, whether it was voluntary or not. His only concern, and a slim one at that, seemed to be the apparently inevitable severe welcome that awaited him at home for being "late".

Was it a good idea, even during daytime, to let these children go home without a serious escort?

Schoolmaster Bourru had reached that point in his reflections when he heard a certain commotion in the yard.

He recognized the mayor's voice, that of the police captain and firm barking.

He went out to meet his visitors.

"So, the boy *is* with you," said the mayor in the driest tone, as if the school teacher had pulled a prank and hidden the child in the school.

"Indeed," said the schoolmaster calmly. "Young Jagu came back to school at the regular time, this morning, with his brother. Everyone knew about it and I thought you had been informed."

"Not at all," said the mayor, crossly. "We searched the plain all morning with this police dog. We had him sniff a beret worn by the child and he tracked the boy with prodigious precision. And then the dog brought us here…"

"And we were at the edge of the village when we learned the child had been found," added the captain, furious. "Do people think I have nothing else to do to make me waste my time so pointlessly?"

The schoolmaster thought France was basically a peaceful country and the police must have some free time on their hands. But he politely refrained from raising that issue, particularly since the mayor was giving him a meaningful glance which he did not understand at all.

The mayor decided to change the topic, quite skillfully it is true, by commenting on the dog. "It's a very efficient animal. We were able to track the child's wandering. One single error, in my opinion, and the captain agrees with me. The dog wanted to take us into the cemetery. But we didn't have the key to the gate and it was obvious that, given the height of the gate and the surrounding walls, it would be impossible for a child to climb over! Moreover, after barking for a while, the dog discovered a new trail that brought us here."

"Finally, all's well that ends well," concluded the mayor, obviously satisfied that his "cadaver" had not been discovered.

Schoolmaster Bourru could not believe his ears. Nothing seemed as simple to him as the others were claiming. If the dog was a well-trained animal and had truly followed the route taken by the little Jagu boy, step by step, it was possible to believe that the child had gone to the cemetery and had even gone in. And the schoolmaster knew that was possible since the gate had not been locked... All the police officer had to do was lift the latch and open the gate. He had not done so because the mayor had mentioned a key that he did not have with him... If they had gone in, the dog would have guided them to the tomb. The mayor's secret would have been revealed, of course. But who knows? Maybe at the same time they would have uncovered some clue that would have clarified the child's actions?

The schoolmaster decided to return to the cemetery.

The mayor and the police officer had just eagerly accepted a cup of coffee when Bellière appeared.

"You have good timing," said the maid, smiling. "I just made a fresh pot."

And she placed a cup on the table.

"Thank you," said the veterinarian, looking concerned.

Addressing the police captain, he added, "I was looking for you. They told me you were at the school. I've just come back from Clément's farm. Someone has injured one of his bulls. It happened last night. In his barn. A terrible wound, similar to that of the Dumont cow. I can state it was done in the same manner. The animal is bleeding copiously. There's nothing to be done for it. I advised the farmer to slaughter it immediately. No point in letting it suffer more. The butcher will take care of it."

"I'll go and examine it first," said the captain, gulping down his coffee and standing up. "Good grief! The child's situation took care of itself! Now I just have to take care of this unusual clandestine slaughter. Where is the barn in question?"

"In the Top Part," said the schoolmaster. "It is adjacent to the farm buildings and opens onto a prairie, along the plain"

"Along the plain..." repeated the police officer, thoughtfully. I'll go there right away. Mr. Mayor, would you accompany me?"

"Of course! Mr. Clément is a good man, inoffensive! No one here wishes him ill! Dumont is another matter! He's a rogue. The idea of vengeance is a possibility... but it's much less plausible."

"Particularly since the injuries are so similar, we could deduce that they were made by the same..." interrupted the schoolmaster.

He did not complete his sentence, then added, "Mr. Bellière stated that they cannot have been made by a human being. It's quite the mystery. I would not like to be in your shoes, Captain."

The police officer, who did not enjoy unusual investigations, glowered at Schoolmaster Bourru, touched the visor of his hat with two fingers and left the room, followed by the mayor and Mr. Bellière.

In the schoolyard, the students, who had quickly learned about the new incident, were discussing it eagerly. They felt totally spoiled! Fascinating things were happening in Langrune! This was a big change from the gloomy, endless winters!

Mr. Bourru walked hastily among the groups, discretely supervising the largest ones, where the Jagu brothers reigned, surrounded as always by fans. It was not long before his patience was rewarded.

He overheard the older Jagu boy tell his amazed listeners, "I don't know who is tearing that meat off but, in any case, 'he' is not eating it raw. He's cooking in the Manvieu wood. I know that because we smelled burning flesh just before my brother got lost!"

The schoolmaster glanced furtively at the little boy.

It seemed to him that the child had opened his mouth to say something important. He appeared to be thinking intensely and gave the impression that he was burning to share his knowledge, while also trying to hide it. Finally, the child decided to keep his secret and locked himself away in silence once again.

The rest of the conversation added nothing new.

Fine rain fell intermittently then turned into a downpour.

The children took refuge under the canopies and continued their discussions for a while. Then it was time to return to class. The three o'clock recess brought no news and at four o'clock the schoolmaster released the children, advising them to go straight home.

The rain grew violent and they raced off, protected by their hoods.

CHAPTER IX

Freed from the after-school studies, Schoolmaster Bourru suddenly felt at loose ends and abandoned. He decided to correct the students' notebooks so he could free up his evening for a visit to the cemetery. But he quickly had to admit he was in no frame of mind for the routine of fastidious corrections and he pulled on his overcoat and headed out to the tavern to buy a copy of the *Bonhomme Normand*, a local newspaper he always enjoyed reading.

There were a few fishermen there and they invited him to take a "quick coffee" with them. He agreed although it went against his principles. He considered it incompatible with the dignity of his profession to be seen in a tavern in the company of the most assiduous drinkers in the country. But, all in all, the conversation focused on the recent events and he was not displeased to learn a few details he had been unaware of.

A tall, red-headed fellow, who fished for clams in his spare time, claimed that "unusual things were going on" and since the rum freed up his tongue along with his ideas, he revealed he had never told anyone that he had seen, on two separate occasions, a large man in a sailor's uniform walking along the shore, waving his arms about like a maniac and moaning like a possessed man...

His companions chuckled wryly. They were familiar enough with the speaker's overindulgences that they took his words with a grain of salt. But the schoolmaster, who was reasonable and logical by vocation, was starting to seriously admit that unlikelihood was not a sufficient reason for rejecting testimony. The bizarre events that had been taking place recently made him cautious.

He noted this singular report without, however, making a connection between it and the strange incidents occurring in his village.

He drank his coffee, stoically emptied the glass of alcohol they had generously offered him, thanked them and left, with his newspaper tucked under his arm.

As he left, he was unpleasantly surprised to find himself face to face with the local priest. He had the childish sensation of being caught out. Yet the priest was a good man and, if not for an ancestral tradition that required them to feel like enemies and behave like cats and dogs, they would have got along quite well...

The priest smiled and started up a conversation saying, "I'm pleased the little Jagu boy came back safe and sound. You must have been quite worried. I know how attached you are to your students. The people here are harsh and the children need affection... we all strive hard to give them as much as we can. I prayed nothing unfortunate would happen to the child. I held masses and I had my entire flock pray. The Good Lord heard us since the child came back by some miracle! But the Evil One has not been vanquished! All these stories about cruelly mutilated animals also worry me. What do you think Schoolmaster?"

Schoolmaster Bourru, feeling more moved than he wanted to reveal by the priest's kind sentiments, replied that he initially thought it had been some stupid act of vengeance but that, without really knowing why, he now thought things were more complicated.

He would have like to speak to the priest about his visit to the cemetery, but held back, recalling that the drowned man had not been given a Christian burial and that would surely anger the saintly man.

He did admit, however that, while he did not want to believe in the intervention of the devil, there was something deeply dark in the mystery.

The priest smiled, crossed himself, and said, "The devil is not the hairy, horned creature we describe to children. He has many aspects; he personifies evil in all shapes and forms. Sometimes, he's a very pretty young girl, a hypocritical bigot,

189

a shady politician or even a simpleton to whom we'd give Mass without confession... Right now, Schoolmaster, the devil may be one of our fellow citizens, perhaps the one we suspect least, perhaps one of those men with whom you just shared a cup of coffee..."

Schoolmaster Bourru felt guilty again. Although this entirely spiritual vision of the events did not satisfy him completely, he had to admit that a spirit of evil hung over Langrune and he would have to fight against it valiantly without relying too much on the efficiency of the authorities.

He was thinking about the police, of course.

As if reading his mind, the priest quickly added, "The police, as everyone knows, are complete asses. We can't rely on their science. We should only rely on ourselves. If I can be of any help to you, don't hesitate to let me know... I fought in the great war and not as an ambulance driver. I volunteered for the front lines. If you have to take a risk, I'd be pleased to assist you."

Schoolmaster Bourru admired the intuition of the man in the clerical frock. No doubt the priest was reading his thoughts, accustomed as he was to untangling the tenuous threads of confessions, which were no doubt reticent and clumsy.

He thanked the other man, promised not to anything without seeking his advice or assistance and left.

He walked resolutely back to the school.

After putting on his slippers, he plunged into reading the *Bonhomme Normand*. A short report relating strange incidents taking place in the township of Douvres immediately caught his eye. It mentioned animals cruelly and fatally injured by some mysterious being. Man or beast... No one knew. And the provincial journalist, who knew his readership well, skillfully wielded his pen, stimulating two nerves to which the people of Normandy were sensitive: their concern for their interests and their taste for the marvelous.

He complacently evaluated the value of the losses suffered, transforming peaceful ruminants into valuable, highly prized animals. He also recalled historical and prestigious antecedents, citing, with innuendos, the memory of the horrible beast of Gévaudan. And the journalist, a good politician, concluded his article by honoring the sub-prefect and the police captain who had been able to make prompt, energetic decisions. Curiously, there was not a single word about the disappearance of the child and the schoolmaster deduced that the man behind the article was none other than the police captain himself. It was easier, in fact, to track down someone killing animals than a kidnapper.

The schoolmaster had no doubts. The child had been kidnapped and confined. Skillfully enough that he felt no fear and would not reveal anything he had seen.

The more he thought about it, the more Schoolmaster Bourru was convinced he would find some clue in the cemetery.

In any case, he was going to attempt another nocturnal expedition. His conversation with the priest had made him aware of the role he had to play. He would leave the cattle business to the police, but the danger hanging over the Jagu child and the other boys did not leave him indifferent.

It was *his* business.

Schoolmaster Bourru decided to inform his wife about his decision. She was frightened.

"That's not an undertaking for someone your age," she tried to plead, although deep down she knew perfectly well her objections would fall on deaf ears. She admired her husband's courage and, like him, loved the students as her own children.

She did, however, get him to agree to accept the priest's help and to go with the other man to the cemetery, together. She forced him to agree to this unusual cooperation.

After dinner the schoolmaster's wife made sure her husband was dressed warmly.

The weather continued to be just as detestable.

In the basement, she found the bottle of gas that he had vainly sought the previous day and carefully filled the storm lamp while he checked his rifle and selected the bullets with the least rust.

She kissed him on both cheeks, making an effort to hide her apprehension.

And he set off, leaving her to wait all alone, a wait that would be long and distressing.

CHAPTER X

Schoolmaster Bourru went straight to the presbytery. It was only 9:30 p.m.

He found the priest reading in his library, which was quite remarkable for someone of such modest means.

"I love books. Reading is my vice," said the priest. "I'm convinced the All-Mighty will hold this attachment against me, but it's my only distraction."

He glanced lovingly at the old bookshelves made of carved oak that covered the walls from floor to ceiling.

"They're all bound in leather. Book binding alone will ruin me..."

The schoolmaster was unable to hide his amazement. He owned an impressive number of books himself, but the bindings were quite ordinary.

He pulled out one that seemed to be the oldest to him and cautiously touched the voluptuous leather. Then he opened it and was surprised to find it was written in Latin.

The priest smiled and cheerfully said, "Destiny gives us mysterious signs! I just finished reading a few pages in the book you're holding. It concerns exorcism. Surprising, isn't it? It's an extremely valuable document the bishop has entrusted to me. I'm one of the few rare exorcists in the region... It's a skill that is being lost, fortunately! People no longer need my services in this field, although considering current events such services may, in my opinion, become more important."

Schoolmaster Bourru was dumbfounded. Although he tried to fight it, the supernatural was filling his thoughts.

"Let's get down to business," he said. "I've decided to return to the new cemetery. Not now. It's still too early. But I would like you to accompany me. I went there the first time last night... Don't pay any attention to the extravagant elements of my tale. I'm fully aware of the unlikelihoods. But do treat me with friendship and believe that I'm sound of mind."

"Since we have some time, let's settle in comfortably," said the priest. He pointed at an old, black leather armchair. "Can I offer you a small glass of Chartreuse?"

By the time the schoolmaster had completed his account, he was on his third glass.

Although he had made the priest promise to keep the single tomb in the new cemetery secret, the other man could not contain his anger.

"I know you had nothing to do with this matter since you knew nothing about it either, but you must admit it is all too much. You can't just bury a drowning victim like a dog, on the pretext that he's not from the parish and it serves the mayor's interests! That's desecrating my new cemetery, the eternal home of the dead, myself and you as well no doubt!"

He fell silent for a moment, then added, "In the face of such a sacrilege, how can we be surprised by what is happening to us now? We are going to pay for this and we are paying for it right now! This is how you draw evil to good people, without them even knowing about it!"

Schoolmaster Bourru did not agree with this vision of blind and collective justice that made an entire population pay for a sin they had not committed...

He mentioned as much to the priest who grew even angrier.

"But they're all at fault!" he exclaimed loudly, arms spread as if preaching a sermon. "Of course, they're all guilty. They're behind everything! Why didn't those hard heads agree five years ago to bury their dead in the holy enclosure? Nothing would have happened if they had listened to me, if they had listened to you as well! Aren't we here to think for them? I spoke to them about decency. You spoke to them about hygiene. All those dead bodies stacked up in the heart of the village are poisoning their wells! God forgive me, but they're complete imbeciles!"

The schoolmaster thought the punishment was unjust but he avoided aggravating matters. He had not come to discuss theology...

He replied, "Well, imbecils or not, we have to try to clarify the situation to keep more incidents from happening. I fear for the children! Will you accompany me?"

"Of course," said the priest, suddenly growing calm. "And I'll bring some holy water with me. You never knew, it might be of use..."

"I've brought my rifle," said the schoolmaster. "I left it in your vestibule and I truly hope I won't need to use it."

"Please leave it where it is. We're not in the trenches here."

Deep down, Schoolmaster Bourru was not unhappy about having to abandon his weapon. He recalled the night before. In a moment of panic, the gun had gone off on its own and he did not want a murder on his conscience, even the murder of some evil-doer...

They continued their vigil, talking about this and that. The Chartreuse warmed their hearts. Although a few logs were burning in the fireplace, it was cold in the presbytery. The atmosphere was austere, the air was damp, and the place smelled of mold, perhaps incense, like a church or a tomb.

The wind was striking the windows and the tall black pines were groaning like the masts of a crippled sailboat.

The priest pulled a black sweater, no doubt knitted by one of his parishioners, on over his cassock.

The large pendulum clock slowly rang out 11:30 p.m.

"Let's get going," said Schoolmaster Bourru.

He thought that, although they had not discussed it, they had waited for the approach of midnight to head out to the cemetery. Midnight, the fateful hour, the hour of black plans, crimes, covens, the work of Satan, all those whose villainous actions could only be performed in the shadows...

The priest donned an old army coat, vaguely black in color, picked up a flask of holy water and a lamp lit by a can-

dle usually used for first communion, and they headed out,
shoulders hunched, under the rain, as silent as penitents.

CHAPTER XI

Once they had left behind the precarious shelter of the walls and the last houses in the village, the wind intensified, pushing them toward the plain, forcing them to quicken their pace. They reached the walls of the cemetery quickly.

The road was so narrow they had to walk in single file to avoid the ruts.

"I'll go first," panted the priest. "This is my domain. With this storm, we won't be able to hear one another and we'll have to protect our lights carefully..."

They walked in this manner, slowly, cautiously, along the large wall, as sinister as one surrounding a prison. After a very long time, the priest stopped.

"We've missed the gate," he said. "This cemetery is just not that vast!"

"You're wrong," said the schoolmaster in a low voice. "I had the same impression last night, but we shouldn't be far from the gates now."

The priest set off rather quickly and Schoolmaster Bourru feared he would be left behind. He picked up his pace, worried about the noise his shoes made splashing about in the mud. He caught up with his colleague and advised him to walk more slowly. Someone would hear them...

...And the two men went back to walking slowly, painfully, hesitating, stopping every time they heard something unusual.

Yet, the wind was howling so loudly it was difficult to identify what it was hiding. They now knew something was happening behind the wall, behind the screen of undefinable noises. Schoolmaster Bourru recognized the impression he'd had the previous night, that vague yet real presence, detected by some animal sense, forgotten by man thousands of years ago, showing up so clearly in animals when they sense danger.

Danger was there, lurking around them, invisible, impalpable but so very present.

The schoolmaster had the impression the priest was crossing himself. Did he too feel something was about to leap out at them?

The gate appeared in front of them before they realized it. They glimpsed it, standing like a portcullis, shining bars, like those of a cave, implacable as the gates of hell.

The schoolmaster expected to see it shake at any moment, vibrate over its entire height, but nothing of the kind happened.

The wind fell, as if by magic.

Schoolmaster Bourru examined the iron bars from top to bottom. He was looking for hands. Well. There were none this evening...

He could have felt relief. Quite the contrary. The absence of hands merely increased his anxiety. There was nothing behind the gates, nothing other than thick, silent shadows.

They did not dare speak, but boldly uncovered their lanterns.

And that's when the thing showed itself, as if it had been waiting for them, looking for a signal, the light from their lanterns, to move into action.

It was not abrupt, but slow, very slow, patient, painstaking, like eternity.

The gates started to move on their own. Bit by bit, they opened partway as a very dim, red light, appeared behind the gates, progressively intensifying, transforming into the changing and moving flames of a fire, seeming all the more unreal as a result of its silence.

Their faces lit by a crimson light, they stared desperately, eyes wide, at this incomprehensible spectacle as the gates opened wide.

The priest bent down to place his lantern on the ground. As he straightened up, he calmly crossed himself then, turning to the schoolmaster, he ordered the man, in a loud voice, to make the sign of the cross.

Then he said, "If we cross over this threshold, we'll be entering the demon's domain, where anything can happen, even to a priest... Do you have the strength to come with me? You can still back out."

"Let's go," Schoolmaster Bourru said, taking a step.

The priest followed suit and they entered the cemetery.

They could not hear the slightest breath of wind. The rain, which had been pouring a moment earlier, had transformed into a fine mist, wrapping everything in sight in a supernatural halo.

They walked over soft, supple weeds, on spongy soil, soaked, as springy as a foam carpet.

And the frightening silence continued to isolate them from the world.

They experienced an impression of lightness. They could no longer feel the ground under their feet. Their footsteps were slow, airy, comfortable; a prodigious strength was carrying them. They no longer had to worry about their bodies, which had grown immaterial. Like winged angels, they made their way through the cemetery.

Their anxiety gradually left their minds. They were perfectly aware of it but made no effort to set aside the horrible euphoria... Was it even possible to do so? Did they know where they were going as they made their way deeper and deeper into the bloody, icy inferno?

They were not the least bit concerned. Quite the contrary. They felt liberated, almost happy, their minds so clear, so calm...

Imperceptibly, a tall, human silhouette appeared, remaining indistinct for a long time, with blurry, undulating edges, that grew clearer and clearer, more and more stable.

It was a very tall man. He stood there, legs slightly apart, arms held away from his body, wearing a dark pea jacket, with somewhat short sleeves, revealing long, powerful wrists. His hands were immense, half open, palms facing forward.

His head was terrifying. If not for the altered state in which the priest and the schoolmaster found themselves, they would have retreated in fear.

An enormous head sitting on top of a long neck, a bulbous skull, almost bald, with tufts of sparkling hair, white perhaps, but tinted with enormous coppery highlights cast by the luminous, crimson fog that enveloped the trio. Yet, the light did not affect the pale, gray skin. His eyes seemed filled with blood. They shone, staring, enormous and globulous in deep sockets.

They could not see a nose. No lips either. Just a fixed smile, brilliant, made of long teeth like those of a large carnivore. One incisor was particularly bright, casting a metallic, golden light similar to the reflection cast by a button on the pea jacket or the braid on the sleeve.

The figure was so motionless it looked like a statue, or even a waxwork created by some mad sculptor...

The two men stood there, for a long time no doubt, looking at the giant. They appeared to be frozen in their ecstasy. No twinge of their muscles, no blinking of an eye revealed the slightest fear.

They all stood there, motionless, in the cemetery, like lunatics. In the colored fog, the three monolithic silhouettes evoked a trinity of large, magical figurines.

Inside the rigid bodies, their minds continued to work.

The schoolmaster and the priest saw the monster's arms open partway, lift bit by bit to form a cross with his torso, through small, imperceptible jerks, producing weak cracking noises, the crackling of a damaged machine.

The monster's jaw dropped haltingly, revealing the black hole of an immense mouth.

A voice rang out from the deep chasm, a cavernous voice. First deep sounds, unintelligible. Then words gradually took shape and became sentences.

The statue spoke, "Welcome to my kingdom. I greet you as the friends I never had since I have always found myself surrounded by enemies or traitors... But I have finally returned to the land of my birth, behind the walls of the same village where I was born, Langrune, on March 25, 1636. My name is Vincent Lesabre... I spent peaceful days here in my early years, but the sea demon took me. I wanted to sail, to become a captain. I took the helm of a ship the day I turned thirty and one month later, on April 27, 1666, I raised anchor, leaving the harbor at Havre de Grâce to set anchor that same day at Hogue, along the Cap de Barfleur..."

This time the shock was too powerful. The schoolmaster and the priest could no longer refrain from reacting. The cadaver stood there, stating that he had been born in Lagrune on March 25, 1636...

They regained the use of their limbs and hastily leapt back. Yet they could not tear their eyes away from the emaciated giant who was speaking to them in a voice so confident, so sad, so pathetic... as if the creature carried with it the entire weight of immense and secret suffering. The deep timber emitted by that throat carried a captivating charm that forced them to listen.

"I captained a ship named *L'Infante* that belonged to the gentlemen of the West Indies Company. We went to join Chevalier de Sourdis, who commanded, for the king, the ship named *L'Hermine,* equipped with thirty-six canons. We had orders to escort several of the company's ships to various locations. Some were headed to Senegal in Africa, others to the West Indies in America and still others to Newfoundland.

"All these ships joined ours out of fear of being attacked by four English frigates spotted cruising a few days earlier.

"Three Dutch ships, fearing the same thing since they were at war with us against the English, joined us as well, after obtaining permission from de Sourdis.

"And our fleet, with approximately 40 ships, set sail along the coast of Normandy..."

During this tale, which Schoolmaster Bourru was listening to avidly, almost forgetting the speaker's disgusting appearance, the priest was clumsily and feverishly looking for something in the pocket of his cassock, under his coat. He finally pulled out the vial of holy water and, throwing it at the sailor's face, shouted, "*Vade rétro, Satanas!*"

He made a great deal of noise and they were immediately surrounded by shadows.

The rain pounded on them noisily, the storm shrieked and they almost fell under the force of the wind.

They did not realize immediately that the red light had died instantly, when the calm and the silence that had accompanied the apparition was replaced by the hurricane. They stood there, dumbfounded, for a long time. Then they went to pick up their lanterns that were shining weakly, far behind them.

They retraced their footsteps and went to examine the place where the giant had spoken to them. They discovered the slab of cement there and nothing else.

Nothing in the vicinity. Not the slightest trace of footsteps in the muddy ground, not the lightest mark on the dead weeds...

Suddenly, in the distance far behind them, they heard the dry, metallic sound of gates clanging shut.

CHAPTER XII

The two men panicked. They were trapped, imprisoned in the cemetery.

The priest prayed out loud, "May God, help us!"

And they ran toward the gates, whipped by the wind, drowned by the rain.

At their age, they could not hope to climb over the walls or the fence. The monster had them.

"Why did you do that?" asked Schoolmaster Bourru. "He was treating us like friends. Your actions made him change his mind. Now he'll want revenge. He has us in his power. We can't hope to be rescued at this late hour, in this deserted place..."

Then he continued, "I regret listening to you. If I had brought my rifle, we wouldn't be in this jam!"

"Don't say that," replied the priest. "You know full well your weapon would have been useless against that supernatural being. Let's pray. Only God can get us out of here if that is His will..."

While walking toward the gate, the priest prayed.

The schoolmaster walked in silence, one hand buried in the pocket of his rain coat, the other holding his lantern.

They tried in vain to open the gate, wondered about the noises it made, as they felt death lurking around them.

Schoolmaster Bourru thought about his wife... Would he see her again? He heard her weeping in her bedroom. The wind carried the sounds of her sobbing...

But that wasn't possible! He tried to think logically, to convince himself that it was all only an illusion... the laments and moans of the storm... and yet he heard his wife's laments and moans...

He put his lantern down, leaned back against the gate and dug both hands into his pockets. There was nothing to do but wait...

Would they be buried in the very place they were killed?

Would their bodies ever be found?

The priest prayed next to him, one knee on the ground.

Without thinking, the schoolmaster caressed a metal object in the bottom of his pocket. He started thinking about the children. Would his sacrifice serve some purpose? If they were never found or if their bodies were found somewhere else... there would be no clue as to where the drama took place and no one would think about visiting the abandoned cemetery...

Suddenly, Schoolmaster Bourru shivered so violently the priest stood up immediately and asked in a low voice, "What's happening? Did you see something?"

The schoolmaster did not answer. He stared fixedly into the night, a vague smile on his lips...

The priest observed him. He had no doubt at all that his colleague was going mad. The strange smile provided ample evidence that his mind had not been able to withstand so many emotions and the man was sinking.

Raising his hands in the air, the schoolmaster started to dance, then laugh, a triumphant laugh.

Suddenly, he stretched his hand out in the direction of the priest, who saw what he was holding in the palm of his hand. A key.

It was the key to the cemetery. The key he had been mindlessly caressing for several minutes. The key he had taken the previous evening. It had remained in his pocket.

He inserted it in the lock and the gates opened.

They rushed out and Schoolmaster Bourru slammed the double gates brutally.

"Thank God," the priest said, almost joyfully. "Thank God!"

They fled down the road, running, hearts pounding.

Their return was so rapid, they were surprised to find themselves once again protected in the world of the living.

They stopped to catch their breath under a streetlight, dumbfounded, heads filled with swirling thoughts.

"That key in your pocket! Now that's a miracle!" said the priest.

"I do believe so," replied Schoolmaster Bourru.

They fell silent.

Finally, the schoolmaster suggested they go back to his place for a hot cup of tea and the priest agreed enthusiastically.

Pale and tired, the schoolmaster's wife was waiting for them. Her drawn features revealed the fear she had felt during her endless watch.

She looked at the two men for a lengthy moment, hands dangling against her flannelette dressing gown. She found it hard to believe that they had returned safe and sound, as if she knew about all the danger, all the fear they had just faced...

Finally, she rushed into her husband's arms and rested her head against his chest for a long moment, as if to make sure he was really there, and alive.

Then she took the priest's hands in hers and looked in straight in the eyes, fervently.

He looked back at her, quite assured. Then he smiled, pulled his hands away, and said, "I feel a bit awkward saying this, but I do believe you're one of my best parishioners..."

They laughed, suddenly relaxed, and the schoolmaster's wife helped the two men take their coats off. She ran through the house, looking for warm sweaters.

The kitchen was warm and welcoming. The stove snored joyfully. She prepared steaming cups of grog which they drank straight up, sitting in front of the fire, legs stretched out, like soldiers back from a patrol. They filled their pipes peacefully.

The priest's coat and sweater were hanging on a chair to dry.

They asked for more grog, which they savored slowly.

The clock rang three, but their fatigue had vanished. They had no desire to part ways.

The schoolmaster finally decided to tell his wife about their extraordinary expedition. The priest added a detail here and there.

When Schoolmaster Bourru had completed his account of the facts, the priest added, "I see, madam, that such stories surprise you. Religion predisposes people to believe more in miracles and the supernatural. Today's science denies them, going so far as to ridicule them. And yet, there will come a day when scientists themselves will discover the universe is not made solely of material and concrete things, that our poor human senses, our limited intelligence, hides the spiritual side of the world from us. Our minds, our powers of reasoning are not all powerful and we will soon discover that Descartes was the blindest man to ever walk on this earth…"

He was caught up in his love of preaching sermons, but the couple listened to him kindly, with interest.

Encouraged, he continued, "In your schools, you claim that the Middle Ages was a long period of darkness and stupidity. I think that's a serious mistake. Of course, it was not a time when exact science made great progress, but think of the mystic awareness, the blaze of love and poetry! The human mind surpassed the material world, bursting like arrows from our churches to the infinite world. Beyond the clouds and the heavens. When facing an evil being, people did not see a sick person, as we do now, people saw evil itself. We've regressed since then!"

"When you threw your holy water, you used a material, down-to-earth technique…" said the schoolmaster's wife.

"Of course not!" said the priest, eyes sparkling with enjoyment at being able to talk about matters with such good company. "Of course not. That poor little bottle of water is not capable, on its own, of extinguishing the fire or evil forces. It's nothing by an immaterial support, but an effective one, for belief in the victory of Good over Evil, in life and even survival, against death and annihilation. The battle started a long time ago, implacable, with defeats and victories. But we will win in the end!"

Schoolmaster Bourru shook his pipe and said, "I have an idea... In 1636, the Langrune priest kept the baptismal records. We need to find out if a certain Vincent Lesabre was born in the parish that year."

"I'll check that tomorrow, Sunday morning, after mass and I'll come and tell you Monday morning, before the children arrive. If he told the truth, that would be proof that you can't deny the reality of the hereafter. But that being is most certainly damned. He carried a sin so serious into his grave that God Himself, despite his great leniency, condemned him to such a long sentence. I must admit that I honestly never thought of Purgatory in such a way. Is it even possible to imagine such things?'

"If you had not seen and heard the being together, I would not have believed such a story," said the schoolmaster's wife. "Do you think it would be brave enough to come into our homes?"

Neither the schoolmaster nor the priest replied, but Mr. Bourru suddenly recalled certain revelations made by a certain red-headed man in the tavern... Had he not mentioned a very tall sailor wandering along the shoreline after nightfall? It was just possible that it might be the same person. So, he was capable of walking far from the cemetery... Did the sea still draw him? He had said that in his youth the sea demon had caught him...

"He clearly mentioned a demon," clarified the priest who never missed such details.

The schoolmaster's wife hesitated to ask a question. Against her will, she said, "Do you think your holy water will have chased it away once and for all?"

She felt a little embarrassed about taking refuge behind such measures, about hoping the remedy would be effective... But how could you fight the supernatural without using supernatural means?

"I cannot assure you that my victory was definitive," said the priest calmly. "I'll go back to the cemetery tomorrow to bless the tomb in the daylight of the All-Mighty. We'll exhume that poor body, which certainly has nothing to do with what we saw, and give it a decent burial. The monster is particularly fond of that site simply because of the sacrilegious aspects..."

He stood up.

"I'll be on my way. We both need some rest. Thank you, madam, for your kindness."

And he set out alone, in the night, heading for his presbytery.

CHAPTER XIII

Monday morning, the priest arrived at the school as Schoolmaster Bourru was just getting up.

"I'm just passing through," he said. "I don't want anyone to see me here... I just wanted to satisfy your curiosity. It's completely surprising. On March 25, 1636, Father Segrais, as distant colleague, baptized a certain Marie Lesabre — or Lesable — the records are moldy and in very poor condition, but the text can still be read."

"That's incredible," said Schoolmaster Bourru, dumbfounded.

"And that's not all," said the priest, eyes sparkling with mischief. "That's not all. The good priest at that time acted somewhat as the captain of his village. He kept a sort of ship's log recounting the daily events. He indicated that the baby, born to an unknown mother and an unknown father — and for good cause as you will see — was discovered on the sand beach by a fisherman, in the early hours of the morning, as if he had been tossed up by the powerful tides of the equinox..."

"That's where the name Lesable comes from," said Schoolmaster Bourru.

"And the name Marie," added the priest. "The event took place on the day of the Anunciation to the Virgin..."

The schoolmaster interrupted, saying "No doubt, given his life as an adventurer, he chose the more virile name of Vincent Le Sabre... In those days, people were not very strict about names and they could be changed at will."

"This must be our man," said the priest, and left with a rustle of his cassock.

Schoolmaster Bourru called after him, asking to attend the exhumation.

"I'll keep you informed," replied the priest.

The schoolmaster ate his breakfast quickly, turning the extraordinary matter over and over in his mind. What an astonishing image. That unknown baby delicately carried by the waves onto the fine sand of the beach in the midst of the brutal forces released by the high tides of spring! What connection could there possibly be between the body of the small being rising from the waters, born from foam, like an ancient god, and the body of the drowned sailor recently discovered on the shore... It was quite impossible to know...

The schoolmaster thought that, just a short while earlier, he would have pushed such thoughts aside as perfectly stupid. He would have settled such matters with two words: simple coincidence. He was surprised by the enchantment that now filled him. He was perhaps not quite at the point of accepting the supernatural. Yet, deep down, he could already believe in it...

Of course, there was nothing at all logical about all those so very unlikely events. But that was no longer enough to make him deny them and reject them. Everything he knew, everything he had seen or heard, truly existed within him. He believed in such things as his young students believed in fairy tales...

He was gradually growing aware of this state of things and nothing could take that away from him. He no longer hoped for unexpected discoveries that would allow him to explain these mysteries, to find the thread that would lead him out of the labyrinth...

When he decided to go outside and supervise his students, he found the schoolyard willed with activity. Wasn't that usually the case? However, his great knowledge of children allowed him to discover a particular climate that would have gone unnoticed by someone with less experience...

The children had learned something, a new fact, a new event, but he had no way of knowing what...

The Jagu boys, of course, were the perpetual center of attention, although small groups had formed here and there. All the children were talking passionately.

Schoolmaster Bourru paid close attention but was unable to grasp the meanings behind the conversations, catching only a few words or parts of incoherent sentences. Moreover, he intended to keep his students' trust and did not want to spy on them too obviously.

It was only at the end of the day that he learned the reason for the hustle and bustle. Initially he was disappointed. It was all about a shell, one the size of a snail shell, but very beautiful, pinkish and pearl-like, finely carved, carefully shaped. It would have held a place of honor in an enthusiast's collection.

Shortly before four o'clock, the little Leprêtre boy raised his hand and asked the schoolmaster what the name of the shell was, displaying it after removing it from his pocket, carefully wrapped in a handkerchief.

Schoolmaster Bourru put his glasses on to look at the object closely and the more he studied it the more his amazement grew. He noted the small, tiny blue and green veins in the pinkish pearl, and the scattering of gold specks.

He quickly became convinced that such a splendid object could only come from an exotic world. Upon consulting a conchology book, he discovered an illustration of a similar shell. The legend under the drawing indicated it was a rare specimen, originally from the Caribbean Sea, and more specifically from the waters surrounding Tortuga Island.

The children were amazed, crying out in joy.

The little Leprêtre boy, self-confident as aways, shouted "I told you. It's not from around here!"

In fact, his intuition had not been wrong. The shell was not local, that much was certain...

It came from the Americas. But how? That was the big question for everyone.

"Who does it belong to?" asked the schoolmaster.

"To me," replied the little Jagu boy, hesitating a bit. "But I gave it to Leprêtre because he wanted to start a collection."

"Fine! And who gave it to you?"

"Ummm... a sailor."

"A sailor from around here?"

"No, some guy I don't know."

And the child hesitated visibly. There was no doubt about it. He was lying.

With difficulty Schoolmaster Bourru set aside the anxiety that was washing over him, to ask as naturally as he could, "Was it the foreign sailor, tall, old, with large hands, who has come to Langrune several times in the past few days?"

The little Jagu boy was more and more hesitant. He seemed to be surprised as well, surprised perhaps by the schoolmaster's description. He decided to reply, saying "It may be that sailor. He's rather old, but nice... He gave me this shell because I listened to him politely."

Schoolmaster Bourru shivered in horror. No! It wasn't possible! If it had been the monster, the child would not have listened, he would have run away... And yet, both he and the priest had listened to him speak for quite some time without trying to flee. Did that mean he had a certain charm, the gift of seduction, of enchantment that had kept them there, paralyzed, throughout his speech... like birds charmed by a snake? But that hypothesis was unthinkable. The child could not have been in the presence of that living cadaver without experiencing unforgettable terror!

Finally, he rejected the idea. It was too absurd. The sailor who had given the shell to the child was certainly a good man, possibly the father of a family. Just because he was tall, thin and old did not mean he had to be the apparition...

Leprêtre placed his treasure back in his handkerchief and then into his pocket and there was no further discussion of the matter.

The next day, a Thursday, was just as rainy as the previous one. But the wind had calmed.

At about ten o'clock, Mr. Rigot came to inform the schoolmaster he could attend when the body would be exhumed. The priest and the mayor would be present.

"It will take place on Tuesday," said the gravedigger, in a low voice, although there as no one nearby to overhear him. But he was aware of the importance and secrecy of his mission. He also realized he was the only ordinary person attending the ceremony along with the dignitaries.

Continuing in a conspiratorial tone, he added "We'll meet in the cemetery when the clock rings noon. At that time, the farmers will have all gone home to eat and if we each make our own way to the cemetery, no one will notice…"

Then he added learnedly that this was not the first time he had dug up a body and that he would respectfully advise the schoolmaster to eat a bite "before" since possibly he might not have much of an appetite "after".

With that Mr. Rigot walked off with measured steps, face closed, nodding his head with a knowing air, shoulders hunched, as if weighed down by the burden of his responsibilities.

Schoolmaster Bourru watched — but not for long — as the gravedigger headed straight for the tavern where he went in, to have a drop of his usual pick-me-up, spiced rum...

CHAPTER XIV

The church tower clock had just rung twelve when the schoolmaster arrived at the cemetery gates.

He couldn't help shivering when he looked at them. He wondered if a city police officer would have been able to take fingerprints from the blackened bars. Do dead people even leave fingerprints? And what about ghosts?

He immediately felt cross with himself for asking such stupid questions. Glancing around himself in a broad circle, he realized the plain was completely empty of farmers and animals. Nothing living, not even a breath of wind.

He thought he was the first to arrive, that he would see the silhouette of the mayor or the priest in the distance.

He waited, then suddenly thought as he looked through the bars that the tomb could be located out of his sight, in one of the corners of the cemetery, and he went in, paying no attention to the fact that the gates were not locked.

To his right, just far enough away that he had no clear view through the curtain of rain, he noticed three motionless shadows.

He felt ashamed of his fears when he realized the three shapes were the mayor and the priest, assisted by Mr. Rigot, who had all arrived well before him.

He rushed over to them.

As he drew close to them, the mayor stopped him, grasping his arm.

"Be careful," he said in a low voice. "Don't go any further. Look at the ground around the slab."

He spoke quietly, visibly upset, as if the slightest sound would alert someone. Was he afraid of waking the dead man?

Mr. Rigot, bleary-eyed, head nodding, uncomfortable... He must had had several drinks...

The schoolmaster could not keep from smiling, but his smile froze when he saw the reason for the emotions.

Next to the slab, on one side, there was a perfectly visible semi-circle in the soil. However, on the other side, the soil had been pushed aside, forming a slight mound. The tombstone had been moved, shifted to one side, without being lifted. That was obvious!

Who could have done such work in a closed place where no one was supposed to enter?

Who had moved the cover of the grave and why?

"We'll see to this," said the mayor. "Come on."

They all braced themselves against the slab, shifting it in the same direction as a mysterious and powerful hand had moved it previously It slid over the damp clay soil rather easily.

The hole appeared.

A deep black hole, not half filled with dirt as the four men would have thought, but perfectly empty, rectangular, with cement walls on all four sides like in a family tomb.

It was obviously not the humble grave the gravedigger had dug in the same soil a few days earlier...

Silenced by surprise, the men bent over and examined the shadow. They saw a few stone steps.

Mr. Rigot was unable to contain his indignation any longer.

"For goodness' sake!" he said. "What is this construction? And where's our drowned man gone? I need to get a closer look!"

And he slipped down into the opening, supporting himself on his arms, feeling about with his feet for the first step...

His companions watched in silence, dumbfounded. The priest muttered prayers automatically, but his thoughts were elsewhere. He was searching intensely for a reason for this mystery.

The gravedigger reached into his pocket and pulled out a cigarette lighter, one of those country lighters with a generous flame that rivals that of a lantern. Using it to light his way, he started down the steps in the tomb.

He soon disappeared.

The three dignitaries waited a long time.

"We should not have let him go alone," said the priest.

"What do you think will happen to him in broad daylight?" replied the mayor. Yet it was obvious he did not feel terribly reassured...

"Mr. Rigot!" the schoolmaster suddenly shouted, leaning down over the grave.

But his call went unanswered.

"What can he be doing down there?" grumbled the mayor, growing more and more concerned.

Endless seconds passed.

The schoolmaster decided to go down into the grave. He asked the mayor to help him slip down into the shadowy rectangle. He was no longer young or flexible and it was not an easy task.

When he felt his feet touch the first step, he took out a box of matches, lit one, and started to walk down cautiously.

Just then, a terrible cry tore through the silence, a long cry, coming from deep under the ground, a cry muffled at first then slowly making its way up, bursting at the surface like a bubble of anguish...

They heard footsteps immediately after that, running quickly, and the gravedigger's head suddenly appeared in the grave against the schoolmaster's chest.

Mr. Rigot was out of breath. He was panting, eyes wild, forehead covered with sweat, the cigarette lighter still clasped in his hand.

The three other men pressed him with questions but he seemed incapable of uttering a single word. Finally, he grew calm enough to say a few sentences.

"He's there," he said. "At the end of a long hallway, in a large, low room, lying on a bed with red sheets, still in uniform, with chests all around him, chests filled with golden coins, necklaces, jewels that shine even in the dark. There are other chests full of lace and still more containing shells. And he's lying there like a king, on his red sheets... and..."

Mr. Rigot hesitated, considering the enormity of what he was about to say. He took a deep breath and added, "...and he's sleeping... All of that didn't really frighten me, it looked like a tomb from times past, like in the pyramids... but what frightened me most... is that he's sleeping..."

"Come on, Mr. Rigot, you know full well that your drowned man is quite dead! He's asleep for all eternity!"

"No, Mr. Mayor, he's sleeping like you and me, breathing deeply, even talking a bit. He didn't say much. I ran off, but I think he said, 'I sentence de Sourdis...' Wait. It's coming back to me. He then said, '...to be hanged... high and short... from the yardarm...' He's crazy."

The priest and the schoolmaster looked at one another and the priest simply said, "That's his purgatory."

"Purgatory or not, it's damned embarrassing!" said the mayor. "What are we going to do with the man? If it's true that he's not dead, we can't leave him in this hole..."

The priest looked dumbfounded, but Schoolmaster Bourru knew what he was thinking. He knew there was no urgency. The living mortal remains could be left in the creature's lair and they could take the time they needed to think. In any case, he did not think the mayor's initiatives should be encouraged considering the extraordinary circumstances. And he decided to serve as the devil's advocate to gain some time.

"Mr. Rigot," he said, taking the arm of the poor grave-digger who was shaking like a leaf. "I saw you go into the tavern this morning. Tell me how many glasses of rum you drank this morning."

Mr. Rigot gave the schoolmaster a beseeching glance, then looked at the mayor, then the priest. First there were the emotions of the past few moments and now they were accusing him, questioning him about a small problem no one really criticized him for...

But the question did raise interest since, it is true, people tend to grab on to the slightest explanation rather than believe the unbelievable...

The others waited for his answer. Particularly the mayor. And, given the lengthy silence, the gravedigger made a quick calculation.

"No more than three or five,' he said. Lying brazenly. "I swear I'm not drunk! He's there!"

He glanced fearfully at the gaping hole of the hallway and shouted "Help us get out of here, Mr. Mayor. I may have roused him!"

The mayor burst into laughter, then helped first the schoolmaster and second the gravedigger out of the tomb. He motioned for the three other men to help him replace the slab.

Once that was done, he shouted, "Come on. We haven't cleared everything up, but it seems obvious to me that Mr. Rigot has had a bit too much to drink. Do you want my advice? Time will tell. Let's get somewhere warm."

And addressing the priest and the schoolmaster in particular, he asked them to drop by that evening to discuss matters with clear heads.

"Let's avoid going back together. We don't want anyone to notice what we've just done."

They went their separate ways after the mayor had once again instructed the gravedigger to watch his tongue even more carefully since he had been drinking.

Mr. Rigot set off, sheepishly, not knowing what to think and quite prepared to admit that rum was not good for him.

After performing the benediction of the blessed sacrament, at five o'clock, the priest went to the mayor's office to discuss what was to be done, along with Schoolmaster Bourru. He was not all that pleased about the mayor being involved in the matter. He would have preferred to talk one on one with the schoolmaster but there was nothing to be done and he promised to meet with Schoolmaster Bourru at the presbytery after their meeting with the mayor.

The meeting did not clarify much about the extraordinary situation, apart from the fact that the mayor had consulted certain documents he was in a position to have: the plans for the defense structures built by the Germans in the last war.

The plans showed the locations of various buildings: bunkers, concrete shelters built along the shore or farther into the plain. The three men noted that, according to the old military maps, there had once been an underground shelter at the site of the new cemetery.

"It's simple,' stated the mayor. "Mr. Rigot led us astray. He did not take us to the tomb of the dead man but to the entrance of the bunker. He must have lost his way in the tall weeds in the cemetery, which was abandoned before it was even used. He discovered a few steps and after the oddness of the place surprised him, the alcohol did the rest..."

The schoolmaster and the priest refrained from pointing out that this interpretation did little to explain anything. At the very least, the fact that the slab had been moved recently...

Moreover, that slab was identical to the one the mayor had provided for the clandestine burial.

The mayor concluded that the burial had been done quickly, at night, and that it was possible the gravedigger had not located the tomb properly. He agreed that it should be found then added, "But, there's no rush..."

He was obviously thinking about the upcoming elections and was quite determined to keep the problem of the new cemetery hidden for as long as possible.

Schoolmaster Bourru entered the presbytery behind the priest, glancing furtively over his shoulder to make sure no one saw him. His reputation as a freethinker would have been shaken. But night had fallen and the local people, stay-at-homes by nature, had little inclination to prowl about at night as a result of the mysterious events that had been taking place over the past week. As much as possible, they remained shut up in their homes, next to their fireplaces, and the streets were empty.

They went to the library in the presbytery once again and settled into their armchairs as they had done the previous night.

"I just remembered something," said the schoolmaster. "I left my rifle in your vestibule."

"It's fine there," said the priest firmly. "Give me the pleasure of letting me keep it for a few more days. A wicked rat is getting into my rabbit hutch and I'd like to use your gun to kill the nasty thief."

The schoolmaster was not taken in by the pious lie. He nodded and said, "That matter of the bunker is completely plausible. Is it possible that our sailor has been using it as his home? In that case, should we consider him a being gifted with life? Could he have used the slab to close the opening? If that explanation is accurate, we have little chance of finding the location of his first tomb. The weeds grow slowly this time of year, but the rain will have washed away all traces and the cemetery is vast. We'll have to examine it meter by meter. Moreover, there's no point. What is important is to determine if Mr. Rigot was telling the truth."

"I think he was," said the priest. "He was not drunk enough to make up such a tale. What intrigues me the most, you know, is that the ghost surrounded himself with his riches, his jewels, perhaps the fruit of his pillaging. That attachment to the goods of this world is of no use to him. Quite the contrary. That's not how he'll find the path to salvation!"

"And the shells..." said the schoolmaster, dreamily.

"What shells?" asked the priest.

"Do you remember? When he was describing the chests, Mr. Rigot said one was filled with shells. Well, this morning, the little Jagu boy had an extraordinary shell and I was able to examine it closely. It comes from the Americas and was given to him by an old, tall and thin sailor on the beach. What do you think?"

The brave priest could not contain his emotions. He remained silent for a long time, then slowly said, "Do you know what we have to do?"

He smiled, then continued, "Visit Ali Baba's cave this very night. Although I'm more inclined than you to believe in the supernatural, I insist on obtaining tangible proof. I'm like the Apostle Thomas... for once, God will forgive me for not wanting to believe only the evidence of my own eyes..."

"That's fine with me," said the Schoolmaster. "I'm with St. Thomas as well. We'll go and look into this tonight. But there's no need to wait for midnight. What do you say about going after dinner?"

"No," said the priest, categorically. "If we're going to visit the catacomb again, we have to do so at midnight! Believe me as a man who knows about magic, even black magic! If we want to learn as much as possible through this experience, we have to meet with the dammed man at midnight. I'm convinced that, at that fateful hour, his appearance as a living, human being will be at its peak. That's when we'll learn the most about his secret... And I'd even say that's when I'll the most chances of grasping the meaning of his strange confession... Who knows? I may even be able to help him escape his miserable state."

"I admire your charity," said Schoolmaster Bourru. "I accept your reasons. But do you believe that our monster would have appreciated the way in which you threw holy water at his face? I was quite moved by the first few words he said to us... 'I welcome you like the friends I never had...'"

"That's true," said the priest. "It is perhaps true. It was perhaps a trick of Satan to draw us in better... But if you believe in God as I do, you will know that this holy water could only give him some respite from his suffering, not the peace he hopes for and which it is my duty to give him."

The schoolmaster remained silent for a moment, then stood up, saying "We'll meet at your place at 11:30."

CHAPTER XV

When they opened the large gates to the cemetery, they were no less concerned than during their earlier visits, but they were already growing accustomed to their fear.

The place already seemed les strange to them. The rain and the wind were almost familiar.

The schoolmaster viewed them as usual elements of the winters in the region, elements of an austere nature which had, deep down, stopped being so impressive with their grandeur and serenity.

He thought of children who are always happy, whether it snows or rains, whether the wind blows. They were never truly frightened by the changes of a climate in which they grow tall, strong and straight like sea birds in the midst of storms...

The schoolmaster felt young, swollen with life, as his lungs filled with air permeated with fog, the odors of the sea.

He could face any danger. His thoughts turned fleetingly to the Vikings, on their ships, fearing nothing, facing the wildest storms and hurricanes, with no regard for the sky falling on them. Those were fears for landlubbers!

He wondered what the priest at his side was thinking. His lantern in his hand, drowning in rain, he was no doubt sustained by other powers, his faith unshakeable against the forces of evil, against shadows haunted by evil beings. He did not fear the sky falling on him either. Quite the contrary. It was down below, beyond the waters, in the deepest depths of the earth, in graves, in obscure caves, craters and volcanoes... that was where danger lurked, prepared to grab your feet, to snatch you and drag you down into hell. And that was precisely the orifice they were about to enter.

They walked quietly to the sailor's den — to the evil spirit's den, the priest was no doubt thinking — and easily found the slab they had moved about the same day.

They had no difficulty since it had been positioned to open the entrance to the cave...

Was someone waiting for them?

They were both wondering the same thing. Of course, the gates to the cemetery were not open, welcoming them, but they had the vague impression that they were no longer strangers to the place.

"Well then, let's go in," said the priest in a calm voice.

Then he turned to his companion and added in a slightly nasty tone, "I have not forgotten my holy water!"

Schoolmaster Bourru smiled and the two men helped each other climb down into the tomb.

The priest took the lead. He climbed down a few steps then walked along a long, narrow, twisting corridor. Moisture trickled down the cement walls, reflecting the yellow, wavering lights of the men's lanterns.

The corridor sloped gently down and gradually the walls grew less shiny, dryer.

It seemed to them that they walked for a long time, but they felt no fear until a reddish light, a light they instantly recognized, appeared, blurry at first, then growing more and more intense in the corridor until it absorbed the weak light cast by their lanterns.

When the red light had reached its peak, they entered a room. Initially it seemed immense to them, but perhaps that was just because the narrow corridor had seemed so stifling...

The room was brightly lit although the source of the light was not obvious at first glance.

What struck them first was the impression of magnificence, of gold, of shiny objects, rustling fabrics, bits and pieces of sparkling stones, and iridescent shells.

The two Jagu boys were there, sitting on a chest with iron straps and copper nails. They were listening religiously, silently, calmly to the words of the sailor sitting on his bed draped with red velvet sheets.

They were listening so intently, caught up in the tale, that they did not notice the arrival of the intruders. The sailor did not seem to pay them the slightest attention either. He continued his tale in his calm, deep voice, with inflections that were so captivating, so charming the unexpected visitors were immediately subjugated, without a care in the world, hoping only to enter without making a sound, to settle down on a chest and listen, as the voice with its inhuman, yet sensitive timbre, told stories about another time, about a lost world. Had they not become an audience for a period that was already so distant?

As if enchanted, they listened to the memories of events the man had described to them during their first encounter... They were in the year 1666, Lesabre was at the helm of a ship and three English frigates were lurking of the coast of France...

And the voice continued the strange tale, in a monotone, with no superfluous effects.

The children listened to him, delighted, mouths gaping, eyes shining... Obviously, they were not the least frightened by the unusual cadaver. Charmed perhaps by the beauty of the voice, its chanting rhythm, its power to evoke images, they focused solely on the wonder of the story. They were so caught up in the tale, a story they took for a particular and fantastic form of fairytale, they had not noticed the arrival of the priest and the schoolmaster. Or had they perhaps been hypnotized? It was impossible to know. The two men did not react at all as they would have normally done when finding the two children in such a place at such a time...

Perhaps they had run away from their parents' home once dinner was over and no one had noticed?

But what mysterious call had they received to brave parental authority, their fear of the dark, their aversion of the cemetery to come and listen to the marvelous tales of an old, emaciated sailor, covered with disgusting rags of flesh and fabric, eaten by mildew, covered with mold, whose skin had long lost its tan and had turned ashy, grainy, pale despite the glow of a subdued, crimson light?

But the voice was so enchanting the children heard nothing else. Their fertile, leaping imaginations grasped the story, recreating a world from days gone by and the beings that filled it. The great captain sitting with them was a courageous 30-year-old sailor, in his royal navy uniform, the hero of a thousand adventures, each more extraordinary than the last... They were not in a bunker, but on the forecastle of a great wooden ship, slipping majestically through the green water of the English Channel... The sails flapped overhead, the mast creaked and its inextricable network of ropes swung in time with the swell of the waves and the abrupt gusts of the wind, the three spires of this cathedral of the sea, more living, more vibrant, more powered by faith and hope than any cathedral on land, launched in this manner, driven by the breath of God over the surface of diluvian oceans, toward a promised land, more beautiful, richer, more exalting than any terrestrial paradise imagined up to that point...

"... A few days later...," said the voice. "A few days later, we passed the Raz de Fonteneau, located at the edge of the English Channel. It's a very dangerous zone for navigation since the currents, which are very strong there, cross through a large number of rocks, with only their tips showing through the water. Many ships have been lost there... The danger faced there has given rise to a ceremony that sailors of all nations observe.

"The same ritual is observed in other places people consider just as dangerous, like when we sail across the tropics of Cancer and Capricorn or during the equinox....

"On a French ship, the quartermaster dresses in a grotesque manner. Wearing a long robe, with a cap on his head, a ruff on his collar or rather a yoke made of pullies and wooden balls; his face is smeared and he holds a large book of marine maps in one hand and a stick representing his sword in the other..."

The two Jagu boys were petrified and this disguised quartermaster certainly frightened them more than the speaker.

The sailor continued, "... The book would be open to the page indicating the tides and all of the sailors and officers would place their hand on it as people do with the Bible, and swear an oath declaring whether or not they had already navigated through the zone.

"Those who had never done so would kneel in front of the quartermaster who would tap them on the shoulders with his sword. After that, they would be drenched with water, unless they preferred to bypass this part of the ceremony in exchange for a few bottles of wine and liquor. Those who had already performed this feat were exempt from this punishment...

"As for me, although I was a captain, I declared that I had never navigated those waters for the simple reason that I had mostly knocked about in the North Sea. To the great joy of my crew, I was drenched in a copious amount of water, since it is true that a captain is always entitled to double rations... Then I handed out as large an amount of taffia and other alcoholic beverages, both out of friendship and to show them I held nothing against them for baptizing me so copiously...

"My attitude earned me a great deal of respect and all of those simple, rough people were so appreciative they immediately swore deep allegiance to me and served me faithfully, even in my darkest undertakings..."

The priest blinked imperceptibly. Was he finally about to find the key to the puzzle in this confession? It would take patience. The sailor would eventually unravel his tale, leaving nothing out, apparently, as if he had been sentenced to do so, without passion, by some unknown force, a force that was not blind, since it bent to the sensitivities of his audience. Wasn't this whole story of dressing up particularly likely to seduce the two children? What would follow next?

"... After we had made our way past the Raz de Fonteneau safe and sound and the ceremony had been conducted to the joy of all, a part of the fleet left us and we found ourselves reduced to seven ships travelling the same route to the Americas, still under the command of de Sourdis.

"In a few short days, a good wind pushed us to the Cape Finisterre the most western point of our continent. It was named by Ceasar who, after conquering Galicia and arriving at this cape, ended his conquest, saying he had reached the end of the earth.

"There we were caught off guard by a furious storm. Given our extreme circumstances, I realized the importance of the saying 'He that will learn to pray, let him go to sea…' Everyone prayed, myself included."

"The storm lasted many days and nights. After that, the sea grew calm, the wind settled down and we continued on our way, under full sail.

"But the ships that were with us spread out, we lost sight of them and found ourselves on our own.

"When we were twenty leagues from the West Indies, we encountered an English ship and engaged in a fierce battle. My second and the most hot-headed of my sailors wanted to take the ship, but I forbid the crew from boarding knowing we were limited to a half gallon of water per day and were already exhausted.

"Moreover, the English ship disappeared the next day…"

Schoolmaster Bourru was automatically rummaging through his pockets, looking as if he were about to smoke a pipe. Caught up in the story like the Jagu brothers, he had forgotten about their circumstances...

But the voice continued its tale and the teacher placed his hands on his knees.

"Soon, we were in site of the West Indies and the first island we saw was Santa Lucia. We wanted to head for Martinique but since we were too low and the wind and the current did not allow us to, we headed for Guadeloupe. We were unable to land there as well.

"Finally, four days later, we reached the Island of Hispaniola, which the French called Saint-Domingue. Our landing filled us with joy since every single man had been extremely inconvenienced by thirst and was sea-weary.

"The first day, we dropped anchor at Port Margot, where Mr. d'Ogeron, the governor of Tortuga, the neighboring island, had a very beautiful house.

"Immediately a rowboat carrying six men approached us, greatly surprising most of the French crewmen, as well as myself since we were unfamiliar with the customs of the region.

"Their clothing consisted solely of a small cloth shirt and shorts that came only halfway down their thighs. We had to look closely to see if their clothing was made of fabric or not since it was all drenched in blood. They were dark-skinned. Some had spikey hair; others wore braids. All had long beards and each had a belt with a case made from crocodile skin containing four knives and a bayonet. We knew they were buccaneers.

"Unfortunately, I got to know them well later...

"They brought us three wild boars and we offered them alcohol, which they found particularly delightful.

"The people living in that land, peaceful and welcoming people, brought us all kinds of fruit and we sent our rowboat ashore to look for water. That same evening, we forgot all about the inconveniences of the thirst and hunger we had suffered during our trip... That evening I slept, peaceful and satisfied, but also intrigued by the bloodthirsty men who spoke our language although it would be difficult to consider them Christians..."

The priest blinked. Obviously, the man had a hold over him, but some of his words resonated deep within his soul. The words uttered by the Satanic creature in front of him produced obscure reactions. He felt a desire to eradicate the evil apparition and throw holy water at it, but he felt numb and also wanted to learn more so he remained silent, as the words flowed, as if infinite...

Suddenly the little Jagu boy started fidgeting about.

His brother motioned imperatively for him to stay still, shushing him as discretely as possible. But, after listening for a few more minutes, the younger child coughed, fidgeted again, and finally said, "Captain Le Sabre, what's a buccaneer?"

The priest and the schoolmaster jumped, instantly roused. They both glanced at the child, concerned. His high little voice had penetrated the tale like a supple, sharp blade.

How could he have broken the magical circle they had dived into?

Bit by bit, the adults came to a realization. The monster sitting there, silence and contemplative, did not frighten the children at all. They viewed him as a thrilling yet inoffensive being, a fantastic creature and they believed in the fantastic... In the children, he may have found "the friends he never had...". He could tell them his history, make his confession to them and they alone, were perhaps capable of understanding him and ultimately absolving him.

The priest and the schoolmaster now had only one question: would he answer?

It was not what he would say that was important, but the fact that it was possible to establish a dialogue... and then things would get much simpler. Up to this point, they had been too subjugated by the extraordinary speaker's words to consider, even for a second, speaking with him. Was it going to be possible? Would the little Jagu boy's audacity break the invisible barrier and allow them to establish true contact with the thoughts, the mind of the dead creature that looked mysteriously like a man born three centuries earlier?

The miracle occurred. The answer came, preceded, it is true by a long silence, hesitations, jerky jaw movements that apparently revealed an inner struggle, an immense effort...

"The Caribs, the indigenous people of the West Indies, would cut their prisoners of war into pieces, place the bits on grills and cook them over fires. In French, these grills are called 'boucans' and the word for this cooking and smoking is 'boucaner'. Our buccaneers took their name from that although they settle for cooking only the meat of feral cattle and

229

pigs which they are eliminating from the islands, to sell to the crews of ships of all nations that travel to these lands...

The little Jagu boy, satisfied with this answer, nodded, as if to indicate he understood and was waiting for the rest of the story.

The priest, however, seemed about to ask another question since conversation was possible, but he held back for a few moments.

And Schoolmaster Bourru seemed absolutely captivated; he had no questions to ask for the time being.

The captain continued to talk about his buccaneers.

"Those who hunt the wild cattle are the hardiest buccaneers. They work with packs of 25 to 30 dogs, including one or two excellent hunters to track game in the depths of the uninhabited lands. Each dog is worth six pieces of gold.

"They carry good guns, which they have made just for this purpose in France. The best ones come from Brachie in Dieppe and from Gelin in Nantes. The barrel is four and a half feet long and the mounts are most particular. The buccaneer gun is a large caliber hunting musket. On their bloody, adventurous expeditions, these men would ordinarily carry 15 to 20 pounds of gunpowder, which they had brought over from Cherbourg, in lower Normandy. This was called buccaneer powder. It is stored carefully in kegs sealed with wax to keep it from getting wet."

The priest intervened and it was only then that the children noticed his presence. They turned their heads to look behind them and surprised, frightened expressions washed over their faces. They seemed more afraid of the two men than the monster in this strange place.

The priest realized that the presence of the two children was upsetting. He would have preferred them not to be there. It was obvious to him that the performance was not intended for them and the priest hesitated to allow it to continue any longer. He knew he had the means to put an end to it, yet he wanted to know more about the man. Instinctively, his deep and sincere charity ordered him to try to understand the man, perhaps even help him. He was not certain that, if he ended this contact with the apparition, he would find it again later in any condition to for discussion.

He finally decided to speak, taking the risk that the children would hear something even more horrible.

"My friend,' he said. "You must consider us friends. Although everything you are telling us and even your presence is quite surprising, we would like to understand you better. I have the vague feeling that you are looking for help, that you have been condemned by some evil power to search this world for the confessor you did not have at the time of your death. You have not found him over the centuries but you are already living in eternity... time is no longer important for you, but our time is limited.

"I know I am asking you to make a great effort, but it will save your soul. You no longer need to seek the sympathy of children, but our sympathy, mine and that of God.

"Let's get down to it. The sooner the better. Reveal your faults and hide nothing. I must admit that I have never heard the confession of a dead man. May the All-Mighty forgive me. Let us trust in His mercy!"

Suddenly, with a sinister, almost metallic crack, the tall sailor stood up before them. All of the joints in his skeleton rattled, bones colliding.

The sailor was so gigantic his bald, round head nodded high above them, close to the ceiling of the room.

Something frightening and almost impossible to describe took place. Given the extraordinary effort he had made to stand up, to answer perhaps, to collect his thoughts, his eyes, the enormous sunken globes swelled seeming to jump out of their sockets. His eyes, so unseeing, unblinking, took on an intensity impossible to sustain.

He spoke again. His voice had grown stronger and deeper. It vibrated like a great organ or like the rumble of waves breaking on the pebbles along the shore.

"I have nothing to do with your God," he said. "I have suffered too much and for too long to believe in His mercy.

No one can absolve me of my faults, my sins, my crimes! Not you or anyone else! I will not confess!"

His voice grew quiet, almost impossible to hear.

He said, "I only need friendship, the unconditional friendship of children or perhaps even that of their schoolmaster. Not yours, priest. Your friendship is calculated, a lie... But since you've come here to hear me and to listen to me, I will tell you the end of my tale. It's not a confession, it's testimony. I do not address God because he does not exist, I speak to men, my own kind, and I forbid them to judge me...

"I lived the life of a buccaneer, in the mountains, on sun burnt plains haunted by snakes. I massacred thousands of animals, the wild buffalo that have a reputation for being more powerful, meaner than the most dangerous wild animals on the earth. I gorged myself on their blood under the burning sun for years and I continue to do so even now, miserably, to nourish my poor, human carcass with bits of flesh torn from peaceful beasts.

"But if I lived through this hell, if my clothing was so drenched with blood that it looked like boiled leather, it was all because of an injustice a most terrible injustice...

"In the islands I discovered a wonderful woman. We were young, simple and happy. And my happiness was one you never forget, even in death.

"But it was short-lived since the Marquis de Sourdis decided to steal the woman from me. He was a rich man of good birth. I respected him and he respected me.

"We became implacable enemies."

"First, he wanted to send us, my crew and me, on a perilous, desperate mission from which we had no chance of returning. I refused outright.

"He informed me that he would take away my rank and my ship. I refused to hand over the ship. My sailors supported me and we decided to return to sea, one moonless night, taking my fiancée with us.

"The harbor was guarded and we were betrayed. A broadside by more than 80 canons sent us to the bottom before we had gone even a half mile. The being I loved most in the world, the only one I loved, the only one who loved me, drowned. The night was dark. I could not save her. I swam to shore, a deserted place, and joined the buccaneers, along with a few survivors...

"I was constrained to live an unspeakable life for a fairly long time. I cannot say exactly how long since I do believe that, under the circumstances, I lost my mind...

"I cannot say moreover how or why I found myself one day in the presence of the Marquis de Sourdis. Perhaps it was destiny, perhaps it was a trap... We fought, outnumbered ten to one. I lost the most valiant the most courageous of my men, but I managed to capture my enemy.

"I took him deep into the lands of the indigenous people. They held me in great esteem and I turned him over to them so they could sacrifice him. He was a white man and, moreover, noble. They paid me well for him.

"They burned him alive and the Marquis died in great pain and suffering. The Indigenous people cut him up into little pieces. They grilled the bits and ate them during a sacred festival which was one of the most beautiful they had ever celebrated...

"After that, the medicine man called me over for a discussion. He said, 'I've consulted the spirits. Despite the magnificence of the sacrifice, they are very irritated. I don't know why, but they will hunt you down until you suffer the same fate as your enemy...'"

The priest interrupted, saying "In a certain manner, they condemned you to eternal fire. Hell is for everyone..."

Without seeming to hear him, the monster continued, "Destiny obviously decided otherwise since I died from drowning, after spending a long time with the Frères de la côte and other buccaneers and taking part in the worst carnage the Caribbean Sea has ever experienced...

"My vengeance had not appeased me and the memory of my beloved will always haunt my heart. That's why I am sometimes overcome with rage against the injustice of my fate since, and listen to me well, I already told you. I did not die by fire but by the sea which took me during an unfortunate battle, near Saint-Domingue, a few cable lengths from Cap Tiburon, in a place named Anse aux Ibernois.

"The waves and the currents caught me and I started to wander in that way, neither dead nor alive, victim of I don't know what curse..."

Schoolmaster Bourru who, until that point, had been the most attentive, the most silent listener, coughed to clear his voice and said, "To a certain extent, you have been experiencing a particular form of Purgatory but since you are still alive enough to be able to speak about humans, there is one thing I would to know more clearly. I beg you to answer me, me above all, since I am atheist. Here is my question, to which you have already almost provided an answer: Deep down, do you have any knowledge, as vague as it may be, as to the reason for your punishment?"

The giant remained silent for a long time. The prodigious effort he was making inside could be felt in a certain vibration of his entire dusty carcass.

Under the sheet, his body twitched and jerked, making his ornate gold buttons embossed with fleurs de lys sparkle.

The answer came; it was cruel and sarcastic. The words fell, one by one, like blades.

"Sir, when a criminal is sentenced does he know his judges? And do they make an effort to teach him the Spirit of Laws?"

The priest sighed deeply. In despair, relief, pity? No one knew.

The large body fell silent once again and seemed to slump, to be breaking apart from within. The four listeners could still hear the frightful sound of bones clanking against one another. Then he leaned over slightly on his crimson bed.

The priest approached him, kneeled on the ground, and prayed silently.

He placed the vial of holy water near the bed then went out, pushing the two children, faces pale, eyes red with lack of sleep or tears, ahead of him. The schoolmaster followed. He glanced one last time at the cadaver that was disappearing in the red shadow, as the light itself died...

There was a brief meeting, under pounding rain, at the gates of the cemetery.

The two men made the children promise they would never return to that sinister place. The children made the adults promise they would not tell their parents about their adventure...

The Jagu brothers were taken in secret to the door of their home and the four accomplices separated in silence.

CHAPTER XVI

There were no more visits to the cemetery. The priest and Schoolmaster Bourru avoided one another. They either had too little to say to one another or too much.

A few more cattle were mutilated, but the farmers took defensive measures and supervised their herds so vigilantly that such "accidents" stopped.

The after-school study sessions were still cancelled until the days grew longer. And, given these precautions, the village returned to its usual calm.

The sailor stopped wandering along the shore at nightfall. He was never seen again, except for one last time.

This encounter deserves mention.

Once again, it was Schoolmaster Bourru who found him. Was that by chance? Or had the monster chosen his man? No one knows.

One cold January evening, so cold that at low tide, the sea water froze in puddles, the schoolmaster had gone out to fish crustaceans. Those creatures, numbed by the icy water, were easy to catch and it was a custom, in the region, to take advantage of the harsh conditions of winter to make the most of this miraculous harvest. But night fell very early and fishing continued by lantern light.

It was under these circumstances that Schoolmaster Bourru met the captain, standing on a rock, motionless, feet battered by short, foaming waves.

Overcoming his initial surprise, the schoolmaster approached him, without any fear.

No light enveloped him. In the lantern light, he seemed just as tall as ever, arms outstretched in an attitude of poignant despair.

His coat floated in the wind and revealing his vast, hollow chest, ribs barely covered by strips of torn skin. The iliac bone, poking through a hole in the sailor's pants, was visible on his hips, with an ivory patina.

The head had lost what little human appearance it once had. Two small, bright spots, as large as pin heads, shone in the depths of his sockets. A few strands of hair and whiskers, long and fine, moved with the wind, fluttering over what had once been a face, like small, silvery snakes.

In a gust of wind, one of these strands tore free, carrying with it the bit of flesh to which it had been attached.

Schoolmaster Bourru viewed the man as the very spectacle of desolation, suffering, and deepest despair.

He wanted to speak with him again, but his voice was lost in the immensity of the night, the sky and the water.

He spoke to himself, "When man grows old, when his bodily envelope gradually deteriorates, year by year, bringing new miseries, new failures, new weariness each day... when the heart stops beating its peaceful rhythm and starts jerking in fatigue... when muscles decline, when skin dries, when gaiety vanishes, taking happiness with it... when the world seems to be as dark as it can get, when fatigue accumulates, storing so many small and large disappointments... when the night no longer brings the hoped for rest... man merely aspires to the calm of the tomb. Hoping to abandon his shell of rotting flesh and bone, because his body is already fleeing from life in every which way...

"I know that better than anyone because I experience it constantly with fresh, young children, bubbling with life, children that come year after year, always just as young and eager to live. And each day, I measure the race of time and the implacable rigor of its destruction...

"I can imagine your distress, the terrible suffering you have endured and I know that I am far from being able to picture it in its entirety. Of course, you would not have experienced that if you had not perished by fire, reduced to ashes. You would have been spared this fate..."

The shadow said nothing. No doubt, it no longer had the strength to reply. Deprived of blood and meat, it had come, once again, to seek a pitiful remedy from this living water that has contained all the principles of life, since the creation of the world.

But even that could be of no help...

CHAPTER XVII

On an icy February evening, the children left the school in an unusual rush.

The last hour of classes had passed with distressing slowness and all of the boys were champing at the bit.

Schoolmaster Bourru was not surprised. It was Mardi-gras and, as a result of an inexplicably inhuman government order, the day had not been declared a statutory holiday...

To ease this administrative cruelty, the teacher had decided to dedicate the afternoon to crafts and, more particularly, to making cardboard masks, police hats, crowns, service hats, bicornes, all out of Bristol board and crepe paper, quite innocently competing with the grocery stores in the area that displayed such articles in their store windows.

Their impatience grew minute by minute and the students took pleasure in yelling wildly, somewhat ahead of the sacrosanct hour.

They rushed to their respective homes, grabbed their snacks, knowing full well they would be able to bustle about the streets until dinner time. Mardi-gras traditions were tenacious in Langrune, and scrupulously respected.

By some extraordinary chance, it was not raining. It was, however, freezing cold. That did not dampen the enthusiasm of the children and preserved their paper disguises. One single shadow on the agenda: the Jagu boys had gone directly home to their hamlet.

Faces masked, decked out in costumes both approximate and complicated, the children ran up and down the streets and alleys of their village, trying to make as much noise as possible.

Banging on old pots and pans with sticks, they shouted:
Mardi-gras is dead
His wife inherits

239

A wooden spoon
And an old pot!

It was the time to bang on the shutters of the old Langrune grumps shut up in their homes, the bitter, of the old spinsters who gave them such a hard time, particularly when it came to the catechism...

They dedicated themselves wholeheartedly to the task at hand and no one was spared. In their frantic agitation, the children paid little attention to the cold or the icy wind, coming straight out of the north carrying frosted fog.

The schoolmaster, correcting the students' notebooks, was entitled to a rather particular serenade and the most frightful noises rang out under his window for a good quarter of an hour. He took the situation philosophically.

The mayor was given the same ceremony but the priest, whose presbytery was somewhat set back and surrounded by an orchard, was protected and suffered less... Moreover, he cheerfully tolerated such pagan festivities, which had no impact on his calling.

The joyful tribe could not stay in one place. The boys, accustomed to running about every which way, could not stand to stand about for long and there always one who would point out that they had forgotten someone, had forgotten some old so and so... and they would race off through the village again, in all directions, panting, out of breath, throats sore from shouting as they banged madly on all surfaces:

...Mardi-gras is dead
His wife inherits
A wooden spoon
And an old pot...

But time was passing and the church clock had just struck seven o'clock. It was time to bring an end to these jubilant celebrations so as to avoid getting back home too late for dinner.

In keeping with tradition, the effigy of Mardi-gras was to be burned on the beach, as the participants danced around the fire.

And each year, they very scrupulously respected this tradition that foreshadowed another large nocturnal celebration in the children's minds, the fireworks display, which also took place on the beach, on July 14, in the great happiness of vacations and summer.

Yet, each year the children faced the same acute problem. They had to make a straw effigy to be burned.

Getting the straw was relatively easy. they merely had to steal one or two of the bails stacked in the fields and on the plain. But they also needed clothing and that's when their difficulties became almost insurmountable. It was almost impossible to find an old pair of pants or an old coat anywhere in all of Langrune.

The reason for this is not, as you might think, because the people living in our rural areas are exceptionally economical, mending even the most worn-out clothing over and over again, but rather their love for fishing, which, every full moon, overtook professional fishermen as well as the village's entire population, farmers included.

For this purpose, and to fight off the harsh climate, they used old clothing and old sweaters, preciously stored in sheds, bleached by the weather and covered with salt.

At low tide, every nook and cranny of the rocks would be searched by a group of tramps and ragamuffins carrying hooks...

That goes to show how serious stealing fishing clothing was.

Time passed and it became urgent to decide, to find a solution. They could not allow it to be said that, that year, Mardi-gras had not been sacrificed on the beach.

Death in his soul, a boy removed the main part of his disguise: a captain's hat, decorated with braid and tarnished gold trim and so large for the child that the visor fell down over his nose, forcing him to lift his head to see anything in front of him.

241

He was thanked for his offering by the consideration he could read on the faces of all his colleagues. They were, of course, perfectly aware of the scope of his sacrifice and appreciated his heroic gesture for its full value.

But a head covering is not enough to dress an entire effigy and the discussions grew more and more feverish, more and more worried.

They finally came up with a solution which, although not free of danger, could be acceptable: to go to the plain as quickly as possible and steal a scarecrow. There were still enough farmers who, either rather naïve or solidly attached to traditions, entrusted their seeds to such a derisory protective power although the crows and other birds obviously ignored it completely.

After hesitating briefly, the group galloped off in the direction of the fields.

When they reached the final houses in the village, those in the lead, as rapid as rabbits, but fearful, slowed their pace, breaking the momentum of the entire troop.

The church bell rang out the quarter hour, although some considered it a little late.

"We'll never have enough time to take it to the beach," they said. "We'll get caught...

No one wanted to admit he was afraid of going out on the plain. One by one, they described the brutal punishment that would be applied by an energetic father if they got home too late, Mardi-gras or no Mardi-gras...

Others said that there had been no scarecrows for some time and their undertaking was doomed to failure, that even if there were a scarecrow somewhere it would take a crazy amount of time to find it...

With that, believing they had found a more or less valid excuse, they turned back, in small groups, sulking, disappointed, aware of the scope of their failure... Only four rascals, from among the largest and the most hardened, perhaps better

242

fed on traditions than the others since there was something sacrilegious about missing the ceremony, decided to push on.

They included the generous donor of the cap who did not want to see his sacrifice die in vain...

They walked into the fields, chanting:

...Mardi-gras is dead
His wife inherits
A wooden spoon
And an old pot...

They repeated it over and over to build up their courage.

Their efforts were rewarded.

A quarter moon, in this freezing weather, shone weakly in the starless sky, a light mist formed a circular halo around the satellite and a boy stated, based on this phenomenon, that it was going to rain the next day...

In the bluish light, they saw the scarecrow covered with frost. It shone weakly, like an old silver statue, arms outstretched, like a metal crucifix, standing there, facing the dark sky, seeming to humbly take the moon as a witness for the derisory role they were about to make it play...

The boys shouted in joy, threw themselves on the scarecrow, uprooted it brutally from the ground and placed the cap on its head. Then they dragged it rapidly in the direction of the village, picking up two sheaves of straw from a stack along their way.

At the church square, they encountered a certain number of their friends who, filled with remorse, had decided to wait for them a while.

They were greeted with shrieks of enthusiasm and warm congratulations. And the troop, now back to three-quarters of the size it once had been, raced down Rue de la Mer, pulling their Mardi-gras behind them.

The uproar grew. A few piggy banks, emptied in secret, provided the means to buy sparklers, fire crackers, and even three supremely magnificent flares of a reasonable size and red in color, the most beautiful of all...

Along the shore, they swung the scarecrow over the dikes, above the sand, and each of the boys jumped off the parapets in the dark, at the risk of breaking their necks.... But using the stairs was out of the question...

They finally dragged the scarecrow onto the wet sand that was covered by waves each day and they stood it there, firmly supported by large rocks.

The sheaves of straw had lost much of their substance along the way, but enough remained to build an improvised fire, with the help of a few pieces of driftwood or bits and pieces from shipwrecks, pieces of crates or bins tossed up by the waves.

In a dry area, on flat stones, the three flares were placed in a triangle, around the sacrifice.

Then they lit the fire, awkwardly of course. In the boys' haste, matches were broken or blown out by the wind.

The straw finally burst into light and flames, surrounded by thick smoke, violent red in color.

Mardi-gras appeared, spangled with myriads of small, sparkling droplets formed by the melting frost.

The cap, tilted forward, hid what served as a head, but the flames rose higher and it would have been dangerous to approach and push it back up.

Never before had they burned such an imposing, such a large, such a beautiful man! They would definitely remember that year...

They shouted, jumped, ran about like savages, like demons, like the possessed, laughing out loud, faces turned red in the light of the fire.

"Mardi-gras is dead... Mardi-gras is dead... dead... dead..."

The large carcass collapsed suddenly, projecting sparks in all directions, breaking the circle. The children stepped back, shouting, frightened for a moment, then their circle drew closer.

244

They no longer felt like dancing or singing. The party ended suddenly...

They tried to rekindle the coals, to bring a few flames back to life, but it was a waste of time.

All that remained was a pile of reddish powder.

Using a piece of wood, one boy swept the ashes, scattering them in all directions. The wind carried them away...

Soon, all that remained, among the bits of calcified metal, were ornate, gold buttons, embossed with fleurs de lys...

Kurt Steiner

THE
IMPROBABLES

adapted by Michael Shreve